STO

FIC

A VOICE IN THE DARK

A VOICE IN THE DARK

Claire Lorrimer

CHIVERS
THORNDIKE

This Large Print book is published by BBC Audiobooks Ltd, Bath, England and by Thorndike Press®, Waterville, Maine, USA.

Published in 2005 in the U.K. by arrangement with the Author.

Published in 2005 in the U.S. by arrangement with Claire Lorrimer.

U.K. Hardcover ISBN 1–4056–3342 –5 (Chivers Large Print)
U.K. Softcover ISBN 1–4056–3343–3 (Camden Large Print)
U.S. Softcover ISBN 0–7862–7599–5 (Buckinghams)

The text of this Large Print edition is unabridged.
Other aspects of the book may vary from the original edition.

Set in 16 pt. New Times Roman.

Printed in Great Britain on acid-free paper.

British Library Cataloguing in Publication Data available

Library of Congress Cataloging-in-Publication Data

Lorrimer, Claire.
       A voice in the dark / by Claire Lorrimer.
              p.   cm.
       ISBN 0–7862–7599–5 (lg. print : sc : alk. paper)
       1. British—Italy—Fiction. 2. Nobility—Fiction. 3. Nurses—
Fiction. 4. Italy—Fiction. 5. Blind—Fiction. 6. Large type books.
I. Title.
PR6062.O77V65 2005
823'.914—dc22   2005003423

FOR
CATH STEVENS
WITH AFFECTION

PROLOGUE

October, 1943

The great white house stood shuttered and silent at the end of a long drive of cypress trees. An old gardener was sweeping up the fallen vine leaves scattered over the stone terrace. The uncut lawns surrounding the house were baked and brown after the long dry summer and needed watering. The flowerbeds were ablaze with petals fallen from the parched flowers. Neglect cloaked the once beautiful mansion in a tangle of weeds and uncut hedges. The big house seemed to have closed its eyes against the poverty and shame of its deterioration and lay sleeping in the hot breathless sunshine of the October afternoon. Far across the lawns and hedges, a brown lake, vaporous in the heat, rippled with the wake of two white swans gliding effortlessly across the muddy surface.

Within the house there was also silence. Behind the heavy double doors, a man sat on a torn red leather chair, an old gun across his knees, his head jerking from time to time as he roused himself from the torpor of silence and heat. Across the great empty hall in which the plaster had flaked and dropped in a fine white dust on the marble floor, a servant's soft voice sang an Italian song of lament.

When the song ended it was possible to hear the drowsy buzzing of a bumblebee seeking a way out to sunshine and freedom. It flew erratically up one of the two carved staircases and settled for a moment on the first of a row of portraits hung on the wall of the long gallery. Then it disappeared into a sunbeam which had forced its way through the small shuttered window.

At the end of the gallery, a door stood slightly ajar. Inside the room, a woman knelt at a prie-Dieu, her hands clasped in prayer. The furnishings—if a trifle threadbare in this fourth year of the war—were ornate and very beautiful. A young boy stood with his back to the woman, staring down into the garden below.

The child's eyes were focused on a huge stone bowl beneath the window. In the centre of the bowl a large bronze horse reared its head to the azure blue Italian sky. There was water in the bowl but no glittering shower fell from the fountain that was the horse's mouth. The child leaned his forehead against the window and sighed.

From another room came the thin wail of a baby. The boy, careful not to disturb the praying woman, walked past her and out onto the landing. He wandered along the gallery, staring up with large grey eyes at the portraits hanging high above his dark head. At the very last one, he stood to attention like a miniature soldier and saluted the man in his grey officer's uniform. Then he turned and opened the door, letting the full volume of the baby's cries out into the silence.

His eyes searched for the round, dumpy little figure of a nanny nursing the crying baby. The cries stopped with a hiccough and the blue eyes of the nanny met the dark ones of the child.

'Will the Germans come soon, Boney?' asked the boy from the doorway.

The face turned towards him was momentarily clouded by a look of fear. Then the nanny put the baby back into its crib and went over to the child, holding his dark head against her starched white apron.

'Don't you worry, Rodrigo! No one is going to hurt you while old Boney's here to look after you,' she said in English.

The boy pulled away from her, his head lifting proudly.

'I am not afraid!' he said in the same language, which he spoke with only a trace of his native Italian accent.

He went out of the room, back along the landing and resumed his stance at the window of his mother's room. She did not look round or cease her prayers until the boy, stiffening suddenly, called out:

'Look Mama—they're coming!'

The woman rose slowly from her knees. She joined the boy by the window and together they watched the thin column of soldiers moving down the drive towards the house. The sound of their heavy jackboots pounding on the gravel came like an assault upon the soft silence of the afternoon. The noise increased as the platoon of soldiers came nearer. Their rifles glinted in the sunshine. The boy left his stance by the window, darted back into the shadows of the room and returned with a full-sized old-fashioned gun which he could barely lift to his shoulder.

The woman looked down at him. In her eyes there was a look of pride, of approval; but she shook her head and laid a restraining hand on the boy's arm.

'No, Rodrigo! I'm afraid not!'

She allowed him to continue to hold the gun, however.

'Halt!'

The officer's command was in itself like a gunshot. The men's boots stamped the ground in unison. The rifles clinked metallically. The gardener came slowly round the corner of the house wheeling a barrow in which lay a sharp pruning knife, its blade glinting, like the rifles, in the sun. He watched the soldiers. The officer stood the men at ease and marched up to the front door accompanied by a sergeant. The man lifted his rifle butt and hammered on the closed doors. The old gardener spat, the spittle reaching nearly to the soldiers now watching their officer with interested, hopeful eyes.

The doors opened suddenly, revealing the old servant barring the entrance with his gun.

The German sergeant pushed him aside and as the officer walked in, kicked the doors shut.

High above his head, in the gallery, the woman and the boy watched. As the servant tried once more to bar the men's way, the woman called out sharply.

'No, Mario! Let them come in!'

She came down the staircase, one hand resting on the shoulder of the boy, her back stiff as a ramrod, her head high. If she was afraid, she showed no sign of it. Reaching the last step, she inclined her head very slightly and said:

'I am Francesca, Contessa dell'Alba. You desire to see me?'

The German officer clicked his heels and bowed.

'Kapitän Ludwig von Spieler! I regret the disturbance but I must order you to your room. My men will search the house.'

'You will not order me, Kapitän. No one gives me orders!'

At the imperious tone, the officer bowed again. His face tightened perceptibly.

'You forget, Contessa, that you are no longer our ally. You are now an enemy alien. You will do as I say!'

The boy stepped forward between the woman and the officer.

'Don't talk to my mother like that!' he cried.

The sergeant moved towards him, his hand lifted, but shame-faced, the officer pushed down the man's arm with his cane.

'He is only a child. Leave him!'

'I am not a child. I am ten years old. One day I will be il Conte dell'Alba like my father. Then I shall shoot you!'

The woman pulled the child back against her. The officer smiled.

'We shall see. At least, unlike the rest of your fellow countrymen, you have courage. I admire that, especially in one so young. Now, Contessa . . .' his voice became sarcastic '. . . *if you will be so kind* as to retire to your chamber, together with our fine young aristocrat, I shall search the house.'

The Contessa bowed.

'Very well! But you are wasting your time, Kapitän. Perhaps you are unaware that my husband was killed last year in North Africa. There is no one here but old men, women and children.'

Taking the boy's hand, she went back up the stairs. They walked unhurriedly but as soon as the bedroom door closed behind them, the boy broke away and ran over to the window.

Down below, the soldiers had been given permission to break rank. They had propped their rifles along the edge of the stone bowl. As the boy watched, the hot, red-faced men began to dip their hands and splash their faces in the water. The quiet of the afternoon was broken now with their heavy gutteral voices; their jokes, their laughter. One of the men picked up a stone and aimed it at the head of the bronze horse. The boy's face flushed and he reached once more for the gun that was far too heavy for him to aim.

But there was no need. The old gardener was ambling along the drive, mumbling to himself as if he were half-witted. The boy, puzzled, frowned. The wheelbarrow, wobbling from side to side, caught one of the rifles. Like a row of ninepins, each one toppled its neighbour until they were all lying in the pools of muddy water beneath the fountain. The corporal in charge waved his hands furiously and then swore at the men who sheepishly began to pick up their guns.

The boy, his grey eyes dancing with laughter, saw that the gardener had disappeared. The soldiers were still grouped round the fountain. Suddenly the mouth of the bronze horse spurted out a great jet of water. It rose into the air and began to fall outwards like a silver umbrella. It covered the soldiers as they fell over one another in their attempt to avoid the shower.

'Take note, Rodrigo!' said the Contessa as she joined him at the window. 'Never forget your first glimpse of The Master Race! They are cruel, stupid, ignorant. They have no breeding, no intellect, no manners. Worst of all, they have no God.'

The laughter faded slowly from the boy's face.

'Yes, I know, Mama,' he said, frowning. 'But we have surrendered to them, have we not?'

'No Rodrigo! Not to them. Our armies surrendered to the British. The Germans are no longer our allies.'

'I thought the dell'Albas *never* surrendered, Mama,' said the boy sighing.

'Only . . .' pronounced his mother slowly '. . . when it is the will of God. Mussolini's reign has ended, Rodrigo, and pray God, the war will soon be over. Only then can we hope that the dell'Albas will be great again.'

Down below the German officer came out of the house. The soldiers stood once more in military order. They were brought sharply to attention. The officer resumed his place at their head and as the sun beat down on them, they about turned and marched off down the drive. The fine dry dust rose in a cloud, covering their uniforms, their muddy boots, their rifles.

The old gardener stood leaning on his spade, staring after them. Then he looked up at the window, grinning.

'I'll turn the fountain off now, Signora Contessa,' he said with a chuckle. 'Mustn't waste water!'

The Contessa nodded.

'They might have shot you for that,' she reproved him. But there was the glint of a smile in her eyes as she left the window and returned to her prie-Dieu.

The boy remained alone, watching the fountain fall more slowly until it had ceased altogether. The last ripples of water in the bowl spread outwards and the surface became smooth and still again. High overhead a lone plane was dividing the blue sky with a white vapour trail. The great bronze horse stared upwards, at one with the boy.

CHAPTER ONE

My first glimpse of the Villa dell'Alba was from the end of a long, straight drive, flanked on either side with tall dark green cypresses pointing up to a postcard blue Italian sky. The great house we were approaching was three-storeyed; balconied; stone-carved; like a palace, or a Stately Home.

In front of the house lay a round green lawn, in the centre of which stood a fountain. Water, diamond-bright, splashed into a huge basin and cascaded down the flanks of a bronze horse—a mythical creature with wings, its two front hooves raised as though in recognition of its own power.

The winged horse was the dell'Alba crest and linked to it was the family motto TERRAM SPERNO, SIDERA PETO. *I scorn the earth, I seek the stars!*

But I was unaware of this as I was driven towards the house that was to change my whole life; to change me too, so that nothing would ever be the same for me again. I had no inkling of this, no presentiment, no instinctive forewarning of what lay ahead. As far as I was aware, I was unlikely even to enter the big house outside which we had now stopped.

Beside me in the back of the luxurious saloon car, an elderly Italian lady was seated. I had met her quite accidentally when I was in Calmano's Antique shop in Florence, hoping to find an inexpensive present for my sister. Betty had not been lucky enough to come on the two-week all-in coach tour of Italy with me. She had had to remain at home to look after Father who was partially paralysed and spent his days in a wheelchair.

Just as I was about to purchase a butterfly brooch for my sister the old lady had come into Calmano's. The antique dealer made such a fuss of her I realised at once she was someone of importance. Then suddenly she swayed and fainted. Being a trained nurse, I naturally offered my assistance. That was when old Calmano told me that she was the Signora Contessa dell'Alba. The name meant nothing to me, of course, but the shopkeeper's concern for her was considerable. She soon recovered consciousness but I thought it best to offer to accompany her home when she confessed, in impeccable English, that she still felt a little dizzy and that the Villa dell'Alba was several kilometers out of Florence.

At first, the old lady refused to accept my help. She was a tiny, frail-looking woman but her fierce pride would not readily permit her to accept help from a stranger—a young rather untidy looking English girl and a tourist at that. I was in no doubt about her poor opinion of me. Not that it bothered me very much just then, but in spite of myself I was curious about

2

her. She was dressed completely in black, with a tiny square of black lace covering her piled up snow-white hair. Her face was olive brown, scored with wrinkles and she had deep-set, heavily lidded eyes, black, penetrating and sad. I think it was the look of intense suffering on her face which deepened my curiosity.

The Contessa had barely spoken a word to me during the drive out from Florence but now, as the chauffeur came round to the side of the car to open the door for her, she suddenly smiled at me.

'You must permit me to offer you some refreshment before you return to Florence. It is very hot and you must be thirsty, child!'

I was twenty-four and a fully qualified Staff Nurse. The word 'child' seemed inappropriate until I reminded myself of her great age. She must be over eighty, I thought as I accepted her invitation.

I was deeply impressed by my first sight of the house and longed to see more of it. The fine old stone of its façade reminded me of some of the magnificent architecture I had seen last week in Rome.

Six great pillars supported a wide portico over which hung a mass of brilliant purple bougainvillea. I counted at least twelve long windows, six on either side of the entrance. The double front doors were dark polished wood, studded and hinged with antique ironwork. Two lamps on iron stands stood on

3

either side, like sentinels, or footmen. Over the upper windows there were striped sunblinds and beneath were wrought iron balconies of exquisite design. Along the terrace stood rows of glazed pottery tubs and urns full of bright flowers. Below, the flowerbeds were massed with scarlet carnations. On my left, I could just see more formal gardens surrounded by hedges clipped to the shape of peacocks. An old gardener was busy spraying water on to an English-looking lawn. It looked deliciously cool and green after the dust and heat of the city.

I was overcome by the beauty of it all and seeing my face the old lady said proudly:

'The Villa dell'Alba has no equal!'

'Is it very old?' I asked, understanding her pride in her home. I was also impressed by the mere thought of having one's house named after one—or was it the other way round?

'Most of it was built in the sixteenth century. It has been in our family ever since. Only the front terrace and a new wing for servants have been added but that was at least a hundred years ago.'

'And the winged horse?' I asked.

'As old as the house. The horse is the dell'Alba crest, which was given to our great ancestor, the first Conte dell'Alba, for services rendered to Catherine de Medici. He was of her household.'

With the chauffeur, whom she addressed as

Guiseppe, I helped the Contessa out of the car and into the house. A small round old woman in a blue linen dress with white collar and cuffs, came hurrying towards us. She wore spectacles. Her hair was white, short and curly. The eyes regarding me were still a bright forget-me-not blue.

'Ah, Boney!' said the Contessa in her perfect English. 'I'm afraid I have had to return earlier than expected. I had a slight attack of giddiness in Calmano's . . . nothing much, I assure you.'

'Oh, Contessa, for mercy's sake . . .'

'Now, Boney, do not get excited. I am perfectly all right. It was just the heat. Allow me to introduce you to the Signorina, Nurse . . . ?'

'Laura Howard,' I filled in, holding out my hand.

'And this is Miss Bone, our English Nanny.'

The pink scrubbed face that had been smiling a welcome at me turned suddenly grey. Tears filled the blue eyes and spilled on to her cheeks.

'You mustn't call me that, Contessa—you know you mustn't!'

The voice sounded so agonised I took an involuntary step backwards knowing I had blundered into some personal grief that was not my concern. I glanced at the Contessa's face and saw that it held a mixture of anger, fear and pity.

'Be quiet, Boney!'

5

She turned to me and with a visible effort, spoke as if nothing had happened.

'Miss Howard is a trained nurse, aren't you, my dear? She was good enough to look after me when I fainted.'

It was a moment or two before Miss Bone had herself under control. She took hold of my hand and shook it warmly.

'A blessed bit of luck you were there to help,' she said, the smile returning to her lips.

My trained eye noticed a slight trembling of the Contessa's hands although her stiff, upright figure had not relaxed since we had entered the hall. I said in a professional voice:

'I think the Contessa should go straight to bed and that a doctor should examine her— just to be on the safe side,' I added, seeing the look of worry on the old nanny's face.

'Yes, of course. Oh, my goodness! What will Niko say when he hears about . . .'

'He will not hear!' The Contessa's voice was suddenly sharp and filled with cold authority. I thought that I, for one, would not like to arouse her anger.

'I forbid anyone to mention this to Domenico,' went on the Contessa. 'I will not have him worried. Now, Boney, if you will help me up the stairs? No, Miss Howard, Boney and I can manage. If you turn to your left, you will find the *salotto grande*—the drawing-room, I think you call it in your country. Mario will bring you something refreshing to drink.

6

Goodbye, Signorina, and thank you for your assistance.'

I murmured goodbye and stood where I was, watching the old English nurse—obviously a privileged person here—help the Contessa up one of the magnificent staircases. There were two of them curving up to a minstrel's gallery. The panelled walls were hung with oil paintings. I had no time to examine them in detail but could see that they were mostly of men in richly coloured historic costumes—obviously the dell'Albas of the past, I thought entranced. On my right stood a long oak table bearing two great silver tankards and an immense alabaster Greek urn filled with lilies. Dazed by so much grandeur, I moved towards two tall ebony doors with gilded handles. I found myself in what I presumed to be the *salotto* where the Contessa had told me to wait. It seemed even darker in here than in the hall. All the windows were partially shuttered, allowing only faint glimmers of light to drift through the slats. But once my eyes became accustomed to this religious gloom, a sight of such beauty and elegance gradually unfolded before me that I gasped.

I could not take in so much loveliness all at once. I tip-toed over the black marble floor, set in squares, on which lay one or two fine silken rugs. Six tall windows led out to a terrace. They were framed in violet brocade curtains, shot with gold. Two sofas, of the same colour, with carved gilt backs, stood at right angles to an enormous fireplace carved in pure white marble. On the mantelshelf stood a pair of gold candelabra, each with tall ivory candles. There was also a Venetian clock decorated with china Cupids and gold, pink and turquoise blue flowers. Over the mantelpiece there hung a mirror of such fragile glass, so delicately carved and embossed, it looked as if it might shatter at a breath. That, I was sure, must have been made in Venice.

The ceiling seemed abnormally high. It was painted with a scene from the Bible—angels, madonnas, saints; like the roof of the Sistine Chapel which I had seen in Rome. Dazed by so much beauty, I stared around me and glimpsed even further magnificence—rich walnut and ebony cabinets full of old glass, ivories and china; gilded chairs; pedestals bearing marble busts. Then, at the far end of this glorious room, I saw a piano.

A concert grand! My heart leapt. I hurried over to it. The case, like so much of the furniture, was painted and gilded. I looked for the name and saw that the instrument was a Bechstein. I sat down and lifting the lid, I dared to touch a note. It was perfect.

Once, music had absorbed my life. Father said I had inherited my talent from his Spanish mother. It had been my ambition from girlhood to become a concert pianist. But that was several years ago. First my mother died and then, just after I had obtained a scholarship to study at the Royal College of Music, my father had a stroke. Although he recovered, he was partially paralysed and since neither my elder sister, Betty, nor I wished to abandon him to a Home, I felt I must share with my sister the nursing care Father required. Albeit reluctantly, Betty agreed that I should give up my dreams of a musical career and undergo nursing training instead. Father never knew what the sacrifice cost me as I insisted that since I had grown up, I had changed my mind, preferring a career I could pursue anywhere in the world. Because I had spoken to him so many times of my longing to travel, he accepted my reasons.

But after I had qualified, between caring for Father and part-time nursing there was no opportunity for travel. Nor was there time for music, except when I played at hospital concerts or on the still fine old upright at home, which Father cherished and kept in good order.

I struck another note and then let my fingers run lovingly over the ivory keys of the Bechstein. Soon I was lost in my own harmonies. The tone of the piano was rich and resonant. The fine accoustics of the big, lofty room added to the magnificence of it.

I tried out the slow movement of

Tchaikovsky's *Pathétique* Symphony. Soon the *salotto* was filled with the glorious sorrowful sound. Delighted, I drifted into the haunting strains of the *Prize-Song* from the *Meistersingers* and from that into the rippling music of Liszt's *Lieberstraum*. It sounded to me like the water cascading from the splendid old fountain outside.

Despite my lack of practice I found myself playing well. I thought I was quite alone and abandoned myself to the luxury of playing so perfect an instrument. There was nothing to warn me that the music was reaching other ears than mine.

But as I paused and flexed my fingers a voice behind me suddenly spoke in a rapid flow of Italian. Startled, I swung round. I saw a young man standing just inside one of the long windows. One hand lay lightly on the violet brocade of the curtains, the other held a walking stick. I looked into his face and remembering that moment now, I think it was exactly then I fell in love with him.

It was a handsome face—sun-tanned, sculptured. He was tall and thin but with wide shoulders set off by a pale blue towelling shirt open at the throat. The neck was firm, muscular, reminding me instantly of Michelangelo's *David.* He wore dark glasses so I could not see his eyes but I noticed his mouth—wide, beautifully shaped.

He addressed me once more in rapid

Italian. His voice had become imperious, almost angry and only then was I aware that I had no right to sit down at this piano as though it were my own.

'I'm awfully sorry,' I said stupidly. 'But I'm English and I can't understand what you are saying. *Mi Inglese,*' I tried desperately. 'I'm very sorry I touched the piano. *Mi scusi!*'

To add to my confusion my companion suddenly laughed. He began now to speak to me in near perfect English.

'Certainly I will forgive you—if you will go on playing.' I breathed a sigh of relief. I was not to be thrown out of the place after all.

'Continue, please!' The voice was dictatorial and yet filled with an urgency I did not fully understand.

I was about to obey when a servant came in carrying a large silver tray. He spoke to my companion in an unintelligible flow of Italian which I could not begin to follow. But when he departed the young man came over to me.

'I understand from Mario that I am in your debt. He has told me about the accident this morning and how you assisted my grandmother. It was very kind of you, Signorina.'

'How is she?' I asked. His gratitude made me stupidly shy.

'I am glad to say, quite all right. Our family physician has called to see her and says that a day or two in bed is all she requires. We are fortunate that he lives in the neighbourhood and is close at hand to deal with such emergencies. Mario asked me to apologise for keeping you waiting so long for your drink. He has put lime juice and iced water on the table. Please help yourself, Signorina . . . ?'

'Howard—Laura Howard.'

I held out my hand but he seemed not to see it.

'I am Domenico dell'Alba. Now please take your drink, Miss Howard. As you have no doubt noticed, I am blind and cannot perform the service of pouring it out for you.'

As a nurse I had long since become accustomed to shocks but now I was deeply shaken to learn that this charming, handsome young man was blind. I should have guessed, I thought stupidly. His walking stick was white. I felt a sensation of deep, personal sadness.

A crystal jug stood near me on the silver tray, a bucket of ice beside it. I helped myself to a glass of fresh lime juice.

'May I pour *you* a drink?' I asked. I was unsure how to address him. If he was the Signora Contessa's grandson, he, too, must have a title.

He shook his head.

'I want nothing but that you should play to me again,' he said briefly. 'You cannot know what a pleasure it was for me to listen to you just now. Miss . . .' he pronounced it Mees '. . . Howard, I beg you to spare me more time in

12

your generosity and play again.'

I was flattered and at the same time, nervous. I was dreadfully out of practice and playing to amuse myself was quite a different matter from playing to a critical audience. I put down my glass and sat down once more at the piano. His voice behind me said:

'You play professionally, Signorina?'

I explained as briefly as I could the circumstances that had forced me to abandon my hopes of becoming a concert pianist.

'So I became a nurse,' I ended my dull little story from which I had omitted the terrible heartache the end of my musical career had caused me.

'That is tragic!'

There was so much genuine pity in his tone, I looked up at him surprised and suddenly grateful for his intuitive understanding. Betty, who lacked any musical appreciation, had said with grim practicality:

'It's probably all for the best, Laura. Music could never be a nice steady job like nursing!'

Nevertheless, I loved my elder sister who was as much a mother to me as a sister. She was fifteen years older than I and since Mother died, she had looked after me. Security to her meant everything . . . which was just as well since Father and I were hopelessly impractical.

'I minded it terribly at the time,' I answered. 'But these things happen. Anyway, looking

13

back on it, I don't think I would ever have been good enough to make the top grade. I worried about appearing in public for one thing and for another, I got tired of practising scales. I just wanted to play—to spend my life playing the music I love.'

I broke off, realising that I was probably boring my companion. A strange uneasy silence filled the room: I looked down at the keyboard and felt a great longing to touch the notes just once more; yet I had the feeling that I was expected to leave. I had certainly outstayed my welcome, I thought. Good manners demanded that I go. But I sat still, clasping my hands together, waiting without quite knowing what I was waiting for.

Suddenly my companion spoke.

'I do not expect you to understand, Miss Howard—how could you?' he said. 'But just as you enjoy the playing of music, so I enjoy listening. You play with your heart—not just with technical ability. I have an excellent tape recorder and stereo record player to which I can listen but to me, music always loses something essential in this form of reproduction, no matter how brilliant the performer.' He paused and when he spoke again, he seemed under some kind of strain. 'Since I have been unable to see, my hearing has become doubly important. No one in this house plays the piano. That is why I was enthralled by your performance.'

14

'You don't play yourself?'

'Very indifferently. I do have a balalaika on which occasionally I strum. But I have the wrong fingers for a pianist.'

He spread out his hands in front of me. They were long and beautifully shaped. On one finger was an onyx ring with a crest. It stood out remarkably against the brown skin. They were the hands of an aristocrat but, as he had said, not of a pianist. I remembered my teacher telling me that short, square hands, strong and flexible, were the best—like mine.

I looked up at his face, trying to see his eyes hidden behind the dark glasses. I was suddenly intensely curious about his blindness. It wasn't a nurse's professional curiosity but a personal one. Before I could stop myself, I was asking him how long he had been blind. He did not seem to be offended.

'When I was quite a small boy, I lost the sight in one eye following a stupid accident when I ran into a thorn bush. Unfortunately, I developed some trouble with my good eye last year and I have been sightless for over six months now.'

He gave the technical reason for his affliction in Italian but from the little I knew about ophthalmics, I guessed he was describing a detached or damaged retina.

'Surely there is a remedy? An operation?' I faltered. 'One day you will be able to see again?' I felt absurdly anxious.

15

His mouth curved into that strange half smile.

'I hope so very much. I am to have the operation in a few weeks time. Meanwhile, I must stay quiet and do nothing and I find this torture. Mine is not the nature to stay still. I am a restless creature.'

I could believe it. Already I had sensed that this young Italian was highly strung; certainly not the type to sit and dream away his life.

'Now that we have exchanged the stories of our lives, Miss Howard, will you please continue to play for me?'

It was not so much a request as a command. Clearly, he was used to giving orders and to getting his own way. It was hardly surprising. It was obvious the dell'Albas were rich. The Villa, the gleaming car belonging to the Contessa, the beautiful objets d'art and paintings in the room all suggested the kind of wealth I had read about but had never thought to come in contact with. It was as if I were living momentarily in a fairy tale.

Expressing my strange excitement and happiness, I let my hands fall in the opening bars of Strauss' *Tales from the Vienna Woods*. I felt like laughing and dancing with the music as it poured from the piano. It was such fun to be alive—just as I imagined it had once been fun for the Austrians waltzing together in the romantic light-hearted days of the old Vienna.

'Niko, Niko, stop this girl at once. Your

16

grandmother says she must be stopped—*at once!*'

I was jolted rudely out of my dazzling dream world. This time the interruption came from Miss Bone—the nanny. She had rushed into the room and was clinging to the young man's arm, her wrinkled face white with worry.

'At once, at once!' she kept repeating.

I did not understand what all the fuss was about. I just felt a shiver of apprehension which increased as I saw a look of intense sadness come over that handsome young face. Silently, breathlessly, I watched him lean over the old woman and put his strong young arm round her shoulders.

'Don't upset yourself, Boney. It is perfectly all right for Miss Howard to play. I have ordered her to do so.'

'But the Contessa says . . .'

'I know, Boney, I know it has always been the rule, but I have decided it is time the rule was broken. My mother would have wished it, I am sure, since it brings me such happiness. Please tell Nonna that this is the way I wish it to be. Tell her, *cara mia,* that her *nipotino* is happy—yes, happy, for the first time in years.'

The old woman, still wringing her hands, left the room, mumbling to herself. I looked up at my companion uncertainly. I was very confused. Why was it wrong for the piano to be played? It did not make sense. Why had my playing angered the Contessa? Why was the

17

old nurse so upset?

'Pray continue!'

I was becoming accustomed to that command, but this time I knew I could not obey. My gay, irresponsible mood had given way to one of utter perplexity. I could sense something in the atmosphere which had not been there before and which, without my knowing why, frightened me.

'I . . . I can't!' I said stupidly.

Suddenly I felt his hand on my shoulder, warm, reassuring, comforting.

'I am sorry—I'm afraid you are upset. If you can spare me a little more of your time, and if you will promise to play for me afterwards, I will explain why my grandmother sent poor old Boney to stop you. That is, if it would not bore you?'

'Oh, no!' I gasped. I was finding it difficult to collect my thoughts. Apart from the mystery he had promised to explain, I was further disturbed by the strange emotions the touch of his hand on my shoulder aroused in me.

I was trembling. He must have felt it for he said gently:

'Do not be afraid. It all took place a long time ago. Now I am—and always will be—very grateful to you, Signorina. You have dispelled tragic memories and revived happy ones for me.'

Then he turned and moved across to the French windows where he stood silently staring out into the sun-drenched grounds.

I sat still, holding my breath, waiting for him to speak.

CHAPTER TWO

'My mother's name was Sofia. She was a very beautiful woman. On that little satinwood table beyond the Bechstein, you will see a hand-painted miniature of her.'

I reached out and picked up the purple velvet and silver frame from the table near me. I looked at a young woman, perhaps thirty years old. She stared back at me with large grey eyes in which there seemed no hint of a smile. In fact, there was an expression in them of intense sadness which was accentuated by the sorrowful droop of the beautifully shaped lips. At once I saw the likeness between this woman's face and that of her son. His was but a more masculine edition but the features were identical. Did that mean that his eyes, too, were grey? I seemed to remember reading that many Florentines had grey eyes; that it was the Sicilians whose eyes were nearly always dark. Sofia dell'Alba's eyes were lovely—wide apart, fringed with long straight black lashes. The nose was small, Grecian.

'She was indeed very beautiful!' I exclaimed.

'She died when I was ten years old and

Paolo, my brother, was seven. She was only thirty-one. She was playing this piano on the afternoon she died. My father had come in to listen to her. Mario had just handed the afternoon mail to them when my mother had a heart attack and fell across the keys, crashing them discordantly. She never recovered. My father ordered that the piano should be locked and that no one should ever play it again. He threw the key into the lake. The piano tuner had his own key and not knowing of my father's order, came as was his custom, to tune the Bechstein. No one stopped him, so he continued to come. He must have left the piano unlocked on his last visit, otherwise you would not have been able to open it.'

I looked down at the slender black and white ivories, then back at Sofia's picture. I could visualise the shock her sudden death must have given everyone in the household that terrible afternoon.

'Your father must have loved your mother very much,' I said quietly.

'He died a year later. The doctors said it was pneumonia but my grandmother has always said it was of a broken heart. I was too young to understand anything but the fact that I had lost the person I loved most in the world. But since I have been . . . how do you say in English . . . adult? . . . I have often wondered about that day. My mother loved to play the Bechstein so much. I do not think she would have wanted it locked as my father ordered and never touched again.'

'Perhaps he was afraid the sound of the piano would remind him too poignantly of her?' I suggested.

He turned away from me, sighing.

'It is possible—yet he clung to every other memory of her. As a child I would find him sitting here alone in the evenings, holding her picture, his face full of sadness . . . of grief . . . of something more, I think, but I was so young, I did not really understand. When I grew up I asked my grandmother many times to tell me more about it, but she would not speak of that terrible day. She forbade old Boney to speak of it either, so my father and mother are seldom mentioned now by any of us. I am happy to be able to talk of her to you.'

A dozen comments rose to my lips. He had a right to know all there was to know about his parents, I thought indignantly. The old Contessa was being unfair, to say the least, to try to suppress the past. Her silence must have raised doubts in her grandson's mind—it did in mine—as to whether there was something more behind the story of Sofia dell'Alba's sudden death. But I knew I could say none of these things to the young man by the window. It was not my business. He looked so sad, I tried to lighten the moment.

'Your mother played well?' I asked him.

'Beautifully!' he replied, his voice full of

21

warmth again. 'I was never so happy as when I could sit quietly curled up on the sofa listening to her. The moment I heard your music I knew that it had been wrong to keep the instrument closed and silent. My mother would not have wished it. Music was her great joy and mine. Until today no one, least of all myself, had thought to countermand my father's orders. But I am head of the household now. As from today the piano shall stay unlocked.'

'Your grandmother . . . ?' I began hesitantly, but he broke in with an imperious lifting of his head and a set line to his mouth:

'My grandmother lives very much in the past. She is old so it is natural. But I think her attitude mistaken. The world is full enough of that which is bad and evil and sad. To bar music from one's life when it is good and pure and uplifting must be wrong. I am grateful to you, Signorina, for making me realise it.'

I felt my cheeks grow hot, partly with pleasure and partly with apprehension. If I touched the piano again, would the fierce old Contessa create a scene? I felt sure she would not want her orders countermanded—not even by her grandson. I was afraid of her, yet knew I would play again if il Conte dell'Alba told me to.

For want of anything to say, I mumbled:

'I wish you wouldn't keep calling me Signorina. My name is Laura.'

Somehow the childish words broke the

tension between us. He turned away from the window and came back to the piano. His mouth was curved into that half smile which seemed to have the power to set my whole nervous system quivering.

'And my name is Domenico—Niko to my friends. I hope we shall be friends, Laura.'

It was a moment or two before I could stop my fingers shaking. The sound of my name, spoken with that soft Italian accent, had affected me almost as badly as his smile! I told myself not to be so ridiculous. I was behaving like a romantic schoolgirl. It was high time I grew up.

'My full name is Domenico Rodrigo Leonardo dell'Alba. If you prefer to call me by one of those names I shall not object!'

Suddenly I was laughing and he was laughing with me. I was no longer nervous or ill at ease. It was as if the long aristocratic title was so improbable that he became just an ordinary young man making up a list of names to amuse me. He couldn't be much older than I . . . no older than Peter, my medical student boyfriend. The fact that he was wealthy and titled was no reason for us not to become friends.

'Now will you please play to me again?'

'Tell me what you'd like to hear,' I said.

He left it to me. I sat down and inspired by the sound of that glorious piano, I played again Chopin, Schumann, Schubert—anything

23

that came into my head.

The time flew past. Suddenly, the door opened.

'What is it, Mario?' Domenico asked. He sounded irritated by the interruption.

'E ora di cena, Signor il Conte.'

'Lunch time—already! How quickly the morning has gone!'

Domenico stood up and rested his hand on my shoulder.

'I'm afraid I have been very selfish, you have been playing for quite two hours. You must be exhausted. Forgive me, please!'

I was stiff but I had enjoyed every moment of it.

'You will stay and eat with us, of course.'

I jumped up.

'I'm afraid I can't. They'll be expecting me at the hotel. They'll think I'm lost or something.'

'They?' His voice was suddenly sharp.

'My friends, Jean and her aunt. They are on the same tour as myself,' I gabbled. Suddenly the warm easy friendship was gone and I was aware of his extraordinary authority again. 'We usually go everywhere together but this morning we split up because we all wanted to buy souvenirs for our families.' I realised I was talking too fast and that he probably hadn't the faintest interest in what I was saying. 'I really must go. Thank you for letting me play your beautiful piano.'

'But this is absurd. You cannot leave now. Or if you must, then will you return this afternoon? This evening? *Domani?*'

He lapsed into Italian and it was only this which made me realise he was really perturbed by the idea of my departure. I was thrilled and yet I tried not to let him see that I desperately wanted to come back—to see him again.

I might be a romantic, but there was a strong practical streak in me, too—the streak that enabled me to be a good nurse. And I could see that wonderful though the morning had been, it would do me no good to grab just a few more hours with this strange, fascinating new companion. I was already halfway to falling in love with the Conte dell'Alba and tomorrow I was leaving Florence forever— going with the rest of our party to Milan, the last city before we returned home. I would never see him again. The thought was unbearable.

'You do not answer, Laura. You do not wish to come back and play to me?'

The anxiety in his voice was nearly my undoing. I almost confessed how very, very much I wanted to come back and that I hated to have to leave him at all! Surely, I thought, he must see that for himself?

I explained about Milan.

'We leave early tomorrow, after breakfast. The coach goes at eight-thirty,' I ended miserably.

'And *you* must go with it?'

I sighed.

'Yes, of course. You see, it's the end of the tour. I know I shan't love Milan as much as I love Florence, but I want to see it and anyway, on a tour like this, you have to do what is planned for you.'

'It is imperative you continue with this tour? Why not postpone it?'

Despite myself, I smiled. It was obvious this rich young Italian had no idea how package tours were run—everything organised down to the last detail and worked to a close schedule. I tried to explain this to him.

'It has to be like that in order for it to be so cheap,' I said.

'Ah! Then it is only a matter of finance!'

Only! If he but knew how difficult it had been to raise the money for me to be here at all. Suddenly, I was annoyed with him. Cushioned as he was by so much luxury, how could he understand what it meant to be hard up for a few lira. Well, pride could take second place for once. I'd make him understand.

'I *want* to see Milan. I may never have another chance. I'm not like you, Signor— Conte!' I saw his eyebrows lift as I used Mario's form of address. 'I can't just get in a plane and fly to the places I want to see, stay here, go there, when I wish. I've been saving for over a year to make this trip. Really and truly, I shouldn't have come at all.'

Now I could see his lips soften and realised he was beginning to feel sorry for me. But it didn't help. I felt my anger rising and held my head even higher.

'We could do with the money I've spent, at home,' I went on, 'but . . . well, my father was so anxious for me to come. He trained here in Florence as a young man and he was here during the last war. He has never forgotten Italy or how much he loved it. He wanted me to see it all, too, so that we could talk about it when I went home. I suppose you think that's silly!'

'No, no, I do not!'

I did not look at him. There was a catch in my voice, partly of anger but mostly because I was so miserable at the thought of leaving not just the Villa dell'Alba, but Florence, *Italy*. There was something about the country that had captured my heart.

I had fallen in love with Florence. I knew it was not all hot golden sunlight and madonna blue skies, bells and towers and glorious architecture. There was poverty here, too; frightening grilled doorways, filthy narrow cobbled streets and beggars.

I had read so many books about Italy—Florence in particular. Perhaps it was because my father had talked so much and so lovingly of this city of his dreams when I was a little girl, that I now had this feeling of belonging here. If I had but one tiny part of the dell'Alba wealth, I thought, I would never, never leave the country. But such was my current state of poverty, I doubted I would be able even to afford a programme at the opera we were scheduled to hear that night.

Il Conte's voice cut across my thoughts.

'Please believe me, Laura, when I tell you that I do not think it at all silly. On the contrary, it was selfish of me. I wanted so much to hear you play the piano once more.'

Suddenly I stopped being sorry for myself and with one of my usual violent see-saws of emotion, was filled with pity for him. It must be terrible to have so much and yet be blind and unable to enjoy it; to be dependent upon a stranger's playing for a few brief moments of pleasure. I found myself wondering if my music reminded him of the dead Sofia—the mother he had lost when he was still a little boy.

Impulsively I said:

'I could come back this evening for a little while, if you really wish it.'

'*Sono molto felice* . . . I am delighted! Thank you, Laura. Now, I will arrange for Guiseppe to drive you back to your hotel. At what hour shall I tell him to collect you?'

I had never been in a chauffeur-driven car before this morning and now I was to be driven back to my hotel by the uniformed Guiseppe! I nearly smiled at the mental picture I had of Jean, her aunt and the rest of

28

our coach party gaping at the luxurious dell'Alba limousine depositing me at the hotel.

I decided to avoid any comments by asking Guiseppe to drop me at the corner of the street. Hopefully by the time he called to collect me that evening, my friends would already have departed for the opera.

'Could you tell me what time you have dinner?' I enquired, only just preventing myself from saying 'supper'. 'Then Guiseppe can call for me half an hour beforehand.'

I barely noticed the scenery on the drive back to Florence. I had far too much on my mind. Not the least of my problems was how to tell Jean and Aunt May that I wouldn't be going with them to *Rigoletto*. My morning seemed so fantastic and unreal. I wouldn't really be surprised if they thought I was making up the whole story. I wished I need not tell them about it. I liked Jean. She was a plump, round-faced Scots girl in her thirties, a senior nurse at 'my' hospital. She was always jolly and good natured but not very intellectual. Her mind was limited to romantic novelettes. She read True Life Romances and talked about 'Mr Right'. She was always telling me that one day 'Mr Right' would come along and I would fall in love and get married. Every boy I went out with was, in Jean's mind, a possible husband. I simply could not bear it if she started saying that il Conte Domenico dell'Alba was Mr Right at last. The thought was so ridiculous that I laughed aloud. Guiseppe turned his head, grinning, and said:

'La Signorina e molto felice.'

Yes, I was happy—happy because I had the whole magical evening to look forward to, even though it would end, like Cinderella's ball, at midnight. Which reminded me, what on earth would I wear on such an occasion? I had no long evening dress. What did the Italian aristocracy wear at home for dinner? I had a short white nylon jersey dress which I had bought at Selfridges just before I left London. Perhaps that would do. I had brought nothing else but cotton shifts, a jump suit, casual 'tops'—and a pair of jeans. I laughed again, imagining myself trailing through the exotic Villa dell'Alba in jeans.

Guiseppe dropped me at the corner of the street in which the Albergo Castello was situated. The dining-room windows overlooked the front door. I couldn't face the curious glances which would greet my arrival. I crept into the hotel. I was late for lunch. Jean and Aunt May had nearly finished their meal when I arrived and seated myself at the table. I tried not to make comparisons, but the Albergo seemed so bare, so badly furnished after the Villa dell'Alba.

'We were worried to death about you, Laura,' Jean said. 'What on earth happened?'

Suddenly, I could not tell her. It was my secret. I crossed my fingers under the table and said:

'Oh, I got lost somewhere near the Duomo and I lost count of time. I was fascinated by the architecture on the other side of the river. I just couldn't tear myself away.'

Neither of my companions pressed me for further explanations. They were both far too anxious to tell me about the presents they had bought. I was allowed to eat in silence. As Aunt May pointed out, I must hurry up or I'd be late for the scheduled visit to Sita after lunch.

I don't think I really took in the beauty of the wonderful treasures in the Museum we visited that afternoon. I kept seeing instead the treasures in the Villa dell'Alba. The only time I really paid any attention to our guide was when he showed us some of the old musical instruments. Amongst them was a balalaika. Immediately I thought of Domenico and wondered how well he played. I was suddenly reminded of a magnificent old film *Dr Zhivago* I had recently watched on television. The love of the hero for his Lara had made a profound impression on me. Sad though the ending was, I felt that to share so deep and wonderful a love, however briefly, must make one's life seem well worthwhile. The theme song was played on a balalaika, a haunting melody which inevitably brought a lump to my throat. I wondered if Domenico knew it, if he could play it. I thought of his long, tapering fingers moving over the strings of the instrument I saw in the Museum and suddenly I was wondering how I would feel if he were to touch me with those beautiful hands.

'Come and look at this, Laura!' Jean's voice brought me back to the present like a douche of cold water. I remembered rather grimly the hospital, the long corridors smelling of antiseptic; the wards with their polished floors, the trolleys, the screens, the vases of flowers, the rows of narrow beds and the patients waiting, hoping to get well again. Not for them the excitement of this Italian tour. And even if they achieved it once they were well again, maybe they would never have the incredible good fortune to go inside a *palazzo*—for that was what the Villa dell'Alba resembled. Not for them the chance to meet a real live Italian count. Domenico Rodrigo Leonardo. *Niko*, Miss Bone had called him. I found myself wondering if I would see her again tonight. Suddenly I was cold, filled with strange apprehensions. Why had the old woman been so upset when the Contessa had described her as the 'English Nanny'? What had the poor woman said that could possibly invite the Contessa's anger? The thought of meeting the Contessa again made me less certain I wished to return to the fabulous Villa. Yet it seemed absurd to be afraid of that tiny frail old lady.

'Come *on*, Laura. Everyone's gone!'

I followed Jean's impatient figure into the next room, but I couldn't concentrate on the guide's droning lecture. It was a wasted afternoon. I was back in the Villa in thought— I might as well have stayed there in person. I wondered what Domenico was doing? Listening to his stereo? Walking in the garden? Upstairs, perhaps, talking to his grandmother? Was she angry with him for countermanding his father's orders about the piano? Could she impose her will on him and have the piano locked again before I returned? That would be awful! I must face the possibility here and now that Domenico might greet me this evening with the words:

'I am sorry, Laura, but after all you cannot play to me.'

Impossible to say which of the two of us would be the more disappointed. Impossible for me to know whose word was the last word in that strange household. Both Domenico and the Contessa dell'Alba spoke with voices of complete authority, yet one must govern the other. I did not know enough about the traditions of Italian aristocracy to be sure whether the elderly Contessa was head of the household, or the young Conte himself.

I looked at my watch and saw that it was nearly four o'clock. Although desperately impatient for the time to pass, when later that evening the moment came at last for me to leave the Albergo, I was a bundle of nerves.

For the second time that day I entered the Villa dell'Alba. I understood from Mario's flow of Italian punctured with gestures, that Miss Bone would be down directly and that I was to wait in the great hall.

I stood nervously clutching my green shoulderbag. If only I could be sure I was correctly dressed! The white jersey dress looked very nice. But it was cut away at the back, revealing quite an expanse of golden brown skin. Suppose it was considered improper by an old lady like the Contessa? I had no way of knowing. At home everyone lived very simply. No dinner, only high tea at night, fish and chips or sausages or kippers, and fruit and custard or cheese.

Would there be other guests, I wondered suddenly, in a fresh panic. My Italian was so bad I would never be able to talk with strangers. Why *had* I come? I wished myself a million miles away.

Miss Bone came hurrying down one of the two great staircases.

She was wearing a plain, shapeless black dress and her grey hair was scraped back into an old-fashioned bun.

'I'm so sorry I have kept you waiting, dear. The Contessa asked me to give you her apologies but she is remaining in bed and trusts you will understand. She is still a bit shaken up, you know.'

'But of course!' I said. I was glad to see little

Miss Bone and held out my hand to clasp hers. At this moment the old woman seemed a veritable lifeline.

'How sweet you look, dear!' she said kindly. I think she guessed my nervousness. 'Now, you mustn't be shy. There will only be you and me, Domenico's secretary, and Paolo, his brother. Domenico will be down in a minute. We'll go into the *salotto*, shall we?'

I followed Miss Bone into the room where I had played to Domenico—could it be only this morning? We sat down side by side on one of the yellow sofas and her little blue eyes twinkled at me.

'You mustn't be shy,' she said again.

'It's just that . . . well, I'm not used to dining out!' I blurted out truthfully. 'And I'd hate to make any social blunders, Miss Bone.'

'Call me Boney, dear,' the old woman said, patting my hands as if I were one of her small charges. 'As to making any social blunders, you just be yourself. If anyone misbehaves, it'll be that Paolo. You haven't met him yet, have you? He's Niko's younger brother.'

The old nanny's face took on a queer expression.

'I daresay he's not so bad as I make out,' she went on. 'But all the same, you being so young and English as well, I feel it my duty to warn you. He's not a *good* boy.'

I smiled. I could imagine a naughty little boy upsetting his bowl of cereal or forgetting

35

to say 'please' or 'thank you'.

But Boney wasn't smiling.

'You can't believe a word Paolo says!' she was muttering, more to herself than to me. Then, as if realising she was being disloyal, she patted my hand again and added:

'Now Niko—he's a fine lad, the apple of the Contessa's eye. "Niko has all the finest traits of the dell'Albas", the Contessa says and she's usually right. Such a lovely little boy he was, too, with those enormous grey eyes and long dark lashes, like a girl's. Not that there's anything girlish about Niko—a will of iron he has, like his grandmother. You should have heard them this afternoon—not that Niko ever raises his voice to his grandmother. All the same, he stuck to his ground and there was nothing for it but for her to give way.'

'You mean . . . about the piano?'

The old woman nodded.

'That's the first time Niko has ever openly disobeyed the Contessa.'

'I'm sorry!' I said. Yet I wasn't. Now that I knew for sure I could play again on that lovely Bechstein, I was thrilled—thrilled, too, to think that Domenico cared enough about my playing to stand up to that imperious old woman.

'Have the dell'Albas *always* lived here?' I asked.

'Since the sixteenth century. I won't go too far back in history—only to the nineteen

36

twenties when I came as nanny to the Contessa's family. There were five children of whom only one survived to marriageable age—that was Rodrigo, Niko's father.'

Momentarily, tears filled her eyes as she recounted sadly.

'Antonio, the eldest, was killed in the first year of the war—World War Two, that is to say. Rodrigo was only a child then and his sister a babe-in-arms. We were all alone here when Italy surrendered to the Allies and the Germans became our enemies. Il Conte—the Contessa's husband—was killed in the fighting, and that's when the family lost near everything they owned, excepting the house—and that they only kept through influence with an old friend, Cardinal Pettrachi. But for him, I myself would have been put in a concentration camp. We all have much to thank him for.'

I was fascinated by this glimpse into the past and Boney, seeing my interest, gladly continued her story.

'Some ten years after the war was over, Rodrigo married a beautiful Italian girl called Sofia da Zacchira. Like the dell'Albas, the war had ruined them, too. Sofia bore Rodrigo two fine sons—Domenico, bless him, and Paolo three years later. Then—then sadly she died, poor soul, and not long after Rodrigo passed away. Neither was born to poverty and they suffered a great deal, not caring for the new ways of the country either.'

Puzzled, I pointed vaguely round the room. 'But all this . . .' I faltered. 'The family must have made a lot of money since the war?'

'Not *made* exactly!' The old nanny gave me a speculative look, as if sizing me up. Obviously she decided that I could be safely confided in for she went on:

'One of the boys had to make a good marriage—for the sake of the family. Domenico was the eldest and we counted on him.'

I felt suddenly faint. It wasn't that I had eaten little or no lunch and had nothing since. I was honest enough with myself to realise that I was suffering from shock. I had never imagined Domenico *married*. I didn't want him to have a wife. Somehow it spoiled everything. Then my common sense prevailed. How ridiculous of me! What difference could it possibly make to *me* if Il Conte Domenico dell'Alba was a married man? This morning when I'd climbed out of bed, I had not even known of his existence. He was little more than a stranger. After this evening I would never see him again, so why should I care? I was no better than Jean with her silly romantic True Life Stories.

'Of course, Paolo was on the young side to be married. Not yet twenty, but . . .' the old woman paused and shrugged.

I nearly laughed in my relief. So it was not Domenico but his brother who had married, and I had imagined Paolo as a little boy spilling his cereal! It was obviously time I stopped being so imaginative!

I concentrated on Boney's quiet English voice.

'At first the Contessa was against the marriage. Not only was Helen five years older than Paolo but her father, William Lennister, was only a car manufacturer from the Midlands. You understand, dear, that in an aristocratic family like the dell'Albas, breeding counts. They say Helen's father was once a petrol pump attendant—years ago, of course, before he made his millions. Just fancy!'

I sat silent, trying to make up my mind if the old nanny were the snob or if she were merely repeating the Contessa's views.

'I believe Helen's father is on the short list for submission to the Prime Minister for a peerage now,' Boney went on. 'Things aren't what they were, are they, dear? Anyway, as I was saying, Paolo married Helen Lennister and suddenly there was all the money in the world to restore the Villa to its former glory. I'll say this much for her, she has been generous and she has perfect taste. Of course, she'd been well educated—her father sent her to the best schools and she speaks any number of languages. She's able to hold her own as the wife of an Italian nobleman, not that I'll ever like her, no matter how much she's done for the family.'

'Why not?' I asked, intrigued by the whole story.

'Treats me like dirt!' old Boney said, too resentful against Paolo's English wife to be reticent with me, a stranger. 'Oh, she's pretty enough if you like red hair and green eyes. But she has a temper to go with that hair of hers and I'd as soon not be around when she lets go, I can tell you. Still, she got her deserts when she got Paolo. It wasn't him she really wanted, you know; it was Niko. Paolo was second best.'

Once again my hands began to shake. I was shocked to discover how the mere mention of Domenico in connection with Helen could have this unsettling effect upon me. I felt I ought not to be listening to the old nanny's gossip. As if she, too, suddenly had the same sense of guilt, she added:

'I do run on so. I dare say as how it's you being English. I can't sort of feel you're a stranger. Still, now you're staying here we'll be able to get to know each other better, won't we?'

There was something rather pathetic about the old woman's desire for companionship with one of her own countrywomen. I squeezed her hand and as gently as possible, said:

'I'm afraid I shan't be *staying*, Miss Bone— Boney. I'm just here for dinner.'

The periwinkle blue eyes stared into mine

40

with a peculiar certainty in them.

'No, dear, it's all been fixed. Niko arranged it this afternoon with the Contessa. You're to stay a month and play the piano to him whenever he wants. It's all settled. The Contessa has agreed.'

A hundred protests leapt to my lips.

'I can't—I'm going to Milan tomorrow—I have a job at home at Bartlington Hospital and I have to be back next Monday.'

I broke off. I saw Domenico standing in the doorway.

'That was very naughty of you, Boney! You've spoiled my surprise,' he said in that soft voice that so enthralled me.

Boney clambered stiffly off the sofa and went over to him. She put her gnarled, freckled hand on his arm.

'I'm sorry, dear. I thought Miss Howard already *knew*. I wouldn't have spoiled your surprise for anything.'

I remained seated. I couldn't speak. Domenico's voice was gentle as he said:

'Never mind, Boney. It doesn't matter. All that matters is that Miss Howard—Laura, should agree?'

'But I can't . . .' I launched once more into my reasons.

Domenico came towards me, finding his way with his white stick. He seemed to know where I was sitting by the sound of my voice. As I stopped speaking, he hesitated and spoke rather irritably.

'I cannot see where you are. You have not run away, Laura?'

'No, no! I'm still here.'

Weakly, I got to my feet and moved towards him. I could not bear to see that proud haughty figure prevented by blindness from taking those imperious steps towards me.

I touched his arm and he reached out and caught my hand, holding it tightly in his own. My heart lurched.

'You *must* stay! It is all arranged. My grandmother has agreed and I might say it took me nearly all the afternoon to persuade her. You are not to worry about money. That, too, is all fixed. You are to receive four times the salary you get as a hospital nurse. If this is not enough, then you have only to say so.'

For a moment I could not find my voice. I was conscious only of his fingers holding mine, his grasp warm, vibrant.

'I would love to accept your very generous offer but you do not understand. My father . . .' I began.

Once again I was not allowed to finish.

'You can telephone your father after dinner and request his permission. He need have no fears for your safety—Boney will be your chaperone.'

'But I have been greatly looking forward to seeing Milan. I may never have another chance to go there . . .' I protested.

'Then go you shall—and return here afterwards,' Domenico broke in. When I made no reply, he added frowning:

'There is something else? Tell me, Laura!'

'There is the far greater problem of my job at the hospital . . .'

'We shall telephone them. I will make whatever recompense is necessary.' Domenico sounded unconcerned. 'As for the manager who arranged this complicated coach tour of yours. All these things are mere technicalities—small obstacles that can be overcome, Laura. What is important is that you *wish* to stay. *M risponda. La prego.*'

Answer me. I beg you . . .

I did not know what to say. I desperately needed time think. How could one make on the instant so momentous a decision? Of course I wanted to stay, of course, *of course!* But I had been so long a victim of my duty towards others that automatically I thought of them now. Father—how would he feel about this? And Betty? It would mean she could rarely get out because Father could not be left alone in his wheelchair. On the other hand, with so much money, most of which I could send home, Betty could, perhaps, find and pay a sitter-in. The hospital seemed the greatest difficulty. What would Matron say if I just threw up my job like that? Her anger at my irresponsibility would be entirely justified. As for the future, I could doubtless obtain another job easily enough but it might mean a change of hospital and Bartlington was so conveniently near home and I liked my friends there . . .

'Laura!'

I looked into Domenico's face and wished desperately that I could see his eyes. The thought was irrelevant and absurd.

'Laura, we have an Italian proverb—*Potea non voile, or che vorria non puote*. I will try to translate for you. It means, I think, *who will not when he can, is willing when he cannot*. You said this morning that you love Italy, especially Florence; that you are sad to be leaving. Now you have the chance to stay another month. If you go home, will you not wish you had stayed?'

It was a question to which, as he had known, there was only one answer.

CHAPTER THREE

'Vincenzio, come and be introduced to Miss Howard. I spoke of her to you this afternoon and I'm happy to tell you she has just this minute agreed to stay with us for a month. Laura, this is my secretary and companion, Signor Vincenzio Guardo.'

I looked up at the man who had just come into the room and was now standing at

Domenico's side. He was a little taller than il Conte, who I thought must be at least six foot—unusually tall for an Italian. Signor Guardo was darker skinned too. He had brilliant agate eyes and heavy dark eyebrows that seemed to meet across a high-bridged, arrogant nose. A hard face, was my first impression, but then as he held out his hand and bowed slightly in my direction, he smiled. I realised I had judged him too quickly. The haughty face softened almost to handsomeness with that curve of his mouth.

'*Come sta*, Signorina Howard!' His voice, too, was soft. I resolved in that moment to improve my Italian whilst I had the chance. It was the loveliest, most melodious language of all.

'Vincenzio has always been my right hand man. Now since my blindness, he is both right and left.'

Domenico's voice was full of warmth towards his employee. Perhaps Vincenzio Guardo was also a friend. He did not have the look of a servant. His face had the same indefinable aristocratic quality as Domenico's. Nevertheless, I still was not sure that I was going to like this man.

'Vincenzio spoils me, I'm afraid,' Domenico continued. 'Today he should have been off duty but see, he returns this evening to offer his assistance. I find such small details as putting in my cufflinks or knotting my tie strangely difficult.'

A moment later we were joined by Paolo, Domenico's younger brother. He stared at me with frank admiration.

'Well, well, well, now I understand the reason for my brother's fracas this afternoon with Nonna! Aren't you going to introduce me to this exquisite creature, *fratello mio*?'

Paolo was as much of a surprise to me as I appeared to be to him. Maybe he had expected someone older, a formal starchy sort of hospital nurse. His glance was complimentary. I, in my turn, had expected him to be very different—a younger replica of Domenico, perhaps. Instead he was not only a head shorter, but he had light brown hair which was thick and wiry and his eyes were a bright sky-blue, fringed with long dark lashes. He might have been very handsome but for the wide, sensual nostrils and too-full lips.

'Laura, this is my brother, Paolo.'

Domenico's voice was no longer warm and friendly. It was obvious that he and his brother did not like each other. I remembered Boney's remarks about Paolo and raised my eyes to take another look at him, only to find him staring boldly at me with a glance that embraced my whole figure in a rather repellent way. There was a look of amusement on his face which brought the colour to my cheeks.

'My poor Niko,' he said to his brother with

46

mock sympathy. 'What a shame that you cannot see how charmingly our little English pianist is blushing. You have no idea how young and beautiful she is—or did Boney tell you, Niko?'

Domenico's mouth tightened.

'I am sure Miss Howard has no wish to hear you discuss her in this ill-mannered fashion, Paolo. Will you please pour the drinks and make yourself useful for a change?'

But Vincenzio had already stepped towards the big heavily embossed tray which one of the servants must have left there, with bottles and goblets, before my arrival. Paolo turned back to me.

'You speak Italian, Miss Howard?'

'Only a little, I'm afraid. I want to learn much more.'

Again he gave that disconcerting smile, half patronising, and deliberately provocative. I knew now I was not going to like him.

'Then please do me the honour of allowing me to give you some lessons,' he said. 'Nothing would bring me greater pleasure. Of course, many Italian phrases are very dull, such as *"ho mal di gola!"* my throat is sore! But much is interesting such as *"lei ha bellissimi occhi"*— you have wonderful eyes . . .'

'Paolo!'

There was real anger in Domenico's voice— enough to frighten me and apparently enough to deter Paolo, for he turned away from me

47

with a shrug of his shoulders. I was glad he could not see the renewed colour in my cheeks; almost glad in this moment that Domenico was blind and couldn't see me at all. My face must be fiery red.

As if aware of my discomfiture, Vincenzio Guardo came towards me again and began to question me about the coach tour. Grateful for a safe topic of conversation, I broke into a description of the trip. My voice carried across the room to Paolo who came over to stand beside me.

'If I may ask, what exactly *is* a coach tour?' He spoke English nearly as well as Domenico but with a more decided accent.

'Don't be silly, Paolo,' Domenico said sharply. 'You know very well how such tours make it possible for many people to see a great deal of Italy in a short space of time at a price possible for the limited purse.'

Paolo seated himself on the piano stool and looked at me over the rim of his sherry glass with his glittering, teasing eyes.

'And what "great deal of Italy" have you seen so far, Miss Howard?'

I launched into another rather too rapturous account of Rome, of the beautiful drive along the Autostrada as far as Sienna, that wonderful burnt-red walled city with its tremendous gateway and doors and the square where the famous races took place; thence to the glorious city of Firenze itself. The City of

48

Flowers. I was fascinated by it, I told my listeners.

Paolo gave a low, scornful laugh.

'Tourist Italy. I'm afraid you have not seen the real thing, Miss Howard. You should permit me to become your guide from now on. I will show you Florence at night—the fascinating underworld—the heart of the city where the genuine Italian lives, loves and dies.'

'Paolo!' Domenico's voice was sharp. 'You talk nonsense. The underworld, as you choose to call it, is far from being the heart of our city. It is merely the other side of the coin—the ugly side that every city possesses. I'm sure Laura has not the slightest interest in night clubs and strip-tease. I might remind you *they* are more for the tourists' benefit than for the Florentines, anyhow.'

Paolo laughed. His voice was insolent as he retorted:

'You mentioned them, Niko, I didn't. I was thinking of the little back streets, the cafés and the amusing people who frequent them. Don't you think this might interest you, Miss Howard?'

I bit my lip. I could sense the hostility between the brothers and knew that I was really not part of this argument. There was a decided undercurrent I did not understand. In one way, of course, I agreed with Paolo. On a coach tour, one saw only what the promoters meant one to see. It would have been interesting to be taken behind the scenes and to see the old part of the city. Yet at the same time, I had no particular wish to see the seamier side.

As if he understood my unwillingness to become involved in their argument, Domenico turned to me and said:

'There is still a little time before dinner, Laura. I have not had my customary walk down to the lake to feed the swans. Would you care to accompany me?'

'Yes, of course! I'd love to.'

I wasn't quite sure if I should offer to assist him but he held out his arm quite naturally, and I led him out through the French windows onto the terrace. Above our heads the vine leaves made a canopied protection from the sun, casting a soft shadowy green shade which was cool and caressing. But beyond the terrace the gardens shimmered in a brilliant golden light that sparkled over the flower-beds, making them blaze with colour. I caught the strong musty scent of geraniums and the rich sweet spicy odour of carnations.

'How lovely it all is!' I broke out as we walked arm in arm across the green, English-looking lawns. I could hear the faint sound of breaking glass which a moment later I identified as the noise of the water falling into the fountain in the front drive. 'It's so terrible to think that you can't *see* it all as I can!' I ended on a sigh.

He laughed gently.

'Do not be sorry for me, Laura. I know every inch of this garden—in fact when it was remade a few years ago, I helped first to plan it and then to supervise the planting of each flower, each tree. I can see it in my mind.'

I remembered what Boney had told me about Paolo's wife, Helen, generously providing the money to restore the Villa dell'Alba to its former glory. The gardens must also have needed restoration. I wondered where Helen dell'Alba was now. No one seemed to talk about her, except Boney, and I did not want to appear too curious by asking questions. Perhaps Paolo's wife was away on a visit.

Domenico and I continued our walk in silence, past a magnificent display of roses, past the formal Italian garden with its dark green cypress trees and white marble statues, until we reached a little stream which, Domenico informed me, came from the hills and fed the big lake. I could see the water shimmering in the haze of the evening and reflecting the brilliant golden-red of the sun that was so soon to set.

'You will find a small bridge here, to our right,' Domenico told me. 'We can cross to the lake by it.'

He knew his way so well, he really had no need of me as a guide. But as he moved a step ahead to show me the way across the little wooden bridge, something nameless inside me made me run forward and cry out childishly: 'No, me first!'

I had no time to feel ashamed of such stupidity nor to analyse why it was so important to me to cross the bridge before him. As I passed him and placed my foot on the plank, there was a sudden creaking, tearing noise like silk being sharply ripped. The next instant, the handrail was wrenched from my grip and as I stepped back horrified, the whole structure collapsed in front of my eyes. I heard Domenico's voice, high, nervous:

'*Che cosa è? Perche non mi risponde,* Laura? Are you all right? For the love of God, tell me what has happened?'

Trembling, I stood staring down at the broken bridge, more frightened now that I knew I was perfectly safe than when I had felt the first premonition of a disaster.

'It's the bridge,' I told him as he gripped my arm. 'It has given way. It must have been rotten. I'd no sooner put my weight on it than it collapsed—just like that!'

'*Non e possibile*—it is not possible,' Domenico corrected me. 'It was only rebuilt a few weeks ago. The timber is new and it was perfectly sound. It cannot have given way like this.'

I felt an hysterical desire to laugh. It wasn't in the least funny but I couldn't stop thinking—if I hadn't run ahead of the blind man he would most certainly have fallen with the bridge. I knew enough about his eye condition to be horribly aware that though such a fall might not have been fatal, it could certainly have ensured permanent blindness.

He knelt down, feeling for the bridge with sensitive hands. Hurriedly I leaned down beside him and drew him away from the edge. As I did so, my eye caught a curiously even circular mark on one of the bridge stays. It had remained upright when the cross bars had collapsed. Leaning over I felt with my fingertips the roughened edge and involuntarily, I gasped.

'Someone must have sawn through the support,' I cried. 'Someone *meant* the bridge to collapse. Domenico, someone *meant* you to fall!'

To my intense surprise, he laughed.

'My dear child, such an idea is too ridiculous. Of course no one tampered with the wood and intended that I should fall. What a fantastic idea! It was an unfortunate accident, that is all.'

We were both standing now. Domenico's white stick had fallen to the grass. He gripped both my arms.

'You have had a fright—it is only natural you should be upset. Come—let us return to the house. We both need a drink. I will send someone tomorrow to repair the bridge.'

I shook myself free of his grasp and then in

my effort to make him understand, caught both of his hands.

'I know I had a fright,' I said as quietly as I could. 'But that has nothing to do with what I am trying to tell you. Someone deliberately cut one of the stays. It is perfectly obvious. Someone *meant* you to have this so-called accident.'

Again to my intense irritation, Domenico laughed.

'Who could possibly wish to harm me? I have no enemies, Laura. I think you have been reading too many—how do you call them—thrillers? I am quite willing to accept your word that someone sawed through the support if you can actually see proof of this, but it can only have been an accident that it was left in such a state. Maybe one of the workmen did not finish his job and the foreman failed to check it. But that anyone should have deliberately made the bridge unsafe, is ridiculous. Everyone knows that Vincenzio brings me each afternoon across this bridge, so that I may feed the swans.'

'But . . .' I broke off. As a guest of the dell'Albas, I could hardly persist in my irrational presumption that someone living on their estate wanted il Conte to die or be badly injured. Perhaps Domenico was right—it was just that a careless workman had used a bad piece of timber and the foreman had not noticed the mistake. It *could* have been an accident. *Why was I sure—so very sure—that it was not?* I had not one valid reason for supporting my theory that the wood had been deliberately cut. If I went on saying so, Domenico would obviously think I was out of my mind—doubtless I would be sent away.

Gently, he released his hands from mine. I had not realised I was clinging to him so tightly.

'If it will reassure you, Laura, I will ask Vincenzio to come down immediately after dinner and look at the bridge—he is an astute man. He will soon find out what actually happened,' he said. 'I am indeed full of apologies that you should have had to suffer such a fright. You are not hurt at all?'

'No, I'm perfectly all right.'

I stooped and picked up his stick and returned it to him. We began to walk away from the lake, back towards the house. Every now and then, I seemed compelled to turn and look back at the bridge. The sun had dropped suddenly behind the hills. The tall, graceful cypress trees, so friendly on our walk down, had taken on the sinister shapes of spectres shadowing the black grass. I felt my skin turn to gooseflesh and shivered. Far in the distance, in the heart of Florence, a bell was tolling. The sound no longer intrigued me. I was afraid of it. I wondered if I was being excessively foolish—over-imaginative. Betty chided me for living in a dream world. Yet I knew I wasn't dreaming. This was real. Domenico was real. The broken bridge was all too real. I had an absurd longing to hear Jean with her Scottish burr, telling me to take another helping of spaghetti! Or better still, Betty's slow placid voice reminding me she did the washing on Wednesday mornings and not to forget to strip my bed. I would settle even for Sister complaining that I had been slow in handing her a bowl. But instead it was Domenico who brought me back to life and warmth and reality. As we reached the house, he said:

'You saved me from an accident which might have been very unpleasant. Thank you, Laura. I am happy and grateful that you are here to stay with us.'

The hot colour rushed into my cheeks and only just faded in time for me to go back into the *salotto grande* with some degree of composure. Paolo was there, holding a half smoked cigar. He looked at me through narrowed eyes, as if wondering what his brother had been saying to me to make me look so distraught. Domenico explained about the bridge, but I think Paolo, watching my face with those searching eyes of his, guessed that I was not afraid for myself. I think he knew, even then, that I was falling in love with his brother, and I hated him for making me conscious of something I was not yet prepared to accept.

I was thankful when Mario announced

dinner and the discussion ended. Miss Bone joined us and we went into the dining-room. The meal was formally served and prolonged. Everything I ate was strange and exciting—like the dining-room itself. The food was delicious, starting with fried scampi, followed by veal cooked in claret and a crisp salad, served with a chilled white wine. After this came a cream-ice sweet and fresh peaches soaked in brandy.

Like the *salotto grande,* the floor of the dining-room was of black and green marble with a lofty domed ceiling within a circular gilt frame. The walls were panelled with black polished wood. The whole room might have been gloomy but for the glorious sea-green tints of the round marble dining table and the twelve high-backed chairs, gilded and cushioned in velvet of the same colour.

There was a bowl of yellow roses in the middle of the table and in two tall heavy silver candelabra burned six green candles. Table-silver, glass and napery were all beautiful. I had never even imagined anything so delicate as the hand-embroidered napkin spread across my lap.

Over the high marble fireplace hung a large oil portrait of a young woman in evening dress. Lace covered her dark brushed-up hair and she held a black fan. Domenico told me this was his grandmother, the Contessa Francesca dell'Alba as a young woman. The almond eyes, the haughty nose, the proud lips, were recognisable.

I sat on Domenico's right, Vincenzio on his left. Paolo sat at the far end of the table and the privileged Miss Bone opposite him. It was Vincenzio who cut up the food for Domenico. It upset me strangely to see him having to feel with his fork for the pieces and fumbling for his glass. He spilled a little wine which Mario at once mopped up. Paolo did all the talking, making light, frivolous conversation which seemed to me out of keeping with the gorgeous dining-room and dignified atmosphere.

Mario wore a livery coat and waistcoat and was assisted with the serving by a young Italian maid. Boney talked to me about the domestic staff. Mario was the major-domo, Guiseppe the chauffeur. Maria, his wife, was the cook. These two servants and Georgio, the gardener, had been with the dell'Albas all their adult lives as had she, herself, she told me. The rest of the staff came daily—young men and women from the surrounding countryside, not yet spoiled by modern life. They kept the great house clean, polished the furniture, cleaned the silver, did the washing, ironing and mending. There were five of them altogether.

I was impressed. Nine servants to look after four people! It was as well the dell'Albas were rich!

At the end of the meal Boney told me that

the Contessa had asked me to take coffee with her upstairs.

'She wishes to have a little talk with you, Miss Howard, and to thank you again for taking care of her this morning.'

'Don't be too long, Laura,' Domenico said as I rose to follow Boney out of the room. 'I shall be waiting in the *salotto* for you to play to me.'

The great hall was ablaze with lights from the two big chandeliers high above our heads, but the gallery was in darkness. I felt suddenly cold. Without knowing why, I clutched the old nanny's arm and held on to her comforting warmth as we went slowly upstairs. The gallery seemed full of shadows. I had the feeling I was being watched. At my side, Boney said in a thin quavering voice:

'*You* don't believe in ghosts, do you, dear?'

'No, of course not!' I replied a little too sharply.

'No, no more do I!' she said but I knew she was as nervous as I. It was not surprising we felt as we did, I told myself, seeking comfort from logic. In the dim light the faces in the long line of portraits running the length of the gallery, were pale formless shapes, bodiless, expressionless, like ghosts.

Then Boney turned on the landing light and I let out my breath. My silly fears vanished. The dell'Alba ancestors regained their arms and legs and bodies, the rich warm colours of the paints glowing beneath each individual strip light. The carved, gilded frames were beautiful. I paused to admire one, but Boney pulled my arm.

'The Contessa will be waiting!' she reminded me.

I realised then that the old nanny at my side was nearly as afraid of Francesca dell'Alba as I was.

'You're being silly, Laura Howard!' I told myself, straightening my back and lifting my head.

There was no single reason I could think of to be afraid.

CHAPTER FOUR

I sat down by the Contessa's bedside waiting for her to speak. Despite Boney's knock, she seemed to be dozing as old people do. I took the opportunity to look around and was instantly struck by the utter contrast between this bedroom and the rooms downstairs. The Contessa Francesca dell'Alba's personal suite had elegance but of a simple, even severe nature. There was almost a religious convent-like austerity here, with the simplicity of white walls, bare waxed floors and only one big white fur rug beside the four-poster bed. Miss Bone told me later that in this bed all the dell'Albas for the past two hundred years had been born.

It was a high, hard-mattressed bed with fluted columns. The frills and drawn back curtains were of faded Madonna blue silk, shabby and darned in places, like the brocaded bedspread. Equally shabby yet also with a faded elegance, were the blue damask covered chaise-longue by the window and the armchairs.

Over a tall, brass-handled chest of drawers hung a colourful painting of the Madonna and Child, surrounded by cherubs. A prie-Dieu stood near one of the three tall balconied windows and over it, an ebony and ivory crucifix hung against the wall. On a bracket stood a silver bowl full of Parma violets.

It was obvious, I concluded, that the Contessa was a devotee to her Faith and that in her old age she liked to pray and read her books of devotion; to shut out the modern world which I suspected she felt to be sadly lacking in either Faith or dignity.

Yet the signs of her youth when she had lived a rich, exciting life as the young wife of one of the most influential men in Florence were still evident. The wall opposite the four-poster bed was hung with a mass of gilt framed photographs of all shapes and sizes, mainly of children. Family groups, gay, smiling, happy, were pictured on the lawns in front of the Villa. There were several enlarged snapshots of relatives or friends down by the lake. I could see that lake from one of the windows, shining in the moonlight, with a pair of swans gliding across the mirrored surface. Yet for me, its beauty would always now be marred by fear.

I shivered suddenly. This room, so full of memories, seemed sad and cold—full of the echo of sighs and prayers. How sad it was to think of the passing of the years; the growing old; the lost passions and loves, the deaths. Yet in the Contessa herself, I was sure there still burned a fire I imagined to be unquenchable— her love and pride in her family.

Suddenly the old lady addressed me.

'Miss Howard, thank you for coming to see me. I believe my grandson has invited you to stay with us here at the Villa dell'Alba for approximately a month. I take it you have accepted. Tomorrow I will write a letter of explanation to your Matron.'

My face burned. It was true that on a moment of impulse I had accepted Domenico's request that I should stay, but now, face to face with this imperious old lady, I was no longer sure it was wise to do so. I knew nothing about this family; they were strangers to me as I was to them. Did I really want to spend a whole month alone in this great house where anything might happen? I thought of the bridge by the lake and shivered. I was still far from convinced it had collapsed accidentally. Suppose there was someone here who really did wish to harm Domenico dell'Alba? I might become involved . . .

'Miss Howard.' The Contessa broke in on my thoughts. 'Perhaps my grandson failed to explain your duties. You are to play the piano whenever he wishes. In a few weeks' time he is to have an operation. The waiting is hard for him. He is young, very active and cannot easily tolerate the passive existence the doctors demand of him. He found great pleasure in your playing this morning. He came to me this afternoon and told me that the days would pass far more quickly for him if he could indulge his passion for the music you can provide. You will probably be constantly at his call. It will not be a holiday. You may have to work hard for your salary.'

I saw the dark eyes raking my face and was reminded of sessions when I was called to the headmistress's study at school. One simply did not argue with Miss Beresford. Now it was proving almost as difficult to argue with the Contessa. She gave me no opportunity to explain that playing the piano for her grandson could never be termed hard work.

'I have not yet asked my father . . .' I began, but she broke in at once:

'Naturally you must do so. I am pleased that you should think of it. Few young people nowadays consider their parents. Please telephone him when you go downstairs. Domenico will instruct you how to use the instrument. And when you do speak to your

63

father, assure him that he need have no worries about your well-being. Miss Bone shall chaperone you. Her references are impeccable, and I am always here.'

'Really, Contessa, I don't need a *chaperone.*'

'But of course you do! It may no longer be the custom in your country but I shall concern myself with your reputation here in Italy, Miss Howard, just as I do with the reputations of my two grandsons.'

For the first time I felt myself bordering on an hysterical desire to laugh. The old lady was not really worried about *me.* She was afraid I might try to compromise her grandsons! The laughter reached my mouth. I felt my eyes crinkling at the corners.

'We will no doubt be seeing a lot of each other,' said the Contessa.

If she noticed my efforts not to laugh she made no comment. 'Thank you again for coming to see me, Miss Howard.' She held out her hand, coolly dismissing me.

The small wrinkled hand lay in my own. Suddenly, without knowing why, I lifted it to my lips. The skin was cool and dry. Without understanding myself I left the room, full of misgivings and no longer laughing, as I walked downstairs.

The madness of the moment when I had promised Domenico to stay had suddenly passed. But in the Contessa's presence I had been too weak to say I knew I couldn't remain after all.

I remembered how stubborn and difficult some of my older patients could be, and how frailty and strength could be combined. Francesca dell'Alba exerted an even more extraordinary authority. It was almost hypnotic. In a way Domenico was like her. I could hear the echo of that word 'Continue!'

Thinking of Domenico, I forgot about his grandmother. Tonight, at least, I would play for him. It was, after all, thrilling to know he found my music so acceptable. It was flattering, too, to think that I was allowed to play the beautiful Bechstein, untouched since his mother had died.

As I went into the *salotto grande*, I heard Domenico's voice, imperious, impatient:

'Is that you, Laura?'

He was standing by the piano. The lid was already raised. He was alone.

There is no twilight in Florence—only a transient purple quivering of the sky before the stars came out and the luminous darkness of night descended. I drew nearer to Domenico. I could see that the ivory keys of the piano held a strange violet tinge. Not that he would know for his world was dark whatever the hour. He was unaware that the lamps had not been switched on.

'Yes, I am here.' I answered him.

'You have talked to my grandmother? It is agreed you will come back and stay with us after your visit to Milan?'

The anxiety in his voice was acute. It made me reluctant to shatter his expectations. I skirted round the question.

'Not altogether. It's all very difficult. I am supposed to telephone my father and talk to him. She—the Contessa—said you would assist me in obtaining the number.'

'Later! You can speak to your father later— after you have played to me. I have been waiting all day. We can talk to your father afterwards . . . convince him of the necessity for you to remain here.'

I found myself obeying him without further comment. I sat down on the piano stool. Domenico tapped his way across the floor and seated himself on a sofa nearby. I flexed my fingers nervously. I did not mind playing in the dark. I could play by ear and did not need to see the keyboard but I feared I might strike a wrong note just because he was there, waiting, listening so intently.

I began to play and my confidence returned. The rich tones of the instrument thrilled me again . . . so totally different from that tinny horror in the nurses' Common Room or the upright at home. It was sheer joy to make music on this perfect instrument so responsive to my touch.

I forgot the man listening in the dark; forgot the old Contessa, my father, Jean, Aunt May. I ceased to feel overawed either by my audience or by the palatial splendour of my surroundings. I played Chopin's *Raindrop Prelude* as I had so often played it to my father when I was a girl. I could almost hear his voice:

'Gently, gently, now, my pet. Think of the raindrops falling on the keys. Can't you hear them? Touch those keys as delicately as they would do. Wrists, hands up, dear. Softly!'

I smiled and lived my own private world of harmony. From Chopin I slid into the stirring *Rhapsody in C Major* by Dohnanyi and was surprised and pleased to find I could remember it without faltering. I followed this with a Chopin *Nocturne* and then went on to something less intellectual but still harmonious and exciting—Richard Addinsell's *Warsaw Concerto*. After the Concerto I played *The Legend of the Glass Mountain* and the *Dream of Olwen* and finally, the strangely haunting melody from *Evita*:

'Don't cry for me, Argentina . . .'

I found myself humming it and then, without thinking, I began to sing.

'You have no real voice,' Father had once told me 'but what you do have is so delightful one likes to listen to it!'

In the shadows, Domenico dell'Alba sat still, like a man in a trance. I was only just aware of his presence and yet in a way I was playing to him—for him—as much as for myself.

At last I stopped playing and stretched my arms, feeling stiff and cramped. How long had I been here? For one hour? Two? I could not see the hands on my little wristwatch. But now the brilliant Italian moon was flooding through the tall windows, silvering the great *salotto*, illuminating the keyboard and the dark handsome head of the man stretched out on the sofa.

'Continue! *Per favore!*'

I had been expecting the command, but I answered;

'Excuse me, I cannot. I must get back to my hotel. What time is it, please?'

He ignored the question.

'You will come back, Laura, after Milan?'

'I don't know. Perhaps. Please may I turn on the light? I must look at the time. Don't you understand? My friends think I am in my hotel room with a migraine.'

I explained that I had invented this story so that I need not accompany them to the opera. When Jean returned and discovered I had not even been to bed, she would be frantic with worry.

'Then turn on the light.'

I did so. Turning back to him, I saw his mouth curving into the attractive smile I had begun to look for.

'I would be interested to know, if you will

explain, why you could not tell your friends you were dining with me?'

Once again I was glad he could not watch the hot colour flame in my cheeks.

'It is difficult to explain. Perhaps I thought they would never believe my story.' I looked at him with sudden impatience. 'You won't understand. This has always been your life, your home—this magnificent house. You take it all for granted. But to people like myself, to my friend, Jean, this is a sort of fairy tale!' I sighed. 'I don't suppose you understand what I am talking about.'

'Strangely enough I do. I have not always been rich. There were all the years of my childhood when the house was almost a ruin. Just because I am wealthy now, and a dell'Alba, I have not lost all sense of proportion, nor my understanding of human beings.'

He was close to me now. I felt his hands touching my shoulders as he had done this morning.

'If it seems a fairy tale to you,' he went on, 'why won't you consent to stay in your fairy world a little longer? Please do not go back to England yet.'

I sighed. The thought of England seemed indescribably dreary at this moment. I had a horrid vision of the endless hospital corridors, the patients, the casualties, night duty in the wards, and the odour of antiseptics and ether!

I could picture, too, our little semi-detached house among a row of others in the road. Betty and I had tried to make things bright and cheerful in the square ugly little rooms. But we had so little. A vase of cheap daffodils in spring; artificial roses from the packets of soap powder in winter. I could almost hear Betty banging her iron on the kitchen table, chattering whilst I was trying to listen to a Prom concert on the radio or TV.

For the first time in my life, I had stepped out of that world. Now I understood Father's wish that I should come on this tour. He had said it would broaden my horizon and answer my eternal question: What is life all about, Dad? Is this all there is to it?

'Life won't come to you, my pet,' he had told me. 'You must go and search for it.'

Dear old Father! He had never been practical nor had any money sense. With only his pension and what I could spare from my salary to keep us all, there was little left with which to go searching for life! I'd felt so guilty when I'd agreed to come on this tour.

But if I did return to the Villa dell'Alba after Milan, I could earn four times my usual salary. With that I could perhaps save enough to give Betty and Father a holiday, too. Betty wanted to go to Brighton or Worthing and Father would be happy anywhere where there was a garden and some sunshine. He loved the country. How he would love this garden—the fountain—the beautiful flowers!

'You have not answered my question, Laura.' Domenico's voice brought me back to the present. 'Must you go back to England? Has your change of mind something to do with the accident this evening? Was it something my grandmother said to you? Please tell me.'

'I don't know. It just seemed impossible. I *could* stay. I will stay—if it matters so much to you.'

'Thank you!'

I was surprised and touched to hear that proud, imperious voice strangely husky with gratitude.

'Now I really do have to go,' I said. If I didn't leave I would be changing my mind again—or did I mean losing my nerve?

'I've rung for Guiseppe. He shall drive you back to your hotel,' Domenico said briefly.

'Thank you. It is after ten o'clock. I must think up something to tell my friends. I don't know why I lied in the first place. It was silly of me. I'm sure Jean won't believe me if I say I went for a walk on my own after dark. She thinks all . . .' I broke off, once more flushing at the *faux pas* I had so nearly made.

Domenico laughed with real enjoyment.

'That all Italians are waiting to seduce foreign ladies?'

'I didn't say that!' I protested.

Domenico laughed again.

'But your friend Jean did! I should like to

71

meet her. On thinking it over, Laura, perhaps it would be a good idea if I drive back in the car with you. I can introduce myself to your friends and make explanations.'

Now it was my turn to be grateful.

'Would you? Would you tell them about your grandmother asking me to come back here after Milan, too?'

'I shall be pleased to do so. Think no more of it, Laura. I imagine the proprietor of your hotel will speak well of the dell'Albas. This might reassure your friends. I do not want you to lose your nerve whilst you are in Milan and never return here.'

His words made me wonder if he had read my thoughts.

Suddenly I gasped.

'I have forgotten to telephone my father! He and Betty will think me mad, spending all that money on a long distance call. Perhaps I should write, instead.'

'No!' Domenico's voice was sharp. 'I would prefer you to obtain your father's permission at once.'

So the call was put through to our little house and I found myself talking first to a thrilled and amazed Betty who answered the telephone, and then to Father.

'It all sounds wonderful, my pet!' he said. 'But what about your hospital job?'

'Yes, I know, it's awful to let them down, but I . . . I would *like* to stay.'

I explained further about the job I'd been offered. I was conscious of Domenico standing behind me, leaning on his stick. Perhaps he was amused by my efforts to explain tactfully that the dell'Albas were respectable, titled people! I felt annoyed at this unusual breach of good manners. He had no right to listen.

'I can't explain any more now, Father—it's a Continental call. I'll write and tell you everything in detail. Do you think Betty could go and see Matron on my behalf and explain?'

'The hospital may refuse to take you back in a month's time, Laura.'

'I know, Father. I'll have to take a chance.'

Suddenly, as I spoke those words I felt again that longing within me to take what the gods offered and live my life in this Villa for one whole month. It had become the most powerful temptation in the world. I wasn't going to try to resist it.

I spoke for a few more moments, trying to reassure my father as to my safety; promising also that the Contessa herself would write to him. Father replied that he trusted in my good sense and I should stay if I wished. After all, hadn't he always advised me to search for adventure and not wait for miracles to come to my door? Betty could manage without my help for a month.

I said goodbye and replaced the receiver. Then I followed Domenico back into the *salotto*.

73

'Now that is all arranged,' he said quietly. 'Would you play to me just once more before you go home to your hotel?'

I nodded my head. His insatiable desire to listen was no greater than my desire to play. But suddenly the doors of the *salotto* were pushed open. Paolo came in, smoking a cigar. He took it from his lips and eyed his brother and me through narrowed lids.

'Forgive me for intruding,' he drawled. 'I'd no idea you were still here, Miss Howard. If I had known, I wouldn't have dreamt of interrupting.'

'Miss Howard is just leaving,' Domenico said sharply.

I sighed. It seemed to me as if these two brothers were always at loggerheads. Perhaps Paolo was jealous of his elder brother's good looks; of the fact that Domenico was the heir. I wondered.

'I am about to accompany Miss Howard to her hotel,' Domenico added.

'I imagined you would!' Paolo replied with a meaningful half-smile.

I heard Domenico say something in Italian. I guessed that he was angry but I did not understand his rapid Italian.

Paolo gave me a mocking smile.

'The dell'Albas have excellent manners, Miss Howard. They were drummed into us by Father Guillio. One of his frequent instructions to us as boys was: *Aver pieta dei*

74

poveri.'

'Paolo!'

Domenico took a stumbling step forward in the direction of his brother's voice, one hand raised as though to strike him. Aghast, I looked at the two furious faces. I could feel Domenico's desperate frustration because he could not see to hit out at his brother as he wished.

Still smiling but with open cruelty now, Paolo said in a soft drawl: 'It means, Miss Howard, "Have pity on the poor". My dear brother, I hasten to say, has always been charitable to the needy!'

Domenico lurched forward, this time beside himself with anger. He lifted his white stick to bring it down upon Paolo. I just had time to see Paolo step nimbly to one side. Then Domenico's stick fell heavily on the side of my head.

The great *salotto* reeled around me. I felt an instant of agonising pain before I lost consciousness.

* * *

'Well, dear, how are you feeling?'

I opened my eyes. The room was shuttered and dim. I did not know what time of day or night it was.

'Shall I open the jalousies for you?'

'Yes, thank you!'

75

I eased myself upright and blinked as Miss Bone opened the shutters. My head throbbed and my forehead felt sore. For a moment, I did not remember where I was.

A breakfast tray was put on my lap. Of course, I was not in the Albergo Castello in Florence—I was in the Villa dell'Alba, wearing a borrowed hand-embroidered silk nightgown, lying between smooth linen sheets, with a pile of soft feather pillows, lace edged, behind my head.

I thought suddenly of Jean and Aunt May, on their way to Milan by now. A moment of panic engulfed me. I ought to be with them! I should never have allowed myself to be persuaded to stay here last night.

I remembered Paolo dell'Alba's leering face and insulting words and how his elder brother had tried, despite his blindness, to come to my defence. I did not particularly mind being called 'poor' but I knew as well as Domenico that Paolo had been trying to insult me by his remarks. That someone with his background could be so rude astonished as much as repelled me. I felt sure I could never like him. At the same time, Domenico's concern for me and his wonderful manners more than outweighed his brother's impertinence. It was at his request, for his sake, I was staying. I had not had the heart to refuse him when, horrified that he had hit me in mistake for Paolo, he had begged me to let his old nanny take me to the spare room and stay the night. He had been so anxious to make amends, it seemed churlish to insist I should be driven back at once to my hotel. Moreover, the blow had left me dizzy and sick. I let out a deep sigh. Everything was happening so fast I could not get a firm grip on events. It was too late to go to Milan now. The coach must have long since left. Whether I wished it or not, I was committed to remaining here for a month.

I was not altogether sorry to have my mind made up for me so irrevocably. My surroundings were sufficient to make any girl excited. The room was vast. Corner windows led to two balconies with sunblinds. The walls were painted a soft blue. The furniture was light, silvered wood. White rugs were on the parquet floor and a white satin spread lay on my bed. The decor was modern. On the dressing-table, which had been built into the wall, were silver candlesticks and crystal jars. A gleaming triple mirror reflected the strange sight of myself in the big bed, framed by the blue shell-shaped padded satin headboard. Dazedly, I went on staring, trying to take it all in. On the table beside my bed there were flowers and fruit and a pile of magazines.

'It's a Continental breakfast, dear. No eggs and bacon, only coffee and rolls. But I daresay you've become accustomed to Italian ways, haven't you?'

'It's fine—I love it,' I said, watching the old woman pour out my coffee into a fragile china cup. There was a rose on the folded napkin. 'It's very kind of you to spoil me like this. I could have gone down to breakfast.'

Boney seated herself on the chair beside the bed and smiled at me.

'The Contessa gave orders that you were to breakfast in bed,' she said simply, taking it for granted I understood that the Contessa's orders were never disobeyed in this household. 'Now drink your coffee, dear, before it gets cold.'

I did as she told me. The old nanny's voice also held a note of authority. I could well imagine her saying: 'Don't get your feet wet, Niko. Wear your warm vest, Paolo!' I smiled. Did the two brothers quarrel when they were little boys?

'I've a note for you from Niko.'

Boney handed me a large white envelope. As I drew out the letter written on thick creamy coloured notepaper, my fingers were not quite steady.

'Of course, Domenico didn't write it himself. He asked me to write it for him as soon as the doctor left him this morning.'

'Is he ill?' I asked anxiously.

'Oh, no, dear. It was just a precaution in case last night's little upset had affected his eye. But there was no damage done—except to your poor face. How does it feel, dear?'

I put a hand to my cheek. The bruise felt tender.

'It really doesn't hurt unless I touch it,' I told her.

I unfolded Domenico's letter and began to read:

'My brother and I are so ashamed of our behaviour last night. It was the height of bad manners at the best and unforgiveable in view of your kindness in entertaining me earlier in the evening. I would like you to know that I shall fully understand if you have changed your mind and wish to return to England. Guiseppe could drive you to Milan if you are well enough, so that you may catch up with your coach party.

I have, I am all too well aware, no right to ask you to remain here. Nevertheless, I do so. You must be aware of the anguish I felt when I realised that it was you I had hurt. I can only beg of you to forgive me, not to go away. I will not give you the embarrassment of refusing me in person. Just send me a message.

With deep concern,
DOMENICO DELL'ALBA.'

'There is no need for him to apologise,' I protested. 'It wasn't his fault. It was an accident.'

Boney's mouth was pursed in disapproval.

'So you kept saying last night when Domenico called me in to attend to you. After I had put you to bed, I had the two boys in front of me and told them to tell me what had really happened. Domenico wouldn't speak—he never was a tell-tale—but that Paolo! He spoke as though it was all a joke that had ended unfortunately. Between you and me, Miss Howard dear, the Contessa would be that horrified if *she* knew about it. I dared not tell her. I said . . . I hope you will understand . . . that you slipped and fell against the sharp edge of the table. I . . .' the wrinkled face looked suddenly humble and strangely touching '. . . I'd be more than grateful if you'd keep the truth from the Contessa.'

I caught the old woman's hand and squeezed it.

'Of course, I wouldn't dream of upsetting her. All the same, Miss Bone, I don't know if it *would* be right for me to stay now. What do you think?'

'I think you are a very nice girl!' Boney said. 'And since you ask me, I think you should stay. Apart from it being so good for Domenico—he was bored and depressed until you played that piano—there's the difficulty of explaining *why* you won't stay to the Contessa. She's that sharp, she'd soon guess there was more to it than a mere accident. I've spoken to Paolo and so, I know, has Domenico. That boy!' She ended sighing and shaking her head. 'Always in

80

trouble!'

'He's not like Domenico, is he?' I said, glad of the chance to discuss the dell'Albas. It seemed that Boney was my friend. My willingness to protect Domenico had warmed the old nanny's heart towards me.

'Not a scrap like his brother. Domenico is a good boy. I won't say he wasn't a bit wild, too, in his youth. But then any young man worth the name has to sow his wild oats. But Domenico never hurt anyone in his life, intentionally or otherwise. It's not in his nature—he's too soft. Not his will, mind. He is as stubborn as his grandmother. But he can't bear to see anyone unhappy—that's a fact. Now Paolo . . .'

I bit into a crispy golden croissant. I felt better. My headache had gone. I began to enjoy my breakfast while I listened to Boney's chatter.

'Paolo's always been jealous of his brother—right from the earliest years. He knew the Contessa's feelings towards Domenico. Mind you, I don't hold with anyone having favourites but things are different with the aristocracy. After all, Domenico is the heir, the head of the family. The Contessa never let him or Paolo forget it. I suppose it was only natural the younger brother should be resentful. And things weren't easy when they were boys. There wasn't any money then. But there . . . I mustn't stay and gossip all morning.

You're to stay in bed if you feel like it, dear. I'll come by later and see how you are.'

'Oh, but I'm fine, really,' I cried. 'I'd like to get up. And please, Miss Bone, do call me Laura. Miss Howard makes me feel I'm back at the hospital where I'm Staff Nurse Howard. I don't want even to think about it.'

The old woman smiled and patted my hand.

'Very well, dear, and you really must call me Boney like the others. I don't usually let any outsider take the liberty, but . . . well, I think you're a good girl and I don't mind admitting I'm glad you're staying. It's nice to have an English person around.'

When she had gone I slid out of bed and walked over to the window. The room overlooked the bronze horse in the fountain. It was splashing merrily, the water sparkling in the sunlight beneath a totally cloudless, postcard-blue sky. The geraniums and carnations in the flowerbeds below sent up their hot, pungent scent. It was going to be a glorious day.

I curled up on the window seat and hugged my knees. I wondered what Jean and the others were thinking. Last night Domenico had gone with Guiseppe to my hotel in order to explain everything to them and to ask Jean to pack my luggage. This morning Guiseppe was going to collect it.

I looked down at my nightgown again. How beautiful it was—rich and creamy, the feel of the silk smooth against my body. Whose nightgown was it? I wondered. Not the old Contessa's, for it was cut low at the bosom and had a revealing panel of cobwebby lace at the waist.

I felt curiously excited. The memory of last night's horrible scene and the thought of missing Milan cast only a small cloud over my mood. Perhaps I might find the time to see Milan on my way home. The Contessa had promised me an air ticket. Would this allow me to fly from Milan airport?

Something compelled me to look out of the window again. Down in the garden below Domenico was walking slowly and carefully towards the fountain. I watched the lean, graceful figure. He wore a white sports shirt and dark blue slacks. Obviously he had not suffered any ill effects from last night. It was awful to think he might have brought permanent blindness on himself through the exertion of striking that blow at his brother—and in my defence, too. The memory made me faintly uneasy. I found myself thinking about the collapse of the bridge yesterday evening. *Had* it collapsed accidentally? It did not seem possible anyone could want to harm Domenico—unless it were Paolo. Although they obviously disliked each other, I could not believe Paolo's resentment could go so far as to wish his brother blinded for life.

I watched Domenico touch the edge of the

fountain with his stick, pause and sit down on the carved stone ledge that ran under the great bowl. He let one hand trail in the water. I had a sudden memory of those long beautifully shaped fingers. They were appealing, like Dürer's famous picture—only younger, more supple.

I struggled to halt the trend of my thoughts, as I hurriedly drew back from the window. I must be careful. It would be all too easy to become romantic about il Conte Domenico dell'Alba. I must remember that I was an employee here, nothing more, and it was dangerous to think of Domenico as an attractive man—one who could stir my senses and my heart.

But nothing I could say to myself would dispel the strange aching longing to feel Domenico's hands holding mine. I felt ashamed, yet at the same time I knew there was nothing wrong in finding him attractive— so long as I kept my feelings to myself; so long as I didn't do anything crazy like falling in love with him!

'Stop it, Laura!' I reproached myself again and tried to laugh. This was too ridiculous. I was being over imaginative. I had to stop allowing my feelings to run away with me. I must think of something, someone else, at once. Pete—dear nice Pete for instance, who imagined he was in love with me. He was always saying he wanted to marry me. Of course, he knew that I didn't feel that way about him. I didn't object to a goodnight kiss, but that was as far as I meant it to go. He just wasn't my type. I had never really met anyone who was, until . . .

'Laura Howard, go and have your bath!' I ordered myself sternly.

This time I managed to behave in a more sensible fashion. My mood became light-hearted once more as I explored the bathroom leading out of my bedroom. I relished the luxury of having my very own bathroom—and a thickly carpeted one at that. The bath itself was green marble with a gold dolphin's open mouth gushing hot water. The towels were green with white fringes; fleecy, thick, large enough to envelop my body completely. The soap was perfumed, a famous Paris make.

I thought of the letter I would write home. Betty just wouldn't believe it. How could she, when I myself found it hard to credit. If Domenico did not want me to play to him, I would begin my letter this morning.

I was still in the bathroom when the maid, Lucia, knocked on the bedroom door and came in with my two suitcases. Wrapped in a bath towel I undid the larger of the cases and looked for something to wear. I chose a short pink and white flowered dress, low necked and sleeveless. Lucia also brought a letter from Jean:

'We are all agog! Needless to say, we are eaten up with envy, too. What a fabulous boyfriend you seem to have landed yourself with. A Count, too! After he had left, Signor Martell went into rhapsodies about him. Apparently the dell'Albas are one of the oldest families in Florence, and frantically rich!

We don't exactly understand about the job but good luck to you, Laura. We shall all miss you but doubt you'll miss us. If you can't be good, be careful, and don't let Romeo break your heart. I'll never forgive you if you don't write and tell me all about him.

Everyone sends love, Aunt May in particular.

JEAN.'

I smiled, imagining Jean and her aunt discussing everything in detail after Domenico's visit. I wondered what he had said to them and hoped that the girls wouldn't jump to the worst conclusions. Jean was totally wrong describing him as my 'boyfriend'. Domenico wanted me here only because he wanted to hear me play. There was no more to it than that. He didn't even know what I looked like—not unless he had asked Paolo or the Contessa or Boney to describe me to him.

'There I go again!' I told myself. I must get out of my head any silly romantic notions that

Domenico dell'Alba had the slightest personal interest in me.

Hurriedly I zipped up my dress and slipped my bare feet into white sandals. I brushed my thick fair hair, lightly coloured my lips and touched my lashes with mascara. I was reasonably satisfied with the result. I might not be beautiful, but at least I wasn't unattractive! I had a good figure, slim but curved in the right places. My legs were long and well shaped—or so Betty was always telling me . . . Pete, too, when I gave him half a chance to become personal.

'But it's your eyes which are your best point, Laura,' Father used to tell me. 'The eyes are the mirrors of the soul and yours express all that you are, my pet—honest and beautiful.'

I turned away from the mirror sighing. Domenico could not see how I looked this morning or any morning. Nor would I ever be able to gaze into 'the mirrors of his soul'. Perhaps I would be lucky enough to stay at the Villa until after his operation. I wanted passionately to see his eyes, if only once.

I heard a car come to a halt in the drive. Hurrying to the window, I looked out and saw Vincenzio at the wheel. He opened the door and helped Domenico into the seat beside him. A moment later the car had circled the fountain and disappeared down the drive.

'Let that be a lesson to you, Laura Howard!' I told myself. 'Domenico doesn't even want you to play the piano to him this morning.' That should teach me not to waste time thinking about him. He had probably forgotten my existence.

I felt deflated . . . all the sunshine of my earlier mood gone as I went downstairs. Only his letter, clutched in my hand, could give me comfort.

To punish myself further, I went over to the piano and began to play Lara's song from *Dr Zhivago*. I hoped it would work the sadness out of my system. But I found myself quite unable to concentrate. A feeling of apprehension I could not explain kept my thoughts straying. I thought of Domenico climbing into the long black car and saw it suddenly, stupidly, as a coffin. I tried to laugh at myself and this quite unwarranted silly sense of foreboding. But the memory of the accident at the bridge returned and with it a doubt as to whether that dark, silent secretary, Vincenzio could be trusted any more than I trusted Paolo. I wished Domenico would come home and dispel this strange mood. But there was no sign of the car and with a determined effort I forced my mind back to music.

CHAPTER FIVE

My letter to Father was longer even than usual. There was so much to say about the dell'Albas, the fantastic Villa in which I was now living. I had only just finished describing the terrifying moment when the bridge collapsed beneath me when Boney came into the *salotto* carrying a little tray.

'A cup of tea for you, dear. It's real English tea. The Contessa sends to London for a supply especially for me.'

The old woman sat down on one of the stiff-backed chairs opposite the leather-topped desk where I was writing.

'One lump or two, dear?'

It was a little touch of England and one I welcomed. I took the delicate china cup from Boney's hand and sipped the strong brew. I felt a sudden longing to confide in the old nurse. Writing about the accident had brought back all yesterday's fears.

'Did Domenico tell you about the bridge?' I asked.

Boney shook her head. I plunged into the story before I could think better of it. There was a veiled look in Boney's extraordinary blue eyes when I finished.

'I'd say you have a very vivid imagination, dear!' she said in the same placating tone she might have used to a child. 'As if anyone would want to hurt our Niko! What an idea! Why, everyone loves him. Not just the family, mind, but the servants, too, indoors and out. Who could possibly want to hurt him?' she repeated.

I sighed. I knew it must sound absurd yet I could not get the suspicion out of my mind that the wooden stay had been deliberately weakened. I wondered if Domenico had sent Vincenzio Guardo down to look at it. As if reading my thoughts, Boney said:

'Come to think of it, Niko was talking to Vincenzio about the bridge at breakfast. Let me see now, if I can remember what they were saying . . . yes, Vincenzio was seeing the head gardener directly after breakfast and Domenico gave orders for the bridge to be rebuilt. So you see, dear, it's all being attended to.'

'Yes, but . . .' I broke off. What use could there be in harping on my fears. Nobody else shared my anxiety. If I kept on about it I'd get the reputation for being a little mental and I'd lose my job.

'Do you ever go back to England, Boney?' I asked, changing the subject.

She poured us out two more cups of tea.

'What with one thing and another, I never have been back. I've lived here with the dell'Albas for sixty years now and nursed three generations of them.'

90

'*Three* generations?'

To my consternation the wrinkled old face was suddenly contorted with a look of acute pain. I caught the words: 'Yes, Rodrigo, Niko's father, Niko and Paolo and the little one, too.'

I was confused, not just by the tears rolling down her cheeks, but by the time factor. If she had nursed three generations, whom did she mean by 'the little one'?

She took out a handkerchief and blew her nose, attempting a smile.

'There now, I shouldn't let the past upset me!'

'Who did you mean when you spoke of "the little one"?' I asked as gently as I could.

Boney threw an odd furtive glance over her shoulder. It seemed as though she feared someone might be standing there, listening. She leaned towards me.

'Baby Tonio—Paolo's child,' she whispered. 'He . . . he died, you know. He was not quite two years old. He . . . the Contessa has forbidden anyone to mention his name. You'll never let on you know, will you, dear? I shouldn't really have told you but you being English . . . well, you don't seem like a stranger.'

She broke off, regarding me anxiously as though no longer sure she should trust me. I was shaken. I couldn't imagine Paolo in the role of a father. I wondered about the little boy who had died. How tragic for the family.

All the same, I felt that the Contessa was wrong not to allow mention of the baby or of his death. One of Father's favourite proverbs was 'a trouble shared is a trouble halved' and I was sure the psychology of that was sound. I'd noticed in hospital how much better some of the patients were after they had poured out their personal problems to a sympathetic ear. I thought of a dozen questions I wanted to ask Boney—who was the child like, his brown haired father or his English mother? And how had he died? But the dell'Albas' private lives were not my business. I knew I ought not to encourage Boney to gossip about them even though she could trust me not to repeat anything she said.

To bring the conversation back to happier ground for her, I said:

'I suppose as their parents died young, it was you who brought up Domenico and Paolo?'

Now Boney's face became wreathed in smiles.

'That I did. Who else? Nor ever left them once, though I always did mean to go back to England for a visit. But in those days the family hadn't much money and the Contessa couldn't afford high wages and expensive fares so there just wasn't enough for my ticket home. Now . . . well, I'm very old now and my only sister died years back, so there doesn't seem much point in going home. I've grown

92

more Italian than English, anyway. The Villa is my home.'

I laughed.

'Oh, Boney, you haven't really stopped being English. Sitting here with you seems to me like being back in my own home or in the hospital where I work. In a funny sort of way, you remind me of my nice Ward Sister—she's little and chirpy and kindly, like you.'

'Fancy that, dear! Well, you may be right. I *am* still English. But this is my home.'

'Tell me about Domenico and Paolo when they were little,' I begged.

'Beautiful little boys they were!' Boney scratched her ear vigorously and smiled. 'Niko so dark with those great grey eyes and long lashes. I never did see such eyes on any child. Sensitive, he was; imaginative, too. He could be strong willed, mind, but kind as anything. He used to pick me little bunches of wild flowers if he thought he'd done something to upset me. It's not so different now he's grown up, either. It's always Niko who says "Go and put your feet up, Boney, you must be tired!" Nor ever forgets my birthday. He's a good boy. He doesn't deserve his misfortune.'

'You mean—his eyes?'

'Well, that first accident to his left eye was a terrible misfortune,' agreed Boney. 'It lost him half his sight when he was only ten. But this upset to his other eye . . . I can't sleep at night for thinking about how terrible it would be if

93

he never could see again.'

I shivered. The thought was unbearable to me, too.

'And Paolo?' I quickly changed the subject.

'Oh, Paolo—well, he was a difficult child with a violent temper and always so jealous of Niko. But clever and sharp as a monkey. You couldn't tell truth from lies with Paolo he was that skilful at colouring his stories. You could never be quite sure you were punishing the right child. Looking back, I'm not sure Niko didn't get the blame for a lot of young Paolo's mischief. Still, as the Contessa says, Paolo did do the right thing by the family when he married Helen. Not that I hold with marrying for money and I told the Contessa so.'

Despite myself I was listening to gossip again. But I couldn't stop Boney now.

'Perhaps I shouldn't speak of it,' she said in a worried little voice. 'I don't know what's come over me. I must be getting old. Or perhaps it's you being English and that. I remember when I was a girl in service in England—a long time ago now, of course. I was under-nursemaid to the Honourable Mrs McArthur. After supper Cook used to make a big pot of tea and we'd all sit round the kitchen table. Nanny, too, though she could be starchy enough other times!—and we'd have a good old gossip. How we gossiped! But there wasn't any harm in it, not really. None of us would have said a word against the family

94

outside. I can remember Cook telling off the next door's parlourmaid because she said something Cook herself had been saying only the night before. There, but I'm rambling on again. What were we talking about, dear?'

'Paolo!' I all but whispered. 'And his marriage.'

'Oh, yes!' Boney said, more to herself than to me. 'I said to my dear Contessa at the time . . . it's as clear to me as if it were yesterday . . . I said: "It'd be wrong for Paolo to marry Helen if he doesn't love her, if you'll excuse me being so bold".' She sniffed and looked at me but her eyes seemed not to see me. She went on:

' "It may be the custom to arrange marriages In Italy", I said, "but I don't hold with this one and I'm sure nor does God neither. Paolo doesn't love the girl and not all the money in the world will alter that". Of course, I know they needed the money badly and she was a millionaire's daughter.'

I put my hand to my face. I ought to stop the old woman's chatter. I was a complete outsider and had no right to listen to such intimate reminiscences. But Boney went on:

'I might have saved my breath. I reckon Miss Smarty Helen wanted to have a title by hook or by crook and she won her fight before I ever knew about it—telling my poor Contessa all she'd do for the estate; painting wonderful pictures of how she would devote herself heart and soul to the dell'Albas and to

95

Paolo in particular. She made the Contessa believe Paolo was halfway to being in love with her anyway, and a little push was all he needed to take him the other halfway.'

'So he agreed to marry her even though he did not love her?'

Boney looked up and seemed surprised to see me still there.

'Oh, yes, he agreed. His grandmother told him it was his duty. Someone had to make a good marriage and Niko flatly refused to consider Helen. You've got to try to make yourself think of it all as being like our royalty, dear. *They're* brought up to realise their lives are not their own, like other people's. It's much the same for an old family like the dell'Albas. Mind you, I won't say customs haven't changed a lot since the old days, but our Contessa has never been a one for change. She's fought a terrible hard battle to keep the family's head above water. One can't blame her for wanting to see the Villa and estate grow great again.'

'So all the beautiful things here are Helen's?'

Boney looked shocked.

'Goodness me, no! They're family treasures she bought back for the dell'Albas. She did work hard to get it back I admit, and paid the bills without a grumble.'

'That was wonderful of her!' I said.

'Yes, I'll grant she kept her side of the

bargain just as Paolo kept his. But she asks more of him than he has to give. That's where it's all gone wrong. She knows the family's grateful and she trades on it. "Take me there, Paolo". "Do this, Paolo". "Do that, Paolo". When she's home there's rows all the time. Neither of them knows the meaning of the word love.'

The tea in my cup was cold. I had been so engrossed in Boney's story I had forgotten about it. How unhappy Helen must be, I thought. To have so much and yet in the final analysis, so little. I would exchange all this magnificence if it were mine, for one spark of real love.

Boney was saying:

'So you see, dear, neither Paolo's nor Niko's life is very happy at the moment. Poor Niko is facing this eye operation and it's hard on him. Your being able to play the music he loves is a heaven-sent blessing as I see it. Do you believe in Fate, dear? I do. And I think it was Fate sent you into Calmano's shop when the Contessa fainted. You were meant to come and help Niko through his trouble. Look, it even says so in the tea cup!'

The old nurse had upturned her cup and was staring at the pattern of tea-leaves in the bottom.

'Look,' she said again, pointing a knobbly finger. 'There's a horse shoe—that's luck, of course. And here an L, as plain as could be.

That's you, Laura. And an N close by—that's Niko most likely. But I don't see a journey and that means you're not going back to England yet. The tea-leaves are never wrong.'

'But it's your cup you were reading, Boney, not mine!'

The old woman met my eyes, her own vague and misty.

'It was to be *your* fortune, dearie—I turned it twice so it would be yours. Now, what was it I came to see you about? With all our chatter, I've clean forgotten.'

'You brought me elevenses,' I said as I stood up. I'd heard a car in the drive and by the unsteady thudding of my heart, I felt certain it must be Domenico and his secretary.

A moment later they came into the room and I heard his voice:

'Mario said you were in here with Laura, Boney. How are you, Laura?'

I felt suddenly desperately shy. The matter-of-fact impersonal tone of his voice made me realise how silly I was being. My heart might leap at the sight of him but he was being nothing more than courteous to me.

'Why, Niko, I thought you were going to Fiesole,' Boney broke in.

Domenico tapped his way across to his favourite sofa and sat down. Vincenzio Guardo remained standing by the door.

'So we were but we had a bit of trouble with the Ferrari. The brakes failed. We were lucky not to have an accident. As it was, we had to leave the car in a garage for repairs and hire one to bring us home.'

'An accident!' The words burst from my lips before I could stop them. Domenico turned his head in my direction and I could see his mouth break into that half smile.

'Now, Laura, don't go imagining any more horrors. I am perfectly safe and if you want the truth, we are feeling not a little foolish, eh, Vincenzio? We just rolled slowly along the highway to a standstill with queues of cars hooting away behind us not realising we were quite unable to stop.'

I looked up at Vincenzio and saw that unlike Domenico, there wasn't a trace of a smile on his face. He had not found it a joke. Yet again that sense of foreboding struck a chill in my heart. Then Vincenzio's eyes looked into mine and quickly away again as if he did not like what he saw.

'The car was serviced last week,' he muttered. 'There was no reason at all for the brake failure. It could have been serious. I have demanded a full report on the matter from the garage mechanic.'

'Come, Vincenzio, you are no better than Laura. Next thing the pair of you will be telling me the brakes were tampered with by some villain anxious to have me out of the way.'

I gave an involuntary shiver.

Domenico turned his head towards Boney

and said:

'I suppose you have been indulging in your usual "cuppa", Boney. How about one for me?'

Boney bustled off to make fresh tea. Vincenzio followed her silently from the room. I was alone with Domenico. Impulsively I went across the room and sat down beside him.

'You joke about the car, Domenico, but how can you be so sure no one tampered with the brakes? Signor Guardo said the car was only serviced last week. Don't you see, it's exactly like the affair of the bridge? That was only recently repaired, too. You could have been killed on both occasions. Why won't you *do* something—make full enquiries?'

I was frantic—too frantic to be very coherent. Domenico's calm, smiling face infuriated me. I wanted to shake him—to force him to share my own unaccountable fears.

'What exactly do you wish me to do, Laura? What has started up in your mind this extraordinary nonsensical idea that someone wishes me dead? Would I not look foolish if I went to the Police? If I said: "Two minor accidents have recently occurred and I want you to arrest someone, I don't know who, for attempting to kill me, I don't know why".'

I could hear the laughter in his voice but I felt near to tears.

'You can joke about it, but even if I can't prove I am right to be afraid, you can't prove I am wrong!' I stormed at him, forgetting that he was the head of this noble house and that I was nobody—and almost a stranger.

He laid his hand on mine. His fingers were warm and had the desired effect of calming me.

'Is it not English justice that one has to prove a man guilty, not innocent? Please, Laura, try to put these silly notions from your head. You must have been reading the wrong kind of literature about Italy. Believe me, we Italians do not go around daily trying to knife one another in the back or drop poison in each other's goblets even if such things happened centuries ago.'

I drew my hand away from his. I felt justifiably rebuked and very stupid. Yet I was not reassured. My intuition told me something was wrong here and that Domenico's life was being threatened.

I tried to convince myself that my fears for Domenico were totally unfounded. It seemed that Vincenzio's inspection of the bridge had proved my theories wrong, and he had added certain explanations which might have satisfied a carpenter but were Greek to me. As for the faulty brakes on the Ferrari, mechanical failures could happen in any car.

'But two such accidents in two days . . .' I began again as Domenico finished his explanation. But he interrupted me rather sternly:

'Coincidence, nothing more. Now, Laura, if you are not too upset, please play the piano for me.'

It was obvious he was bored with my 'nonsense' as he called it. As I walked obediently towards the piano, I thought miserably that he was probably growing more than bored with me, too. I felt resentful of this as well as hurt—like a small girl who was being punished for something she had done for the best. I knew I should let the matter drop; that in his polite but firm way, Domenico had told me to do just that. But suddenly I *had* to make one last protest.

I said:

'At least you will tell the Contessa about the accidents? I feel she may share my anxieties and . . .'

'Kindly do not concern yourself with matters outside your sphere, Miss Howard!'

His voice, cold and sharp, reproved me. It cut across my very heart. I was acutely aware once more that this was il Conte Domenico Rodrigo Leonardo dell'Alba and that I was merely one of his paid employees. The colour flared into my cheeks. Tears welled into my eyes.

He must have realised that he had hurt me for he added in a more gentle tone:

'My grandmother is not well, Laura. I do not want her disturbed by ridiculous fears for my safety which you alone are harbouring.

102

Naturally I appreciate your motives, but it is becoming an aggravation to me.'

A tear escaped and rolled down my cheek. I sniffed like the small girl he had made me feel. I sat down at the piano and banged my hands down on the keyboard. Then I gave vent to my feelings by thundering through Rota's *'Glass Mountain'*. When I had finished I turned round defiantly to see Domenico nearby with an amused smile on his lips.

'I shall never tire of listening to you play, Laura,' he said, his voice trembling with suppressed laughter. 'It is as if you were speaking with your heart, your hands. You *played* your resentment. Don't be angry, Laura, and forgive me for making fun of your fears. Really . . .' the laughter left his voice; it was serious and gentle now '. . . I am truly touched by your concern for me. Please believe that.'

I wanted to run to him, to put my arms round him, to tell him I couldn't bear his anger, his rejection of me; that when he was gentle with me there was nothing in the whole world I would not do for him. I'd die for him, if need be. But it was perfectly plain that all he required from me was my music and otherwise he wished to be left in peace!

Boney came in with the tea tray. I controlled my emotions and to amuse Domenico, began to play what I called my 'Palm Court Orchestra Repertoire'. I had to explain to him that this was an old English custom of playing light orchestral music to guests at seaside hotels, at tea-time.

'One day, after my operation, I intend to go to England,' he said lazily. 'I have heard so very much about your country from Boney and yet, amazingly, never been there. Paris, Tokyo, Delhi, Madrid, Geneva, New York—but never yet London. You and Boney must be my guides. I would like to visit your home, Laura—meet your father. I take it for granted he was the one to encourage your love of music. I have much to thank him for.'

I felt better. My heart warmed to his appreciation. I continued to play for his entertainment until Vincenzio interrupted us with a request from the Contessa that I should go up to her room.

'Oh, dear!' I said involuntarily and heard Domenico laugh.

'You sound like a schoolgirl expecting to be given a talking-to by the headmistress,' he teased me. 'You must never be afraid of my grandmother, Laura. As Boney will tell you, her bark is a great deal worse than her bite.'

Nevertheless, I could not face the stern Contessa without some misgivings.

Nothing had changed since my visit yesterday. The room was redolent of some lightly perfumed toilette water. Fresh flowers were on the delicate cream and gilt table by the centre window. The Contessa was sitting up in her big bed, a lavender silk shawl over her frail shoulders. She kept me waiting a moment or two while she finished a letter she was writing. Perhaps she knew this would make me even more nervous—or perhaps, unlike Domenico, she actually thought of me as a servant. However, she spoke pleasantly enough and bade me be seated.

'Miss Bone told me of your accident, Miss Howard. I trust you are suffering no serious consequences?'

I assured her of my good health and enquired politely as to her well-being. The faintest smile hovered round her mouth as she replied:

'Alas, at my age, one does not recuperate quite as quickly as at yours, Miss Howard. Although my fall was slight, my doctor tells me I must rest in bed a few more days. I am sure Miss Bone would say our stars are not positioned in our favour . . . two accidents— yours and mine—in as many days. That is an unhappy state of affairs.'

Her words, almost identically my own, made me sit upright with a sudden jerk.

'*Four* accidents,' I burst out impulsively. 'Don't forget . . .' I broke off helplessly, aware of Domenico's orders that his grandmother should not be informed of his misfortunes. If only I could learn to think before I spoke!

'You said *four,* Miss Howard?' How sharp and quick was this old lady, despite her age!

'May I know about the other two?'

I tried to dissemble, but I might have saved her time and mine. She soon had the truth from me although I did not make the mistake of revealing any personal concern for Domenico's safety. I said only:

'It seems very strange, Contessa, don't you agree? Almost as if someone were deliberately trying to harm your grandson. I cannot understand why he does not call in the police just to be on the safe side.'

I was totally unprepared for her reaction. Her whole demeanour changed. Her lips tightened. Her thin body stiffened. Two jet black eyes blazed at me from under the white, arched eyebrows. She spoke with icy anger:

'I do not consider it any of your business. I suggest you concern yourself with your own affairs, Miss Howard, and leave our family affairs to those who are a part of it!'

She was furious with me, yet I could not see why. However stupid my suggestion, surely she might have been interested and explained to me *why* the police couldn't be consulted. I told myself that it was probably only in England that most of us looked to our bobbies in times of need.

'Domenico . . . il Conte,' I corrected myself quickly, 'did not wish me to tell you about the accidents, Contessa. He was worried about your health. Please . . . I'd be grateful if you would not let him know how you found out.

106

I'm afraid he would be very angry with me, and . . .'

'My grandson has no doubt realised how extremely silly you are being, Miss Howard. Obviously he does not wish me to be bothered by such nonsense.' Her voice softened, however, as she added: 'Nevertheless, I will not let him know you told me. I am—or so I pride myself—a just woman and I realise I forced you to speak when you wished to remain silent. Kindly do not refer to the matter again. Now, if there is nothing more you wish to discuss, you may leave.'

I rose quickly, as anxious to be gone as she was to get rid of me. But as I reached the door, she spoke again.

'Miss Howard, I trust you have made satisfactory arrangements with your father?'

I nodded.

She went on now as though we had had no altercation.

'I am sorry you missed seeing Milan. Perhaps we can arrange a visit when Domenico no longer requires your services. We shall see.'

I felt so like a reproved child, I nearly flung back at her the fact that I now had no wish to see Milan. But it wasn't true and in any event, I did not want to give the old lady the satisfaction of seeing she had made me feel patronised and foolish.

I closed the door behind me and stood for a

moment with my back to it, staring thoughtfully down the long dark gallery at the rows of family portraits—the dell'Albas of the past—Domenico's ancestors, in rich sombre costumes, with haughty handsome faces. One day when I had time, I would study them all in detail. I wondered what it must be like to see paintings of relations who had lived centuries ago. I'd certainly like to see the Spanish grandmother I was supposed to resemble.

Suddenly my heart jolted. In the moment of tension, it seemed as if one of the dell'Alba ancestors had stepped out of his portrait. He was moving away from me with long gliding footsteps, keeping to the deeper shadows of the walls. I was frightened. The nape of my neck prickled and I felt the palms of my hands damp with sweat. But at last commonsense overcame my imagination and I found my voice.

'Who's there?' I called out.

The figure paused, hesitated as if uncertain whether to continue its flight or return.

'Who is it?' I called again.

'Le occorre qualcosa, Signorina? Do you want anything?'

On hearing the soft Italian voice, followed by the English translation, I let out my breath. I could have laughed aloud in my relief.

'Domenico! You frightened me . . .' I began but broke off as I realised that it wasn't Domenico but Vincenzio Guardo. 'Oh, it's you!' I stammered, feeling gauche and silly again. 'I wondered . . . I . . . I'm sorry.'

'*Prego!*' He bowed slightly. I could see the dark eyes searching my face as if he were about to ask me a question. Evidently he decided against it for he bowed again and disappeared down the gallery. I walked slowly downstairs, feeling oddly disconcerted. I was not yet familiar with the upstairs rooms so I could not make out from where the secretary had come. There was no doorway between that of the Contessa's room and the position I was in when I first noticed the 'ghost'. My own room was in the wing leading from the opposite end of the gallery. It seemed that Vincenzio had materialised from nowhere!

I returned to the *salotto* where I found Domenico on his customary sofa, smoking an English cigarette. I noticed again the long slender fingers, brown against the white paper. He must have recognised my footsteps, for he said:

'You've been a long time, Laura. I've been growing impatient!'

As usual, I did not stop to think before I spoke. I told him about my encounter with Vincenzio Guardo in the gallery and how he had seemed to materialise out of the wall.

Domenico laughed. He was always laughing at me. I wished I had kept my mouth shut.

'Vincenzio has been excellently trained to move quietly, to be self-effacing and to keep in the background. My grandmother could not endure the type of staff that intrudes his or her personality upon the family. She is very old-fashioned, I dare say.'

I was speechless—for once. I wondered if Domenico meant to imply that *I* was trying to force *my* personality upon the family. I need not have worried. He continued to discuss Vincenzio.

'He's a wonderful companion as well as a first class secretary. When I am alone with him, he has a great deal to say and he has taught me much. Vincenzio is more or less self-educated. I admire a man who through hard work and ambition and much self-sacrifice can better himself to such an extent. He watches and observes and is always learning. I believe I could pass him off anywhere without difficulty as a close friend or even a relative. Do you not agree, Laura?'

'I don't know,' I mumbled. I wasn't even sure if I knew how the aristocracy should behave! Domenico didn't seem to realise that I myself came from the lower middle classes.

'Vincenzio has been with me a long time now,' Domenico went on, his voice warm and full of affection. 'I have grown very attached to him. I find him a far more congenial companion than my brother, Paolo. You don't dislike Vincenzio, do you?'

'I don't know,' I said again. I think I was a little afraid of the dark, silent man who

110

hovered in the background.

'Well, since you are prey to so many anxieties on my behalf, it may reassure you to know that so long as Vincenzio is near at hand, harm will not befall me. He is devoted to me and I would trust him with my life. It may seem strange to you, and I don't think *Nonna* altogether approves, but Vincenzio has become more than my secretary—he is my friend, my very shadow. I feel a closeness to him I find hard to explain. So you see, I am not likely to meet any more fatal accidents now that he has appointed himself my personal bodyguard.'

'Has he done that?'

Domenico smiled.

'Indeed, yes. He agrees with you . . . oh, not to the extent of believing either the accident to the bridge or to the car were directed at me, but he agrees that whilst I am unable to see, I should have someone with me at all times— just in case any further misfortunes threaten me. To please you both, I have agreed that either you or he will be nearby.'

I felt as if a great load had been taken off my shoulders. Not only was I thrilled with the idea of being one of Domenico's guardians, but I was intensely relieved to know that there was at least one other person in this household who was as concerned for his safety as I was. At least it seemed that Vincenzio did not mock my fears. As soon as I could I would make

111

it my business to establish a friendly understanding with this quiet man. How silly of me to have been so frightened of him just now in the gallery! In a way, he and I were equals in this household—neither of us related to the dell'Albas, both employees, called by our Christian names, eating at the family table—yet still paid for our services. I must try to be more like Vincenzio, I thought—move quietly and unobtrusively; to be seen and not heard. Except, of course, on the piano!

Mario appeared to announce lunch. It was a delicious meal of asparagus and trout and fresh fruit, but Domenico apologised for its simplicity. I wondered what a more formal menu would be like! During coffee I caught Vincenzio's dark eyes staring at me. For once I smiled at him. He smiled back and I knew I would never again be afraid of him. He was almost handsome when he relaxed. Usually his face was lined, taut, even sinister, as though he were permanently under some kind of tension.

When we returned to the *salotto* he deliberately drew me out onto the terrace. Once we were alone he said:

'I do not wish to worry il Conte but I telephoned the garage before lunch. It was as you said, Signorina Howard. Someone had disconnected a bolt affecting the braking system of the car. The bolt is missing and I can only assume that it was loosened and worked itself out during our drive. It is quite

112

impossible that such a thing could have occurred accidentally. The car is serviced regularly by a first class mechanic. He would never make such an oversight.'

My heart jolted. All my happiness fled again. I looked up at my companion anxiously. I suppose I might have been justified in feeling satisfaction that my so-called nonsensical fears had, after all, proved far from groundless. But I could think only of Domenico and how nearly he might have been killed.

'You have told il Conte?'

The dark brows drew together.

'I tried, Signorina. He ridiculed the suggestion and accused me of behaving as foolishly as . . . as you, if you will excuse me for saying so, Signorina. Like you, I cannot prove but only suspect. One is helpless in such a case.'

'But who would want to hurt il Conte?'

He spread out his hands and shrugged in true Italian fashion.

'That I cannot answer. *I* know of no such person.'

'Can we inform the police?' I whispered. But the secretary shook his head.

'Il Conte would not permit it. There is nothing we can do, Signorina, but watch closely. We must both remain constantly vigilant. Perhaps together we may prevent further misfortune.'

I put my hand on Vincenzio's arm, feeling

now that really was a friend.

'Yes! And if either of us sees or hears anything suspicious, we will tell each other?'

'*Si certo!* With certainty, Signorina.'

Domenico came through the French window in the cool green light of the terrace. He turned towards the sound of our voices.

'Good! You two are making friends. That pleases me. When you can spare the time, Vincenzio, you must stay and hear Miss Howard play. It will enchant you as it does me. This afternoon, perhaps?'

Vincenzio looked at me apologetically and said:

'*E impossibile, Conte.* I have much work to do—some letters for the Contessa and the new books from Rome to unpack and catalogue ...'

'Another time then, Vincenzio. You don't mind playing again, Laura?'

'Of course not.'

He could have taken it for granted I would play, not just because that was my job but because I loved to please him. But I was grateful for the courteous request.

An hour of music as usual passed very quickly, I playing and singing a little, he listening in his darkness.

We were interrupted. Paolo, who had not been present at lunch, came in to say that since the Ferrari was in dock he was taking the estate car to meet Helen, his wife, at the station.

'It is very annoying!' he said like a petulant schoolboy. 'I was going to the races but it is Guiseppe's afternoon off. I wish Helen would give longer notice of her arrivals and departures.'

Then as Domenico remained silent, he turned and gave me a mocking bow.

'I must apologise for not having said *buon giorno* to you, Miss Howard. And my dear brother insists that I should also apologise for last night's little incident. I can assure you I meant only to tease you a little—but in friendliness. I had no intention of being rude.'

I could find no fault with that, but his tone was as mocking as his bow, his smile, his eyes. I could feel he was attracted to me. In that brief glance he had noticed my dress, my hair, my make-up, my sandals. I'm sure he could even have told me the exact colour of my nail varnish. He went on, addressing his brother again:

'Such a shame you cannot see how charming your English pianist looks, Niko. So delightfully cool and fresh. Which reminds me, I must go and change. Excuse me, will you?'

The door closed behind him. I felt most uncomfortable. I looked at Domenico and saw that his mouth had tightened.

'You must try, as we all do, to make allowances for my brother,' he said in a hard, formal voice. 'He does not intend to be rude when he makes such personal remarks. It is just his way. He hopes by flattery to put you at ease. I am afraid it probably has the opposite effect. Paolo has always been his own worst enemy.'

'I don't mind what he says.' The words were inadequate but I did not know what else to reply.

'There is a lot of good in Paolo,' Domenico seemed anxious to defend him now. 'At least he put the family first when . . . when it was necessary for him . . . or someone . . . to do so. I—I owe him much.'

'You mean his marriage?'

Once again I could have bitten out my tongue. Domenico's face was raised to mine questioningly.

'So you know about that? Well, I suppose it is no secret. All Florence knows, so why not you, too? Yes, it was Helen Lennister and her millionaire father who restored our fortunes; who supported us all until I was able to get the farms going once more, which I am happy to say now provide adequately for our needs.' Domenico's face was filled with a pride that I could understand. He was not the man to wish to be beholden to anyone, far less to a woman, a foreigner. 'Paolo can never be repaid for the sacrifice he made,' he added thoughtfully.

'Is he very unhappy?' I asked impulsively.

Domenico seemed to have forgotten he was talking to me, still almost a stranger. It was as if he had dammed up his thoughts for so long that, now he had begun to speak, he could not stop.

'Not entirely so. I suppose Paolo gets more from his marriage than I . . . or another man might have done. Wealth is everything to my brother, the mainspring of his existence. Money is his life's blood. He needs fast cars, race horses, gambling, drinking, parties, holidays in expensive resorts. Until he had all these things, Paolo was only half a man. He meant to get them one day and they came in one big parcel with Helen.'

'Then he cannot complain. And his wife . . . is *she* happy?'

'No, Helen will never be content. She was born to want what she cannot get. That is her nature. I fear she will always be a frustrated, discontented woman.'

He broke off, stubbing out his cigarette angrily, as if suddenly aware that he had an audience. I knew he was regretting his outspokenness. I said quickly:

'Please don't feel badly about telling me these things. People often confide in me. At the hospital, my patients come out with personal stories they would never normally speak of to a stranger. Sometimes I feel I'm like a doctor or a priest under seal of confession. I'm used to receiving secrets and honouring them!'

'Are you, Laura? You sound too young to

me to have to carry the burden of so many souls' confessions and confidences. How old are you? Twenty-three? I am nearly ten years older. I feel a hundred years more.'

'That is only because you have so many responsibilities,' I burst out. 'And because you are worried about your coming operation. Once you can see again, you will feel much younger. I'm sure of it!'

I watched the expression on his face change from tension to laughter. It gave me the strangest depth of satisfaction to think that I had the power to do this to him.

'Funny little English girl—so wise a head on such young shoulders!'

I knew he was teasing me but I didn't mind. I loved him—*loved* him; so acutely that it hurt my heart with a physical pain. I knew it was madness. I meant nothing to him. That didn't matter. Nothing mattered now but this longing to keep him smiling and happy; to keep near him, near enough for me to be able to watch his face, hear his voice.

I turned back to the piano and without thinking, began to play the opening bars of Lara's song. I heard Domenico draw in his breath sharply. I paused.

'No, don't stop!' he cried out. 'I love that melody. Sometimes I play that song on my balalaika. It is so sad, so beautiful.'

So now I had this to share with him, too. For me, the song would mean my love for

Domenico, just as in the film it had meant Dr Zhivago's love for Lara. As I came to the end, I felt unbearably like Dr Zhivago. I, too, was destined to lose my love. And Domenico—what would become of him? Who was his love? Some beautiful Italian girl of whose existence I knew nothing? Perhaps tomorrow, or even tonight, the doors of the *salotto* would open and Mario would announce Domenico's *fiancée,* or even his mistress! If such a thing were to happen, I would want to run away from this house and never come back.

'Continue, please.'

I let go my breath, unaware that I had been holding it so tensely; unaware that I had been clenching my hands together in private agony. How silly I was being to imagine the pain of leaving this man before it had even happened.

'Be happy, Laura!' I told myself. 'Be happy while there is still time!'

CHAPTER SIX

My first sight of Helen dell'Alba both surprised and intrigued me. I had not expected anyone quite so impressive. She stood in the doorway of the *salotto,* framed by the lintels like a picture. Despite the long journey from London she still looked cool and chic in a pale, coffee-coloured linen suit. Her wide-brimmed straw picture hat was white, like her shoes and travelling bag. Beyond her, in the hall, I caught a glimpse of expensive-looking rawhide suitcases and boxes.

'Well, here I am—home!' she announced as Domenico rose to his feet and I sprang up from the piano stool.

With her rather Junoesque figure—she had wide hips and full breasts—Helen was decidedly striking, and I think she knew it. She walked over to Domenico and kissed him, not as an Italian might, on both cheeks; not as an English sister-in-law might, on one cheek, but on the mouth. I gazed stupidly but Helen's back prevented me from seeing Domenico's reaction.

'Niko, darling! How lovely to see you. You're looking well—as handsome as ever!'

Her voice was high-pitched. To me, acutely aware of this woman, it sounded artificial, forced. I reminded myself that she wasn't really *nouveau riche*. Her father, so Boney had told me, had given her an expensive, cosmopolitan education. She was a poised woman of the world, the wife of an Italian nobleman.

I noticed Paolo standing watching Helen. His mouth was drawn down, his eyes angry. Catching my gaze, he gave an imperceptible shrug of his shoulders and spoke to his brother:

'Surely you can find a few welcoming words for your ever-loving sister-in-law, Niko?'

I felt the barb behind the words; saw Domenico's expression grow tense and wary. Paolo was jealous. So, for that matter, was I. I'd never seen such glorious Titian hair as Helen's, piled into a shining, curling twist at the back of her head. Her eyes, too, were magnificent—long, slanting, a deep tawny green. No one had told me Paolo's wife was beautiful.

'Welcome home, Helen. You had a good trip, I trust?'

By now I was familiar enough with Domenico's voice to recognise the coolness of his tone. The reunion was not as pleasing to him as it was to his sister-in-law. Hating myself for the satisfaction this gave me, I was happy again.

She turned away, her mouth petulant.

'Not bad, but I'm tired. Tell someone to take those cases up to my room, Paolo.'

She looked across at me, a long critical stare. Clearly I did not impress her. She nodded her head indifferently and said:

'You must be Laura Howard. Paolo was telling me about you and the strange circumstances which brought you to the Villa dell'Alba. Now that you are here, I hope you won't be too bored having nothing to do but play the piano all day.'

The words were civil enough but somehow I

121

knew that I wasn't going to like Paolo's wife, nor would she care for me. She made me miserably conscious of my cheap dress, my simple hair style and lack of sophistication.

'Forgive me, I should have explained that Laura . . .' Domenico began, but Helen cut him short:

'Not now, Niko. I'm tired. Right this minute, I want a bath and to change out of these clothes. I'll see you at dinner.'

Paolo followed her out of the room. I pretended not to see the look he gave me as he left. I felt myself blushing. I was beginning to hate that look. Somehow it cheapened me. It was as if he took it for granted I'd be attracted by him.

I thought about Paolo as I changed for dinner. I had to admit to myself that some women might well find him attractive with those light brown curls, reminiscent of a painting I had once seen of a Greek god, and those incredibly blue eyes. He was palpably sensual by nature and his manner of looking at a woman was instantly suggestive. But I wasn't attracted. I was repelled and now that I had seen Helen, his wife, I could not understand why he should bother with me, an unsophisticated English girl. Helen was strikingly handsome—something I could never be. She was wonderfully turned out and her manner was imperious.

Later that evening I was on my way down to

the *salotto* to await the announcement that dinner was served when Helen called to me from the gallery. I paused and looked up at her where she stood, one hand on the polished banister.

'Come here a moment. I want to see you.'

Surprised and not a little curious, I went back up the staircase and followed her into her bedroom. The sight of it brought a little gasp from me.

Everything in the room was white—the close-fitted, thickly piled carpet, the satin bedspread, the painted Louis XV furniture. Even the flowers were white roses, carnations and madonna lilies. Only a touch of gold design on the furniture, and edging the cushions and bedspread, relieved the immaculate purity of the snow-white decor. The effect was stunning, the more so because of the dimensions of the room. It was almost as big as the *salotto* below and the ceiling was equally high, a masterpiece of moulded white and gilt plaster.

The long windows were framed in magnificent white taffeta curtains, ruched and frilled and looped up with gold tasselled ropes. Even the awnings shading the room from the hot Florentine sunshine were striped white and pale gold.

In the centre of the room stood an antique table with a top of semi-precious stones which glittered and scintillated with every change of light.

But the pristine beauty of the elegant room was spoiled by open wardrobes and drawers, scattered clothes, cigarette ash over the carpet, a coffee stain on the counterpane.

Helen was wearing a white satin dressing-gown. Her hair flamed loose over her shoulders. She was watching my face, amused no doubt by the impression her room had made on me.

'Come in, Miss Howard. Sit down.'

She pointed to a small white and gold satin armchair. As I sat down she went across the room and opened the doors of a vast built-in wardrobe that occupied the whole of one wall. She began to pull out various dresses, ripping them from their hangers and flinging them onto one of the twin beds nearest to me. I was horrified to see all those beautiful clothes piling up in a growing disordered heap.

'Do please let me fold them for you!' I cried, jumping up at last.

'Don't be silly—I don't want them folded—they're for you.' She glanced at me and shrugged her shoulders. 'Don't look so staggered—they aren't new. I've bought a mass of new clothes in London and I need the room in my wardrobe. Don't you want them? That sugar-pink wool is a Mary Quant. It would suit you. And that blue Yves St Laurent, try that.'

I was staggered and my cheeks grew hot as I touched some of those expensive garments so

124

carelessly discarded. Each one was made of some rich costly material. There must have been at least twenty dresses and suits. I couldn't even begin to estimate their value—I just knew I had never in my life had enough money to buy one of them.

'Well, for heaven's sake, *take* them,' Helen said irritably. 'And whilst you're at it, you can have these, too.' She opened a large drawer and threw a pile of jerseys onto the bed. There were delicate cashmeres, soft fluffy angoras, Shetlands . . . in all colours. Scarves and bags and filmy lingerie followed. It was unbelievable.

'Are you *quite* sure you don't want them?' I asked, holding one of the dresses against myself covetously. I wanted them all right, but somehow I didn't like taking them, not from a complete stranger and particularly from Helen.

'Of course I don't. If you don't want them, ring for Lucia, my maid. She can have them, if you prefer, but I must get rid of them. I need the space for my new clothes.'

Hurriedly I bundled them over my arm. There were far too many to carry in one go. I raced along the gallery without even stopping to look at the haughty ancestors. I dumped the lovely things on my bed, then went back more slowly to Helen's room to collect what remained. I was hating myself for being so greedy and yet I didn't really hesitate. I'd so often longed to own just one really expensive garment. Now I would have enough to give something to Betty and to Jean, too. We were all good with our needles. Those clothes that didn't fit or seemed out of date, we ourselves could alter. Anything made from such wonderful fabrics would look good.

'Thank you, thank you!' I stammered.

'Forget it. I don't want your gratitude. You can do one thing for me though . . .' she paused, looking at me with the strangest expression. I stood waiting, wondering what it was she could possibly want of me. Then she turned away so that I could not see her face. Her voice was a little strained as she said:

'Paolo tells me you usually play the piano to Niko in the evening. Well, do me a favour and go to bed early tonight, will you? I want some time alone with my brother-in-law.'

'I must play for Domenico if he requests it,' I said uneasily. I now wondered if, after all, the clothes were a spontaneous gift or if they had been meant as a bribe. I was no longer sure I wanted them. I went along to my room and sat down beside the dresses. I stared at them almost horrified. Unconsciously my hands began to fold them out of their creases. I'd been brought up to take care of the few clothes I had. If only I could be sure these heavenly things were true emblems of Helen's generosity, I would be happy to wear them. But to be bribed—*bribed* by clothes to stay away from Domenico so that *she* could be alone with him . . . that was unthinkable.

Suddenly, I knew exactly what I would do. Immediately after coffee I would suggest retiring and then see what Domenico replied. If he asked me to stay and play to him, I would. I could always return the clothes. No one—least of all Helen—was going to make me refuse anything Domenico wanted of me.

But as I made my way down the stairs for the second time, I was miserably afraid that Domenico might welcome an evening's tête-à-tête with his sister-in-law.

I need not have worried. Domenico was alone in the *salotto* and as I went in, he recognised my step and tapped his way towards me.

'Laura!' he said, his voice urgent, 'I know you may think this a strange request, but will you please play for me after dinner tonight? It doesn't matter if there are others in the room—just play and continue playing, no matter what anyone says. Would you do this for me?'

I was at a loss for words. Obviously Domenico did not wish to be left alone with Helen—yet I had more or less promised her I would make myself scarce.

'You don't want to play tonight? You are tired? Why don't you answer me, Laura?'

'It . . . isn't that! I'd love to play but . . .'

'But what?' Domenico pursued remorselessly.

'Wouldn't you prefer not to have strangers around on your sister-in-law's first night at home?' I stammered.

I got no further for Domenico took a deep breath and said in a cold hard voice:

'There can be only one reason why you are unwilling to play for me, Helen has asked you to absent yourself. Can you deny it?'

I blushed and tried to prevaricate but Domenico insisted upon the truth. Reluctantly, I admitted it, adding that Helen had been very generous. Domenico's frown deepened and his mouth took on a tired, pained expression.

'You are still so young, I cannot expect you to understand what goes on in this house,' he said as if he were years and years older than I. I could not help myself. I cried out:

'I am not too young to know that you are reluctant to hurt Helen because you are grateful for all the money she has poured into the restoration of this marvellous place.'

I could have added that I strongly suspected she was in love with him, but I managed to restrain myself.

I held my breath, waiting for his anger, his reproof, his demands for an explanation as to how I had arrived at such a conclusion. But he said nothing. Instead, he reached out and touched my bare arm, running his fingers gently over my wrist.

'Strange, that you should be so near the truth,' he murmured. 'Strange that you do not seem to be any longer a stranger.'

I dared not speak. His touch and his words were like a strong wind fanning the already glowing embers of my love for him. I had known him only two days and yet I no longer had a single doubt that I loved this man totally, absolutely and irrevocably. My heart was no longer controllable. It didn't belong to me any more. It was his, for always and always.

The door opened. Vincenzio Guardo came in, shattering the silence, destroying the magical moment. He gave me a long searching glance and I knew that he had seen Domenico's hand drop swiftly from my arm. I wondered what he must be thinking and in the same second, knew that I didn't care. Let the whole world think what they liked. I was not ashamed of loving Domenico. I wished that he felt the same way and hadn't taken away the warmth of his fingers so hurriedly, as though afraid to let anyone see how he felt about me.

During dinner that night I found it hard to talk. It was a much more formal meal than those we had had so far, with two servants handing round the dishes, one course after another. Three tall candelabra lit the table. The crested silver, the shining Venetian goblets caught and reflect the candlelight.

Helen sat at the far end of the table, facing Domenico. She wore a peacock blue chiffon dress which seemed both to cling and float around her. Her red hair was tied in a chignon once more and there was a diamond clasp in the thick shining strands brushed to one side of her white forehead. The dress was cut low, revealing the curves of her breasts, unadorned by any jewellery. She certainly knew how to make the best of her looks, I thought, miserably conscious of my simple white dress.

Helen carried most of the conversation. She was vibrant, restless, feverishly alive. But for the fact that I knew she had had only one glass of sherry before dinner and merely sipped her wine during the meal, I would have thought she had been drinking. Her gaiety and rapid, high-pitched speech, her shrill laughter and the occasional long sensuous looks she fastened on Domenico, all seemed to denote that she was not quite in control of herself. Her green eyes seemed larger than ever, glittering and somehow dangerous. I was glad, childishly and jealously, that Domenico could not see her, could not compare her with me.

Paolo, like myself, had little to say. He drank a great deal of wine and only toyed with the food. The only glance he gave his wife during the whole meal was one of intense dislike when she publicly reproached him, saying:

'Don't drink so much, Paolo. It makes you behave like a sex-starved stallion!' The words were spoken in English but loud enough for us all to hear.

I thought Paolo might throw his goblet of wine at Helen. Her words were so insulting that I almost felt sorry for him. I stole a quick look at Domenico's face, but it was inscrutable, as if he had not heard Helen's disgraceful remark. I did not dare to glance at the servants but I could see Vincenzio's hands clench till the knuckles showed white. The atmosphere was electric.

Paolo made the quickest recovery. He finished the remainder of the wine in his goblet and beckoned one of the servants.

'*Ancora!*' he said briefly, and sat smiling to himself as the dark red wine was poured into the goblet still clenched in his fingers.

I felt a touch of admiration for him. Boney had said that Paolo had met his match in Helen. Helen, too, had met her match in Paolo. He showed her with that one word and gesture how indifferent he was to her commands.

If Helen was annoyed she gave no sign. It seemed to me that although she had wanted to provoke trouble, she had already forgotten it. She began to relate a highly coloured account of the racing at Ascot.

Quite suddenly, as I watched her, I realised what had puzzled me about her manner. Of course she had not had too much to drink! Her behaviour was synonymous with that of a drug-taker. I was horrified, fascinated, appalled and absolutely certain that I had hit on the truth. I'd seen people under the influence of drugs in hospital—some old addicts—quite a few teenagers. They had presented the same symptoms; excited, restless, hysterical, living in a mad dream. I'd seen, too, the dreadful after effects. I wondered how Helen coped with the terrible aftermath and ghastly depression, the illness that must surely follow the hours of crazy elation. I wondered whether she was an 'habitual' or if this was just an isolated occasion. Something told me that she was all-too probably an addict. Possibly nobody knew about it. Perhaps they imagined her to be a nervous hysteric and were sorry for her. Poor woman! I too was sorry for her. I wondered if I had any hope at all of persuading her to give it up. I doubted it. As a trained nurse, I could present her with all the grizzly facts as to what happened in the end to people who took drugs, but I couldn't imagine her listening to me. Only someone whose opinion she truly valued might be able to help her, convince her of the necessity for putting herself under medical care. I knew most addicts rejected help and refused even to admit they needed it.

Involuntarily, my head turned towards Domenico. If she was really in love with him, perhaps he could exert some influence over her? Did he know? Did anyone know? Boney? The old Contessa? Paolo? I felt pretty sure Paolo was aware of it. Maybe it was he who had started her on the downward path.

I pulled myself up sharply. My over-active imagination was running away with me. I'd no reason to suppose Paolo was corrupt just because I did not like him. I must stop interfering even in my mind. These matters were simply not my concern.

Now the servants were bringing in two big dishes piled with fruit—peaches, nectarines, apricots and grapes. To me it was a banquet and every meal here like a Christmas spread. Everything was so luxurious, so beautiful. Yet the deeper I delved into the magical pool, the murkier I found the water. At first, the dell'Alba family had appeared so great, so superior, I had been a little afraid even to step inside the Villa. Now that I was in—right in the heart of it, I was discovering all too quickly that the dream had a nightmare quality. I was afraid. I didn't want my dream world wrecked. Only Domenico retained for me the image of greatness, of a being I could respect. But if I got to know him better, would I find this dream, too, was tarnished? I found myself wishing fervently that I was in Milan with Jean and Aunt May—or with Father and Betty.

I longed to leave the place now, this very minute; run away before the bubble burst. I wanted the safety, the familiarity of home, of Father who was too old to change; of Betty who was incapable of change. I wanted the solid earth and rocks beneath me, not the stars and darkness of night that went with them. I didn't want to be in love with il Conte Domenico dell'Alba. I didn't want to go on worrying whether someone was trying to kill him; whether Paolo was going to embarrass me with his unwelcome attentions; whether Helen would find the power to hurt me as she was hurting herself.

I wanted to be waiting in the rain for a 94 bus to Caldicot Road. I wanted the laburnum tree on the cat-scratched dusty lawn outside our house, the taste of kippers for tea. I even wanted the temperature charts, the hospital trolleys, the white shining pile of bedpans. I wanted Pete's voice hoarse with shouting at his favourite football team; the prod of his elbow in my side as he said: 'See that pass, Laura!'

Then I felt a hand on my arm, the merest breath of a touch. I heard a voice beside me saying:

'Are you all right, Laura? You are so quiet. Please tell me you are still there!'

And I knew I had been lying to myself after all. I wanted no one else but Domenico—nothing but that touch of his hand and the sound of his voice saying: *'Please tell me you are still there, Laura!'*

CHAPTER SEVEN

Coffee was served in the *salotto*. Obedient to Domenico's instructions, as soon as I had finished mine, I went to the piano and started to play. I was glad my back was turned so that I could not see Helen's face. She talked loudly as though deliberately trying to drown my music. Vincenzio retired silently from the scene and shortly after Paolo excused himself, saying he had to meet a friend in Florence for an hour or two. Helen burst out:

'Must we have that background noise, Niko? I find it a bore trying to talk through it.'

I stopped playing, my cheeks burning. But Domenico said:

'I enjoy the music, Hclen, but if you are tired after your long journey, would it not be a good idea for you to have an early night?'

If I had been Helen I would have run from the room. But she only laughed, saying:

'Trying to get rid of me, darling? You forget, I think, that Grandmama would not think it very proper for you and your pretty little English pianist to remain here unchaperoned, so until Miss Howard goes to bed, I shall *have* to stay, won't I?'

My cheeks burned an even hotter red. Helen's remark was so suggestive, it could not be misunderstood. Domenico remained unruffled, to my surprise. He made a joke of it.

'You and I both know that in England young ladies do not have chaperones, Helen. My grandmother must learn to accept the modern ideas.'

At length Helen recognised defeat. I suppose I could have retrieved the evening for her by going to bed. But I stayed because *he* wanted me to, despite the request she had made earlier in the evening. Five minutes later, she left the room, bidding Domenico a curt good night and ignoring me altogether. I knew I had made a bitter enemy.

But she was soon forgotten as Domenico and I lost ourselves once more in an orgy of music. Once I stopped playing for a moment to rub my eyes and Domenico asked me what was wrong.

The room was ablaze with lights, I explained and my eyes were hurting me.

'Then turn out the lights,' Domenico laughed. 'I am in the dark anyway. You shall share my world of blindness.'

I turned them off. Moonlight flooded the room and made it look mysterious and enchanted.

'If only you could see how beautiful it all is!' I cried involuntarily, and then, to make him 'see' in his mind, I began to play *The Moonlight Sonata*, my favourite of Beethoven's sonatas. For a little while after the last notes had died away, we sat in silence. Then Domenico said in

136

a low voice:

'Thank you, it was perfect,' and added: 'Do you know the *Bedouin Love Song*? I sometimes play it on my balalaika.' He hummed a few bars and I recognised it instantly as one of my father's favourites.

'The music, yes,' I nodded, 'but I'm not sure of the words. *"I love thee, I love but thee . . ."* ' I broke off as my voice became husky. Then Domenico's voice came out of the darkness:

' *"Till the sun grows cold, And the stars are old, And the leaves of the Judgement Book unfold . . ."* Play it for me, Laura.'

I played, but I could not sing. The words were too poignant . . . too full of truth for me to trust my voice. At the end, I faltered. The tears were running down my cheeks.

'Why don't you go on? What is wrong, Laura? Is it that you arc sad tonight? Or tired? Has something upset you?'

'No, I'm all right—I'm not at all tired.'

'Do continue then, please.'

The words made me smile through my tears. I resumed my playing, but chose a different, less emotional song this time. A band of moonlight lay across the ivory keyboard. I watched my fingers rising and falling. Suddenly, a shadow fell across them. I turned my head. I had time to give one tiny gasp before a hand covered my mouth. My hands faltered.

'Something is wrong, Laura,' said

Domenico. 'What is it?'

Terrified, I met Paolo dell'Alba's glittering eyes. His brows were raised as if in question. He glanced in Domenico's direction, then coolly, deliberately, he touched my breast. I opened my mouth to cry out but in the same moment, I realised what would happen if I did. Domenico would jump to my defence as he had done the previous evening. He might try to strike his brother again and this time hurt himself, damage the delicate nerves of his eye.

I felt sick and tried to twist away from Paolo's hateful touch. He merely sat down beside me, so quietly that he made no sound, and pointed to the keyboard. If I was not to provoke a scene, I had to go on playing. Paolo was running his fingertips over my shoulder, along my neck, down my arm and once more to my breast. My horror was so intense that I nearly screamed in protest. I could not prevent a second little gasp.

'Forgive me, Domenico, but I can't go on. Excuse me, please!'

'But, Laura . . .' His voice, filled with anxiety, followed me as I edged away from Paolo towards the door. Stealthily, without a sound, Paolo followed me across the room.

'Laura, don't go away,' Domenico said more sharply. 'Something is wrong. I feel it. I could hear it in your music. Tell me, please. It isn't fair to take advantage of the fact that I cannot see. Where are you? Have you gone? At least say goodnight to me before you leave.'

I reached the doors first, but Paolo put his arms on either side of me, preventing me from opening them. I felt first his hot breath, reeking of brandy, then his lips coming down on mine in a hard, terrifying kiss. He forced his tongue between my teeth and I ceased to be aware of Domenico's presence in the room. I bit hard on those desecrating lips and felt the man move away at last. I fumbled for the door knobs, wrenched open the doors and ran.

Behind me I could hear Domenico calling:

'Laura, come back. Don't go without saying good-night.'

Up in my room I lay on my bed shivering. At least an hour passed but I could not rest. One moment I decided to leave this place; the next I knew I couldn't go. My love for Domenico was so much stronger even than my horror and fear of his brother. I thought once more of Paolo's extraordinary behaviour. Had he felt no fear that I would cry out, betraying his presence to Domenico? Or that his brother, with his heightened hearing, might have detected his presence by his breathing— or mine? Or was Paolo quite mad?

Suddenly I realised that I had run away leaving a blind helpless Domenico alone with his lunatic brother; that there would be no sleep for me this night if I were not reassured as to Domenico's safety. At last, unable to bear my thoughts, I decided to go back to the

139

salotto. I pulled on a pair of jeans and a sweater and barefoot, I tip-toed out onto the landing. To my surprise, tiny bars of lights showed all along the gallery. No one, it seemed, could find sleep tonight. There were lights on in the Contessa's room; in Vincenzio Guardo's; in Helen's. I did not know where Paolo or Domenico slept.

Making no noise at all, I made my way down one of the two great staircases. Only the moonlight lit the huge entrance hall. I could see the doors of the *salotto* were open and through them, the Bechstein, with its lid still raised. The ivory keyboard gleamed softly. I reached the bottom of the stairs and stood staring into the room. Was Paolo still in there? Somehow, tomorrow, I would have to face him, try to behave as if nothing had happened. He must have been drunk, I told myself. No man in his right senses could behave in that disgraceful way with his blind brother actually present. Disgust overcame my fear of him. It seemed impossible that he could be Domenico's brother.

Suddenly I caught sight of a shadow beyond the open French window. My skin prickled and for the second time that night, I felt an agonising fear. My legs trembled and my hands broke out once more in a cold, damp sweat. The shadow moved again and horrified, I caught the glint of silver in the dark gloom of the vine-covered terrace. Whoever was out there had a knife.

'Paolo!' I thought. He must truly be insane. But almost at the same moment, my mind rushed to Domenico. Was this his unknown assassin? Where was Domenico? In bed or still in the *salotto*?

Full of stark terror for him, I hurried into the *salotto* and halted as I saw Domenico, still on the yellow sofa where he had been sitting when I ran out of the room hours ago. But now his head was resting against one of the cushions and I knew he had fallen asleep. Quickly I looked back at the French window and saw the shadow move once more.

'Domenico!'

I screamed out a warning as I ran forward to throw myself between him and his would-be attacker. Someone came towards me and involuntarily, I closed my eyes, waiting for the feel of the knife I knew was raised above my head. Fear held me paralysed. I heard two voices speaking then, in rapid Italian, felt an arm, Domenico's, round my shoulders, and I opened my eyes. Still immobilised by fear, I looked up and saw Vincenzio Guardo staring down at me. The bright blade of the dagger in his hand scintillated as the moonlight caught the steel.

'Pull yourself together, Laura!' Domenico's calm voice brought back some semblance of reason. I clung to him without realising it, whether to protect him or because I myself felt

141

so badly in need of protection, I don't know. Once again, the two men spoke in rapid Italian. Then, with a little bow, Vincenzio slipped away back into the garden, leaving me alone with Domenico.

He drew me down beside him onto the sofa, keeping one arm about my shoulders. I could not stop trembling. After a moment or two, he said: 'Now tell me what you were doing down here, Laura.'

'I couldn't sleep . . . I came down to see if you were all right. I was looking into the *salotto* from the hall when I saw . . . I saw . . .'

'You saw Vincenzio.'

Suddenly all my fears returned in full.

'He was going to kill you, Domenico. I know he was. I saw him coming towards you with that horrible knife in his hand. He isn't your friend . . . he wanted to kill you . . . he . . .'

'Be quiet, Laura. Stop it. You are hysterical!'

He wasn't far wrong. I was crying without knowing it and shivering violently. With a stupendous effort, I pulled myself together. I saw Domenico feel his way across the room, heard the clink of glasses. Then he came back to me, holding out some brandy.

'Here, drink this. You had a fright. My poor Laura! It seems you live in a world of nightmares and illusions. It astonishes me. Now don't talk, drink this brandy.'

When Domenico spoke in that tone, I

obeyed. But revived by the strong spirit, I couldn't keep quiet.

'It was no illusion. I didn't *imagine* any of it . . .' I began. 'I saw . . .'

'Yes, I know you did!' Domenico broke in, and now I could actually hear laughter in his voice. I pulled away from him angrily. Why wouldn't he take me seriously? 'But you misinterpreted what you saw, my child.' I stiffened at that word. There were times when I hated him—or would have hated him if I didn't love him so much. 'Vincenzio *was* out on the terrace and he was holding a knife. But, like you, he was protecting me.'

'*Protecting* you!' I gasped. 'With a *knife*?'

'Why not with a knife?' Domenico sighed. 'I think this whole house has gone a little mad all of a sudden. Vincenzio appears to feel as you do, that someone wants to kill me, though heaven knows why! He had felt like a walk before retiring and found the French windows open and me asleep on the sofa in here. He did not want to close the windows for fear of disturbing me but at the same time, he did not like the idea of my lying exposed to any prowler. You see, Laura, how you are not the only one with a vivid imagination! So Vincenzio decided to sit out there on the terrace on guard. Suddenly he heard someone approaching the *salotto*. Quite naturally he stood up and unsheathed his knife. He saw a shadow move across the room towards me and

143

sprang to my defence. Really, it has a very funny side, do you not agree? My two defenders defending me from each other?'

I felt the tears drying on my cheeks which were beginning to burn with my embarrassment. No wonder Domenico laughed at me. If I were not feeling such a stupid idiot, I might be laughing at myself.

'I'm . . . sorry!' I muttered, feeling unbelievably foolish.

'Don't be! I am touched by your concern, Laura, and by Vincenzio's. I just do not understand why the two of you should be so certain I have a mortal enemy. I cannot make either of you believe that as far as I know, there is no one who dislikes me enough to want to kill me. Come now, Laura, tell me who you thought my attacker might be?'

Paolo's name was on my lips but I bit it back. How could one tell a man his brother might want him dead? Even I, much as I disliked and feared Paolo, could not really see him as Domenico's murderer. Not that he lacked a motive. According to Boney, Paolo had always been jealous of his brother; always wanted to be head of the family. Now he had married a woman who took no trouble to hide her infatuation for Domenico. That in itself was a strong enough motive for wanting his brother out of the way. Come to that, what about Helen herself? Love could very easily turn to hate and Domenico had rejected her

144

tonight, in front of me. *'Hell hath no fury like a woman scorned!'* I thought. How humiliated she must have felt that I should have seen his utter disinterest in her, particularly when she had given herself away to me earlier this evening.

I pulled myself up, realising that once again I was letting my imagination lead me to ideas beyond reason.

I thought back to Vincenzio Guardo. Domenico's explanation of what had really happened just now made sense. Vincenzio had himself told me earlier that he intended to keep watch over Domenico. If I had recognised him out on the terrace, I should not have jumped to such silly conclusions. 'My two defenders', Domenico had called us. I should derive some comfort from the fact that Vincenzio had behaved as impulsively and stupidly as I had myself!

'Are you calmer now, Laura? Or do you still fear the house or garden might be lurking with cut-throats?'

'Don't tease me!' I cried. 'I know I've been silly but I don't need reminding.'

He must have realised how upset I was for he said gently:

'On the contrary, you were very brave, Laura. I am touched that you should have found the courage to rush to my defence. An Italian girl might have screamed and run away in such circumstances. But then it is well known that English women are brave. I admire you.'

'But not for my intelligence,' I tried to joke, in order to hide my pleasure in his praise.

'You do not lack intelligence either,' Domenico said, standing up and pulling me to my feet. 'All the same, I do not think it would be very intelligent of either of us to remain down here at this time of night. It must be very late. In a moment we shall have Boney down here, sent by my grandmother to see what all the disturbance is about.'

For a moment he stood with his hands on my shoulders.

'Laura, why did you run away from me earlier this evening? It cannot have been Vincenzio who frightened you and yet I sensed you were upset, otherwise you would surely have said goodnight?'

I wanted to explain that it was Paolo's behaviour which was responsible for my sudden flight, but I felt I had caused more than enough trouble tonight.

'It . . . it was just the music . . .' I lied desperately. 'I felt sad . . . I must have been overtired . . .'

Fortunately he did not pursue the subject further. His hands tightened on my shoulders.

'Then we can say goodnight to one another now,' he said softly.

We were very close—his body almost but not quite touching mine. I held my breath, wondering if by some miracle he was going to kiss me. I felt intuitively that he meant to do so. But suddenly he drew away and in that changed, authoritative voice of his, said:

'Off you go to bed now, Laura, and to sleep this time. I command it!'

I doubt if sleep will be possible, I thought, as I went slowly upstairs for the second time that night. But I had discounted my utter fatigue. I was exhausted and no sooner had I undressed and laid my head upon the pillow than I fell into a dreamless sleep.

*   *   *

I woke to find Lucia standing by my bedside with my breakfast. In a mixture of Italian and broken English, the girl managed to convey to me the fact that Boney wasn't well and would like to see me. More trouble in this troubled house, I thought.

I hurriedly drank my coffee, put on a dressing-gown and ran along to Boney's room. The old nanny greeted me with a wan smile.

'It's just a touch of the 'flu I think, dear,' she said. 'But you being a nurse makes all the difference. It means you can look after the Contessa for me.'

'Of course I will, Boney, and I'll look after you, too.'

Despite her protests, I went back to find my own thermometer and took her temperature.

It was a hundred and three. Realising she might argue the point, I didn't tell her I was going to report the fact to the Contessa and suggest the doctor be called. I didn't think Boney had much time for doctors.

The Contessa received me with more friendliness than usual and agreed to send Lucia off at once to telephone *il Dottore*. She even managed a wry smile as she said:

'A *fifth* accident, Miss Howard? I hope you are not bringing us bad luck!'

But there was no venom in her voice and I suspected that she did not believe in luck any more than in horoscopes or Boney's tea-leaf fortune telling.

'Take care of Miss Bone for me, Miss Howard. She is very precious to me—to us all,' the old lady called after me as I left.

I made Boney as comfortable as possible. I saw Lucia and instructed her to bring some lemonade. Then I left Boney to doze until the doctor came, and went out into the garden. Boney had told me that it was she who arranged the flowers in the Villa and that this would be my job while she was laid up. I took a pair of secateurs with me and a large flower basket which she had told me I would find in the cloakroom.

First I cut a mass of anemones, their colours ranging from palest pink to deepest red, from violet to purple. I meant to put these on the bronze console table near the piano where

148

the velvet framed miniature of Domenico's mother stood. Next I cut some wonderful sprays of red lilies for the marble table in the entrance hall.

As I neared the rose garden, I heard old Georgio, the gardener, singing *Santa Lucia* as if he were nearer twenty than eighty. Domenico had told me about him that first evening when we walked down to the lake. He'd been with the dell'Albas since he was twelve years old.

All around me the crickets were chirping. I thought about the story the Florentine guide had related, of the ancient traditional cricket hunt held here in Firenze on Ascension Day. The children and teenagers would set off early for the Cascine, a huge park skirting the wide river for over two miles. They would rout out the crickets from their underground nests. The children would spend the whole day there, picnicking on the grass, dancing and playing and enjoying themselves. For the following week or so, the town would be full of pedlars selling miniature cages, each with its tiny black cricket prisoner. The thought of caging any wild creature—even an insect—upset me but the guide said as often as not the unwilling prisoner escaped or was set free.

I half expected to meet Domenico in the garden but there was no sign of him, nor of Helen, Paolo or Vincenzio Guardo. I dreaded the thought of meeting Paolo but tried not to think about him. Instead I thought about Domenico and how much I loved him. The idea of having to go back to England in three weeks' time, to leave him for ever, was agonising but one I knew I must face up to and keep in mind. If I could prepare myself for the pain of that parting, I might be able to bear it more easily. Nor must I forget that Domenico would soon cease even to remember I had been here. Perhaps he would miss the sound of the Bechstein, or *The Moonlight Sonata* might remind him of me, but his heart would not be broken, as mine must break.

' 'Giorno, Signorina,' the old gardener's voice broke in on my reflections. I returned his smile and he nodded at the flowers in my basket and pointed to some perfect yellow rose buds. He cut them for me. They were exactly what I wanted to put on the table by the sofa where Domenico always sat. He might not be able to see them, still wet from their watering earlier in the morning, but he could inhale that delicious perfume.

I took the flowers back into the house and began to arrange them in their vases in the cloakroom when I heard the sound of a girl sobbing. Looking into the hall, I saw one of the young maids crying as she dusted a table. I went over to her and tried, in my halting Italian, to ask her what was wrong. It was quite impossible for me to follow the girl's argot but eventually I understood what had happened.

On the table lay the fragments of a broken ornament, one of a pair of green and white china birds. They were obviously antique and valuable. I caught the words '*Signora Contessa*' and realised the girl was frightened by the thought of having to confess her crime.

'*Che cosa devo fare?*' she said, over and over again. 'What am I to do?'

'*Niente!*' I said with as much authority as I could. '*Io parla Contessa.*'

The girl shook her head, the tears still running down her cheeks. Obviously she did not understand my attempt to tell her I would speak to the Contessa and say that I had broken the bird. At that moment Domenico came downstairs. In my impulsive way, I ran to him, explained briefly what had happened and asked him to tell the girl to stop crying and that she wouldn't be blamed. Domenico did as I asked and the girl bobbed a curtsey, smiled through her tears and calling '*Grazie, grazie, Signorina!*' ran off in the direction of the kitchens.

'*E molto gentile,* Laura!' Domenico said, surprising me by speaking Italian. And in case I didn't understand, he added: 'That was very kind of you.'

'*Non importante!*' I essayed in my best Italian and was rewarded by his smile.

He went off to the *salotto* where he told me Vincenzio was joining him as he had to dictate some business letters. I finished arranging the flowers and since Domenico did not need me, decided to go up to my room and write a long letter home. First I looked in on Boney and left a little vase of roses by her bed. She was fast asleep. I went back along the gallery towards my room but as I passed the Contessa's door, I heard voices and my own name mentioned. I suppose I should not have done so, but I stopped, my heart thudding. It was impossible not to hear Helen's raised voice.

'I do not hold your high opinion of Miss Howard, Grandmother. I certainly do not trust her.'

My cheeks flamed. What right had Helen to say such a thing of me. I could not catch the Contessa's reply but as I started to move away, Helen's voice reached me once more, rooting me to the spot.

'You could hardly blame Niko if he falls for her. She's pretty enough and young; and Niko's bored and probably lonely. She can attract him through that music he's so crazy about. Remember, Grandmother, I am English too, and I can see through the girl where you, perhaps, are not able fully to understand her type. She is two-faced. On the surface she may seem innocent and harmless but believe me, she has been doing her best to attract Domenico. And why not, if you look at it from her point of view? She is penniless; he is rich, titled, eligible. Why should she not scheme to become part of the great dell'Alba family? You must admit this is a big temptation to any girl of her class and in her position.'

'As it was to you!' I thought with a violence that left me trembling. Hot tempered as I was, I nearly burst in on them but the Contessa's voice, speaking in my defence, halted me.

'As I said before, Helen, I cannot agree with you about Miss Howard. I do not think she has any designs upon Niko and even if she had, I have every confidence in Niko's good sense. He is not likely to be attracted seriously by her and he is too kind to start up a liaison with a young and innocent girl; too sensible to consider for one moment such a thing as marriage with, as you so neatly put it, a girl of her class and position.'

I felt deeply grateful to the old Contessa and furiously angry with Helen as I walked away from the sound of her voice. I had the Contessa on my side and Helen wasn't going to get rid of me as easily as she had no doubt supposed.

'She's jealous of me!' I thought as I reached my room. The thought was like wine. If she were jealous she must believe she had cause for jealousy. She must think Domenico found me attractive. She must be afraid of me, to want me out of the house!

But the thought could not keep me on top of the world for long. In the end, I would have to leave. She had nothing to fear from me in fact. As the Contessa said, Domenico knew better than to fall in love with a girl of my background. Such an idea would never enter his head. I was the first to recognise the utter impossibility of such a thing.

I forced myself to begin my letter home and for a little while I wrote furiously, page after page. But when I stopped to read what I had written, I knew the letter could never be sent. On every line I had mentioned Domenico. We had done this, he had said that, I had played this song for him, he had liked that sonata . . . his name scattered the pages like fallen leaves in autumn. *Domenico, Domenico, Domenico.*

I wasn't ashamed of my love for him but I didn't want the cautionary letters I knew I would receive in return, once Father and Betty realised I was in love with il Conte dell'Alba. I knew already the hopelessness, the pointlessness, the futility of such a love and needed no reminders. The knowledge pierced my heart as if it were Vincenzio's sharp dagger—a continual, mortal pain sapping my life's blood.

I took the crumpled pages over to the little fireplace and kneeling beside the grate, put a match to the blue crested writing paper. The pages curled, blackened, contorted into varying shapes and slowly disintegrated. But nothing, neither commonsense nor fire, could eradicate that name imprinted on my every thought—Domenico, Domenico, Conte dell'Alba.

CHAPTER EIGHT

When I saw Boney again I thought she was a very sick woman. I was not surprised when the Italian doctor told me her illness was no ordinary case of 'flu but pneumonia. He started her at once on a course of antibiotics but despite this, her temperature rose alarmingly in the next twenty-four hours. There was no question now of my playing the piano for Domenico. I was needed as a nurse and I offered my services gladly.

Domenico came repeatedly to the sick room to see how his beloved nanny was progressing. He was desperately worried about her. Over and over again he said to me with deep feeling:

'I'm so glad you are here to look after her, Laura. I feel I can leave her safely in your capable hands.'

The Contessa came also, leaving her own bed to do so.

I was given a white overall and told to make a list of medical supplies I might need. Guiseppe was sent to the pharmacy for everything I wanted. The Contessa asked me if I thought I could manage. If necessary another nurse could be engaged.

I reassured her as to my qualifications and promised I would not leave Boney for a moment. If a night nurse became necessary, I would let her know.

'Really, dear, I'm quite all right,' Boney kept muttering, but towards evening, she became delirious and I knew I would have an all-night vigil. My meals were sent up to me on a tray. After dinner, Domenico visited us again.

'You cannot go without sleep,' he said when I told him I would remain with Boney all night. 'Go and rest for an hour or two now. Lucia can watch Boney. If there is any change in Boney's condition, Lucia can call you at once.'

His suggestion made sense, so when I had once more bathed Boney's frail old body with tepid water to cool the burning skin and she seemed less feverish, I went to my own room. It was nearly midnight when Lucia called me, telling me that the Signorina Bone was awake and asking for me.

I hurried along to Boney's room. She had lapsed into semi-consciousness again and it was only with difficulty that I was able to spoon some lemon juice and glucose into her mouth and make her swallow her tablets. Her breathing was rapid and harsh. Her conversation was, for the most part, unintelligible. I could only catch a word here and there.

'The soldiers, Contessa—the soldiers!' she

cried out once, twisting and turning as if in fear. I placed a cotton pad, dipped in ice-water, on her forehead and wondered if she was reliving the war.

She slept for a while during which time I looked round her simple little room. As in the Contessa's room, there were photographs everywhere. I found a snapshot of two little boys whom I recognised at once as Domenico and Paolo. Domenico was looking straight at the camera. I presumed he was about seven years old when it was taken. His eyes, as Boney had told me, were enormous and very beautiful. I realised that it was the first time I had actually seen them. Paolo was grinning mischievously. I couldn't relate the rather charming little face to his present one.

There were other photographs; of the Contessa with a couple I imagined to be Domenico's parents; of a tiny chubby little woman with a face not unlike Boney's. Her sister, I wondered? And then I found, tucked away behind the others, the photograph of a baby. Underneath was written: *Tonio, 1981.* I studied the little face carefully. No likeness here to Paolo. The child resembled his mother a little, but strangely enough, was extraordinarily like the Contessa as she had been when the portrait in the dining-room had been painted.

I was filled with sadness at the thought of that little lost life. Poor Boney. How she must have missed her little Tonio. Poor Helen, too. I could feel only pity for a woman whose child had died. Was this, I wondered, what had started her taking drugs?

I found another photograph of Domenico, this time when he was a teenage schoolboy; a handsome, proud-looking child with intelligent eyes and the half smile I knew so well now curling his lips. In a youthful handwriting, across the bottom of the portrait was: *For Boney, With love from her Niko.* I felt a moment of burning envy of the old woman. She had known Domenico as a baby, as a little boy, as a child. I knew only the man.

'I didn't mean him to die!'

I shivered at the sudden unexpected sound of Boney's voice. I went to the bedside and smoothed the white hair back from her hot, moist forehead. *'I loved him. God forgive me!'* There was a brief pause; then the voice continued: *'You wanted him dead, didn't you? I've known it all the time. You wanted him dead. I should have prevented it. God forgive me! God have pity on me. Forgive me. I don't want to die. I'm afraid to die. God, the Almighty knows the truth. He will punish me. I killed my darling. I killed him!'*

'Hush, hush!' I whispered. I was appalled. It didn't seem possible that this was Boney talking. People said strange things in delirium, very often things that they would never mention in a state of consciousness. Often these meanderings were fevered imagination or nightmares far removed from the truth. I hoped desperately that Boney was dreaming.

'Is that you, Laura?' Her hand clutched out at mine suddenly and caught hold of me in a surprisingly strong grip. 'Laura, it was my fault, don't you see?' She looked at me with glittering, feverish eyes. '*You* could prevent it. Don't you understand? *You* could stop him going to the lake. You must stop him. *I* can't move . . . I'm ill and I can't move. Stop him, Laura. Promise me. Go quickly and stop him.'

She sank back against the pillows. Now I could not touch her, despite my training. My moral obligations as a nurse were forgotten. I was too appalled by what she had been saying. *'Stop him going to the lake!'* So Boney must have known about the bridge—known all the time! *Boney!* If I hadn't heard it from her own lips, I wouldn't have believed it. Boney knew someone who wanted to kill Domenico. She had helped them to make that attempt on his life. Now, in her delirium, she had lost her sense of time and she was begging *me* to prevent the accident before it was too late.

Suddenly she seemed to fall into a deep sleep. I knew I ought to take her pulse, to reassure myself she was all right; but still I could not touch her. I was shivering and hopelessly confused. *Who?* I kept wondering. It must be someone in this house, but *who*? And why should Boney, who loved her Niko,

159

help in such a ghastly undertaking? What in heaven's name would Domenico think if he could hear what I had just heard. There would be no gentle teasing laughter at my fears then! But of course, I could not tell him. How could I? He loved Boney. His concern for her today had shown just how devoted he was to his old English nanny. I could not be the one to hurt him by telling him the truth. At the same time, I thought, someone should warn him.

I stared down at the old woman and suddenly wished her dead. If she died, Domenico need never know. On the other hand, I would never discover the name of the person whose accomplice she had been.

Her body looked pathetically tiny beneath the bedclothes. She looked old and frail and utterly innocent. I thought of our tea-drinking sessions and her simplicity and I could not believe my own suspicions.

I suppose half an hour passed during which my emotions see-sawed between doubt and certainty of her guilt. One moment I didn't believe it; the next I did. I don't know how long I might have continued in this vein had I not been interrupted in my vigil. Of all the people I least expected to see, it was Helen dell'Alba.

She stood in the doorway of Boney's room, looking like a statue in her long white dressing gown. The gorgeous red hair was dishevelled and hung about her shoulders in an untidy heap. Her eyes were dull, the pupils mere pinpricks. I guessed she was suffering from the after-effects of a drug—or even the need for more.

'Couldn't sleep!' she said, her voice hoarse, her words staccato. 'I thought you might be awake. Only person in the house to talk to.'

She wandered over to the bed and stared down at the sleeping woman.

'How is she?'

She didn't wait for my reply, but walked over to the window. I could see her body shaking. Her hands were in her pockets but I suspected the fingers would be clenched. She was in a state of high tension.

'I can never stand this time of the night—two to three a.m. People are always at their lowest ebb then. Bloody awful life, isn't it?'

I wet my lips with my tongue. They were as dry as my throat. She turned on me like a tigress.

'For Christ's sake, can't you say anything? Are you dumb?'

I found my voice.

'No, I'm not dumb and I think you might feel better if you drank some strong black coffee. If you'd like to stay and watch the patient, I'll go and make some for you.'

'No, I'll make it—in a minute.' Helen stood looking down at me, a long tortured look as if she was asking herself if she could trust me. Suddenly she broke out:

161

'Being a nurse, I suppose you've guessed I'm hooked?'

Her voice was raw. I wondered if she were ashamed and why she had chosen to tell me. Perhaps she just had to confess to someone and I didn't matter. I pitied her.

'Obviously the answer to that is "yes",' she said. 'Do you find it disgusting? Or don't you know much about drugging?'

'I'm not unacquainted with the problem of addicts,' I said as nonchalantly as I could.

Helen drew out a cigarette case. It was gold and very slender. She made several attempts to light a cigarette and finally succeeded.

'You believe it's curable?'

'Oh, yes, indeed. But you've got to *want a* cure.'

'That's the hell of it. I don't really want to be cured. The only time I feel fully alive is when I'm high.'

'But you have so much else to enjoy . . .' I began. She cut me short.

'Don't delude yourself, my girl. I have nothing. A rotten, corrupt degenerate Italian boy for a husband, a million in the bank, and a broken heart.'

I saw her staring at the photographs on Boney's table and my heart went out to her in pity.

'Your baby!' I whispered the words. Helen laughed.

'You think I broke my heart over a kid?

162

How sentimental you are, little Miss Howard. No, it would take more than a child to break Helen Lennister's heart. It took a man like Domenico dell'Alba. I love him, you know. I loved him from the first moment I saw him. "I'll marry that man," I said to myself, "if it costs me every penny I possess." But do you know, he wasn't to be bought? Not with love . . . *my* love . . . and most certainly not with money.'

There was nothing I could say. Helen walked over to the table and picked up the photographs I had been looking at earlier.

'Lovely little boy, wasn't he? *"To Boney, With love from her Niko!"* What wouldn't I give for him to write like that to me. I suppose the poor old dear earned it. She mothered him for years, you know.'

'Earned it?' I repeated. Now, thoughtlessly, the facts came pouring out of me. 'Boney knew someone was trying to kill him. She let them. She wanted him dead! And you say she *earned* his love!'

Helen stopped her restless pacing up and down the room and looked at me as if I had gone mad.

'Are you crazy! *Boney*—wanted Niko *dead*?'

'I know it sounds crazy but just now she was delirious and she begged me to prevent Domenico going down to the lake.'

As Helen made no move to interrupt me, I told her as quickly and as briefly as I could about the bridge episode. I repeated Boney's ramblings. As I ended I saw Helen's derisive smile.

'You've got the wrong end of the stick!' she said. 'Paolo told me all about your hiatus over the two "fatal" attempts on Niko's life. From the sound of it, you've got an over-developed protective instinct—or are you by any chance in my hell? Are you in love with Niko?'

At any other time I might have tried to deny this. But I was still too concerned about Boney.

'If it wasn't Domenico she was referring to, *who was it?*' I asked weakly.

Helen answered without hesitation.

'Tonio, of course. Boney always blamed herself for his death, poor old thing. Not that she could have done a damn thing to prevent it; she was ill in bed at the time and one of the maids was looking after him. But Tonio was her "charge" and she nearly drove us all around the bend, telling us how it could never have happened if she'd been doing her duty and looking after him as she should.'

Helen stubbed out her cigarette and sat down on a chair by the window. She was deathly pale, with red-rimmed eyes, and she was trembling uncontrollably, clutching every now and again at her breast as though she was in pain.

'No one else will tell you—the subject's taboo in this house. My son was drowned in the lake. We'd always known there was a danger of such a thing happening and Niko had a wire fence put right round the garden near the house. There was a gate, of course, so that cars could freely use the drive, and another smaller gate leading out of the rose garden. Well, someone left the gate open, although everyone knew of Niko's strict rule that it should always be kept locked. Nevertheless, *someone* left that gate open. Tonio found his way out—though God knows how he managed to get so far—and we didn't discover him until . . . until it was too late.'

I tried to gather my emotions into some kind of order. Most of all, I think, I felt relieved that it was not from his adored old nanny that Domenico was in danger. I felt pity, too, not just for Boney who blamed herself so unreasonably for what had happened, but for Helen who, no matter how casually she spoke, must have been terribly shocked and hurt by the tragedy of her child's death.

'No one discovered who left the gate unlocked?'

'No! Everyone swore they'd never touched it. The wretched maid was sacked, of course. She'd been flirting with one of the young footmen instead of keeping her eye on the child. It wasn't one of the gardeners because only old Georgio had a key to the inner garden and by a stroke of ill luck, he'd taken a day off to go to his brother's funeral. If he'd been around, it probably wouldn't have happened. He adored Tonio and always kept an eye on him when he was out of doors.'

'But someone . . .'

'Oh, yes, someone!' Helen interrupted. 'Do you think I haven't thought about it! I don't now, though. What's the use? It must have been someone in the house—the second key hung in the hall, you see, so anyone could have taken it. But we'll never know who.' She turned towards the sleeping figure in the bed and shrugged her shoulders. 'That's one person who certainly did not do so. She worshipped the child.'

'But surely everyone did,' I cried.

Helen gave me a long measured look from eyes that could scarcely focus.

'No, indeed! My fond husband, for one. He didn't want a son. He was only a boy himself and he didn't care at all for the idea of carrying parental responsibilities. He was jealous, too, of all the attention the baby got. Paolo preferred Tonio to be kept well out of the way. So did she.'

'She?'

'The Contessa. Obviously you don't know her or you wouldn't look so surprised. She's a fanatic, you know, obsessed with the dell'Alba family line. She eats, thinks, sleeps, dreams and lives for nothing else. Why do you think she allowed one of her precious grandsons to marry *me*. No royal or even aristocratic blood in the Lennisters' veins. But she had to have money and quickly. She couldn't wait for Niko to make a good marriage. It's funny, when you think about it. We all paid a price for what we got out of the marriage—the high and mighty Francesca dell'Alba, too. It nearly killed her when the new son and heir was found to be deformed.'

'Deformed?'

'Tonio had congenital dislocation of both hips. He was in calipers practically from birth and he'd have had to spend his life in them in all probability. That's why I can't feel so badly about his death as Niko does. I said it would be hell for a kid to have grown up like that but Niko said it wouldn't have mattered—Tonio could have found happiness just the same. It's a matter of opinion. But the Contessa, she was glad when he died. Oh, she never said so, of course, but knowing how she felt about him, I could see it behind the veil of mourning she wore so hypocritically. She couldn't bear to look at Tonio. She couldn't bear to be in the same room with him. There are people like that, people who can't stand deformities. And add to that particular quirk her fanatical pride in the dell'Albas and you can understand why she wanted him dead.'

'Oh, no, *no!*' I cried shuddering.

Helen shrugged.

'I'm not accusing her of being responsible, of course. Maybe she would have gone to such lengths to keep the precious line untarnished, maybe not. I don't know. I just say it *could* have been her. And from what you tell me, old Boney could have known it, too; known the old girl wanted the baby out of the way.'

'How can you talk like this! So calmly! You, his mother, must have cared.'

'Oh, yes, I cared. But I don't suppose I was ever a good mother. Boney looked after Tonio entirely. I didn't spend much time with him. But I was fond of him. He was mine. He was someone I shared with Niko. Niko worshipped his nephew. He was as proud of him as if he'd been the father. Of us all, I think Niko suffered the most. More than I did, though Tonio was my one link with him. When he died, everything died.'

I had a strong suspicion that Helen was nearing breaking point. Quickly I told her to light another cigarette. I ran down to the vast kitchen to make coffee. I found what I needed and I wasn't away long. When I returned, Boney was still asleep and Helen was dozing in a chair beside her. She yawned as I came in and said sleepily:

'You know, I sometimes think I'll leave this house. It has a thread of evil running through its very core. Haven't you felt it? I get frightened. Yes, I, Helen Lennister who thought nothing could scare her. When that happens I run away—to Paris, to London, to New York. But in the end, I always come back.

168

It's Niko, of course. I come back to him. I know he'll never love me. Even if he did, nothing could come of it. He would never lay a hand on his brother's wife. But I can't go, at least not until I know about his operation. If he were to be blind for life, he might need me. Maybe *then* he would need me!'

I don't think she was talking to me. Her eyes were closed and it was as if she were thinking aloud. I poured out a large cup of black coffee and took it over to her.

'You'll feel better when you've had this,' I said. She sat up, opened her eyes and looked straight at me.

'You know, Laura,' she said, using my Christian name for the first time, 'I've once or twice wondered of late just what would happen if Niko did go blind.'

'Happen?' I repeated stupidly.

'Yes! How would our fanatical Contessa feel about it? I think she loves Niko far more than she loves Paolo. But how will she reconcile her love with her distaste for the deformed? It's interesting, isn't it? I mean, blindness is a defect if not a deformity. I wonder if the family line would prove more important to her than any one individual. You see, the weakness, or tendency to weak eyes, can be inherited and if and when Niko married, he might pass it on to his children. I wonder how Nonna would work that one out. Fascinating, isn't it?'

'No!' I cried. 'No, it's frightening and

169

horrible.'

And I was far more scared than I dared to admit. The idea was forcing itself into my mind that the old Contessa might already have made two attempts upon her grandson's life . . . not directly, of course, but she could have paid someone to undermine the strength of the bridge; to tamper with the brakes of the car. She was rich and powerful enough.

I poured myself a cup of coffee and tried to concentrate on the one comforting thought— that as far as I knew, it was most unlikely that Domenico would be permanently blind.

CHAPTER NINE

By tea-time the next day, Boney's temperature was down almost to normal. The crisis had passed and her convalescence began. The old Contessa sent me off to bed with orders that I was not to be disturbed. I fell on my bed exhausted. When I woke, I looked at my watch and saw that I had slept the clock round.

I stretched luxuriously in the large comfortable divan. I felt refreshed and knew that in a minute or two the lazy languor of my deep sleep would vanish and I would get up full of energy.

The evening sun was pouring in through the unshuttered windows. Everything in my room seemed bathed in a soft golden light.

I flung off the bedclothes and let the sunlight dance on my naked body. I stared at myself in the long mirror, and came to a conclusion; I was slender—but I was not over-thin.

At the back of my mind the memory of that long talk with Helen fretted to be let loose. But I wasn't going to allow it liberty, not at this moment when I felt so well and happy. I flung out my arms and nearly knocked a little parcel off my bedside table. I picked it up, admiring the gilded paper and golden cord with which it was tied. It was labelled: '*Signorina Laura Howard*'.

Eagerly I tore the paper away from the box, and opening it, found a white leather case. It held a beautiful turquoise brooch shaped like a lover's knot. The tiny stones were set in gold. It was charming. If I had not been naked I'd have pinned it on at that moment. As it was, I held the brooch against the brown skin of my sun-tanned shoulder and then against the white skin of my breast. It looked equally attractive against both backgrounds. I laughed with delight. I had never owned any jewellery, except the chunky kind one picked up for a pound or two. My only antique was my mother's cameo brooch.

I reached for the jewel case and found a card inside.

'With my gratitude for helping Boney so expertly.
FOR LAURA FROM DOMENICO DELLALBA.'

My heart turned a complete somersault. From Domenico! For *me*. I could hardly believe it. Something he had given me; something beautiful I could take home and treasure all my life.

I read the note again and yet again. He had no cause to be grateful. I hadn't done much strenuous nursing; no more than any professional would have offered a patient.

There was a postscript on the other side of the card.

'If you are awake in time, we will be having a small celebration dinner tonight. It would make me happy if you could be there and, if you are not too tired, play to me afterwards. I have missed our music.'

I laughed again. I was so happy I could not stay still. I jumped out of bed and pulling my dressing gown round me, ran over to the window. Of course I'd go down to dinner. Of *course* I'd play to him.

To complete my happiness, I suddenly caught sight of him down in the garden. He was sitting on the edge of the fountain. For a moment, from behind the curtain, I watched him. I wanted to keep this picture of him in my mind always. I needed every little detail—the dark head, lifted to one side as if he were listening to the sound of the falling water, one hand on his white stick, the other arm along the stone. He had not yet changed for dinner and wore dark blue slacks and a white towelling shirt with a wine coloured cravat tucked in at the neck.

'Domenico!' I could not stop myself calling to him. I wanted to see his face, watch for that special smile, hear his voice. 'Domenico, it's Laura. I'm at the window.'

He stood up, not clumsily, but with quick, sure grace.

'Laura? How are you? Are you feeling rested?'

'I'm fine. I want to thank you for my lovely present. It is really fabulous! I'm thrilled.'

At last, his entrancing smile.

'I am so glad you are pleased. You are coming down to dinner, aren't you?'

'Give me five minutes,' I called.

He smiled once more, then, presuming I had left the window, started to walk towards the house. I stood watching him, loving him more than I had ever loved him—and totally unprepared for any fresh accident or danger. No intuitions this time! Nothing whatsoever to warn me as he came closer and closer to the house. I heard a strange crack—not unlike the sound of a gun; had one horrifying glimpse of the iron balcony next to mine, slide away as if in slow motion. Then a huge green pottery urn full of red geraniums fell with sickening speed and shattered on the drive only a foot short of the spot where Domenico was standing.

'Domenico!' I screamed, far too late to be of any assistance to him. He stood perfectly still, his feet covered with earth and geraniums and pieces of green glazed clay. I, too, stood still. It was as if time had stopped.

Domenico suddenly moved to one side and I, too, was able to move. I tore myself away from the window, across my room and I ran out on to the landing.

'Whose room? Whose balcony?' I wondered. There was no room adjoining mine; no entrance to that room. How could I get in to it? Someone must have been there on the balcony—someone who had tried yet again to kill Domenico.

I suppose I was thinking aloud, shouting in fact. I heard footsteps coming towards me and the old Contessa was beside me. She said sternly:

'Pull yourself together, child. What on earth is wrong? What has happened?'

'Domenico!' I screamed at her. I thudded against the wall with both hands. 'There's a room in there. Someone is in there. Someone has tried again to kill Domenico.'

Helen came running along the gallery. I tried to make her understand what had

174

happened.

'But that isn't anybody's room,' she said. 'It's just a dressing-room leading off the second spare room. Come, I'll show you.'

She took me further down the passage and into a bedroom not unlike mine. It had a bathroom on the right and another door on the left. I flung myself at this door. It opened easily. The room was empty. With Helen beside me, I ran across to the window and stared out. There was the broken balcony rail.

'My God!' said Helen behind me. 'You were right!'

'Of course I was right.'

I pushed past her and ran back into the gallery. Now I was determined I would catch whoever had been in that room. In far too much of a hurry to be afraid, I flung open the doors of all the bedrooms, even the Contessa's. They were all empty—all but Boney's.

Frantically I ran back to the gallery. Vincenzio Guardo was hurrying downstairs towards Domenico. On the far staircase Paolo was halfway up to the gallery. Everyone stared at me. I stood there, saying stupidly:

'Someone was in that room. Someone was in there. Someone pushed over the flower urn and the railing came away, too. Someone was trying to kill Domenico.'

The Contessa was the first to speak.

'The girl's hysterical,' she said sharply.

'Over-tired. Take her to her room.'

'No!' I shouted. 'I won't go. I'm going to find out the truth this time.'

'Laura, I assure you I am perfectly all right. No damage has been done to me, I promise. Calm yourself, please!'

Domenico's voice had the desired effect on me. I let out my breath, trying to regain some kind of composure. I became aware of Paolo, of his eyes on my dressing gown. It had come apart at the neck and was revealing far too much of my naked body beneath. Hastily I pulled the collar about my throat.

'Where were *you* just now?' I asked rudely.

He laughed.

'In the *salotto* pouring myself a drink, Signorina Detective.'

I began to feel silly again and yet I had not the slightest doubt that once more someone had made a rather crude, amateurish attempt upon Domenico's life. I was sure of it. I looked at Helen. She had been in her room at the time presumably—*but how long had she been there?* She would have had time to run back down the gallery whilst I was still standing at my window watching Domenico. And the Contessa? I looked at the tiny upright figure in the sombre black dress. Her bedroom was even closer to the spare-room than Helen's. *She* could have done it. Was she strong enough? It didn't take all that much energy to push an urn off a balcony, providing the rail was weakened first.

'If you did it, I'll kill you!' I thought, staring directly into Francesca dell'Alba's jet-black eyes. For the first time in my life, I knew what it meant to feel murderous. I wanted to put my hands on that thin scraggy neck and squeeze, squeeze until . . .

'Go to your room, Miss Howard. At once, if you please!'

Her voice was cold, disapproving and filled with dislike.

I opened my mouth to protest but Domenico spoke first.

'I don't think Laura should be alone, Nonna. She has obviously had an unpleasant shock. It would be far better for her to be with us all downstairs, not left to imagine all kinds of horrors alone in her room.'

'Yes, come down and have a drink, Nurse Howard,' Paolo put in with his derisive laughter.

I watched the Contessa's face. The determination and anger drained slowly out of it. She looked suddenly old and tired.

'Very well, Domenico, if you think it best.' She turned once more to me. 'But no more of this stupid nonsense, Miss Howard. Please get it into your head once and for all, that no one could possibly want to injure my grandson. I won't have another word on the subject. There have been a series of unfortunate accidents. That is all. I will not permit you to magnify

177

them into melodrama.'

Shaken, I went into my bedroom and was surprised to find Helen had followed me. Only now did I see that she was dressed for dinner—this time in a long gold lamé dress. It glittered as she moved and clung to her hips. She looked regal, quite unlike my bedraggled, wretched companion of those graveyard hours in Boney's room.

'Nonna is fantastic, isn't she?' she said, and lazily lit a cigarette as she sat down on the edge of my bed. 'I think the house could fall down about her ears and she would stand in the ruins saying: "Nothing is happening!" Of course someone tried to kill Niko, but who the hell could it be? I don't know. I can't think who'd possibly want him out of the way.'

She gave me a quick look, saw how badly my hands were shaking and held out her cigarette case.

'Have one. I know you don't smoke as a rule but you've had a shock. You need something to steady your nerves.'

'Y . . . yes. I'm not as stoical as the Contessa—or you.'

I began to dress. As I reached for my old white jersey frock, Helen pushed past me and looked into the cupboard where I had hung the clothes she had given me.

'That's ghastly. Try this,' she said, and flung a dress at me. 'I had it cleaned and it has shrunk. It'll probably fit you.'

178

The dress was a pinkish silk chiffon with a matching stole. It was simple yet perfect and fitted me well. It made me look taller, graceful and unusually chic. Helen eyed me reflectively. She muttered:

'God, I envy you your figure and with that hair you look lovely. No wonder Paolo fancies you. Oh, don't blush, Laura. I couldn't care less,' she added.

I looked at myself in the long glass. She laughed as she saw my face.

'Yes, clothes do make a difference, don't they? You look quite sophisticated now. That will make the old dragon sit up and take notice. You know, Laura, you are really lovely. I suppose I'm a fool to help you on the road to beauty. It may not be long before Niko can take his first look at you. I'd hate it if he fell in love with you.'

'What do you mean—"not long before he takes his first look at me"?'

Helen turned and walked away from me towards the window. 'Of course, you were asleep this morning so you missed all the hullabaloo. The specialist rang up to say he can operate on Domenico next week. He'll be going into hospital tomorrow. That's the main reason for tonight's dinner party, that and Boney's recovery.'

I was stunned. I didn't know whether to be pleased for Domenico or sorry for myself. Would this mean that my job here was about

179

to end?

As if she had read my thoughts, Helen said:

'The Contessa mentioned at lunch that Niko would shortly have no further need of your services so she would be sending you home but Niko wouldn't hear of it. You'd be needed to nurse Boney for at least a fortnight, he said, and in any case, he wanted you to be here when he returns from the hospital. I don't think his dear grandmother was any too pleased. She isn't accustomed to having Niko argue against her wishes. You know, Laura, Niko has changed lately. I can't put my finger on it exactly, but he's different. It's my belief that once he has his sight back, he's going to stop pandering to his grandmother and take the reins openly. Until now he has let her go on thinking she is the head of this damned house.'

I had completed my make-up and was ready to go downstairs.

It occurred to me suddenly that Helen and I had been talking as if we were friends. Our relationship had changed subtly and at this moment, I was no longer so sure I disliked her. I didn't think she had taken any drugs recently. She was calm, composed and apart from her chain smoking, showed no sign of the usual nervous strain. Like this, she was quite charming.

She caught my gaze and her thin pencilled eyebrows went up in amusement.

180

'You're wondering if I've had a fix, aren't you *Nurse* Howard?' I coloured, dropping my eyes but she only laughed. 'I'm not totally enslaved yet, you know. There are times when I *have* to have the bloody stuff and times when I can keep going without. This is one of them.'

'Why don't you go into a clinic and be permanently cured?' I pleaded. 'I wish you would. It . . . it's such a terrible waste of a life. You must know how it will end if you continue to give way to it.'

Helen shrugged.

'Yes, I know. But I'm not sure I care. Don't start trying to mother me, Laura. You're far too young to give lectures.' She stood up, obviously intending to leave me but stopped, raised her hand and swore softly. 'I've lost a ring. Help me find it, will you?'

Together we searched my still unmade bed. I stripped it and went down on my knees to look beneath it. The ring was nowhere to be seen. I was worried. Helen said it was valuable.

'Never mind, don't bother, Laura,' she said after a moment. 'I expect it slipped off somewhere.'

She seemed indifferent.

'It doesn't matter. I'll wear another,' she said casually, and left me to go to her room. For a little longer I continued to look for it.

At last, I, too, gave it up. It was getting late and I imagined everyone would be downstairs. I opened my door and was about to go down the staircase when some unaccountable impulse made me turn back to look at the door of the spare room. I felt a strong urge to go back in there, alone.

I looked over the banisters. Down below, the hall was brilliantly lit by three great crystal chandeliers. I saw Vincenzio come out of the *salotto*, the Contessa by his side, one arm supported by Vincenzio as they walked slowly across the hall towards the dining-room. The old lady was as usual in black, but tonight her dress was of lace and she wore a mantilla over her white hair. She looked very regal. I wondered what Vincenzio Guardo thought of her. Did *he* trust her? As soon as I could, I must have another talk to him, see what his views were about that crashing urn.

A door opened down the other end of the gallery and Helen came out of her room. I moved back into the shadow of the wall and she went downstairs without seeing me. The gallery was deserted now. I hesitated a moment longer and then slipped quietly into the spare room and through into the dressing-room.

The shutters were still open. The white muslin curtains were blowing backwards into the room, wraithlike and ghostly in the dim light. I shivered although the air was still warm from the heat of the day. I tip-toed over the deep crimson carpet and stood for a moment staring at the broken balcony rail, at the scattering of earth on the concrete floor of the balcony. I could just see someone down in the drive below, one of the younger gardeners, sweeping up the fragments of green pottery and the crushed geraniums. By tomorrow there would be no sign of the accident.

I shivered again. Would this, like the other attempts on Domenico's life, be swept out of sight and out of mind? The dell'Albas refused to admit to anything ugly or menacing. Why would no one in this house face facts squarely and deal with them? I thought of Helen's story of her little boy's death. That had been another tragedy swept into the dark corners of everyone's mind. No one mentioned Tonio. It was as if he had never existed. That was the way the Contessa wanted it and her household complied with her wishes. Was she, in fact, as aware as I of the danger Domenico was in; trying to keep us all from admitting it, so that she need not admit it to herself? Was she mad? Or was I?

I turned abruptly, longing for the warmth and light downstairs; for voices and laughter in place of the ghosts around me. But suddenly, something caught my eye—a bright glittering object on the dark carpet a little to one side of the window. I bent down but even before I picked it up I knew it was Helen's missing ring. It lay in the palm of my hand, as cold, as unwelcome as a reptile. I stared at it, trying to think calmly, quietly, factually.

Had Helen been dressed for dinner when the accident happened and she brought me to this room? Was it then she had dropped the ring? *Or was it earlier?* Had she been standing on the balcony five minutes *earlier*, waiting for Domenico to finish his conversation with me and move within range of the urn?

I tried desperately to put such notions out of my head. *Helen loved Domenico.* She did not trouble to hide her love. She even talked openly of it to me. Or was that just a blind? I must not forget that she had tried to get the Contessa to dismiss me, behind my back. Her sudden friendliness had puzzled me. But it could be explained if I assumed she was scared of me and of what I might find out. If I could believe my assumption, then her efforts, first to get me out of the house and then, when that ruse failed, to turn me into a friend, added up and made reason out of nonsense.

I shook my head helplessly, unable to reconcile myself to the thought of any woman, even Helen, murdering the man she loved. But I knew it could happen and had happened. A jealous, neurotic, frustrated woman might kill if driven far enough, and Helen had had plenty to destroy her nerves; the death of her child; a husband like Paolo who had never, as far as I could see, even pretended to love her and was obviously unfaithful to her. I knew he would make love to me if I let him. And I must not forget the drugs. People were not responsible for their actions once they were under the influence of strong narcotics. Right and wrong could become distorted. Perhaps love and hate could become confused in the same way. Perhaps the old Contessa already knew what I was only just beginning to suspect, but was desperately trying to protect the good name of her family. It could account for her reluctance to call in the police. How could that proud woman say 'I suspect Paolo's wife of attempting to murder his brother.'

The more I thought about it the more certain I became that Helen was the most likely of all my suspects. She would have realised that as long as Domenico lived, she would be chained forever to this house by her love for him. She had told me herself that her attempts to leave him always failed; that in the end she returned here to an existence she loathed; drawn back against her will because of her passion for Domenico. If he were dead, she would be free. Was *that* how her sick mind worked?

I knew that at the first possible moment I must warn Vincenzio. He could help me to watch Helen. I felt an overwhelming relief at the thought of Domenico's departure to hospital tomorrow. At least while he was there he would be out of harm's way. During his absence I would try to worm some kind of confession from Helen; persuade her to go away on the threat of exposure if she

185

remained. I might even be able to make the old Contessa understand that no scandal could be so terrible as the loss of Domenico's life. Thoughts of the old Contessa reminded me that Helen had tried to throw suspicion on *her*. Ever gullible, I had accepted what she had told me about the Contessa's obsessions and potentiality for evil. Helen had all but accused her of engineering the child's death. She had also suggested the old Contessa had a motive for killing Domenico. I had had no reason to doubt the story about her fear of inherited deformity.

I heard someone calling my name. It was Paolo, from the stairs. No doubt dinner had been served and he was on his way to tell me so. Quickly, silently, I crept out of the room and along the landing. I started down the other staircase. He called my name again and only then did I answer him, surprising myself by being able to speak so casually.

'I hope I haven't kept everyone waiting!'

'Ah, but how well worth waiting for!'

We reached the hall together and now Paolo stood facing me, his blue eyes both surprised and admiring as he took in my appearance. I remembered that I was wearing Helen's chiffon dress, and looked attractive in it.

I resolved to keep away from Paolo. My nerves were raw enough without having to cope with his open advances.

Domenico and Helen came out of the

salotto together. I was disappointed that Domenico could not see the change in my appearance, for where was the pleasure in looking beautiful when he could not appreciate it? But he moved across and touched my arm, saying:

'I do hope you are feeling all right now, Laura. The celebration dinner would have lost its pleasure for me if you had not felt able to attend.'

I knew he was probably just being his usual courteous self; knew, too, that the evening would not really have been ruined for him if I had been absent. But because of those words I could not stop the hammering of my heart nor the feeling of joy that revived my spirits. It made me forget, just for a little while, all the terrible suspicions that had been occupying my mind.

Domenico took my arm and led me in to dinner.

CHAPTER TEN

'Quanta costa, per favore?'
'Cinquantamila lire, Signorina.'
'Oh, dear!' I lapsed back into English in my disappointment. I was in Calmano's antique shop in Florence. The Contessa had given me a day off which, she said, I deserved after a

week of nursing poor old Boney. I had come back to the lovely old shop with my first two weeks' pay in my pocket, hoping to buy a present for Domenico. Later in the day I would go to the hospital to visit him. Not that I had told the Contessa of my intention. I was afraid she might forbid me going.

I looked at the leather-bound cigar box I was still holding and had been discussing with old Calmano. Reluctantly I put it down. It was much too expensive. I would have been perfectly happy to spend so much money on Domenico but I was afraid he would not accept such a present from me. I did not want to take him flowers or fruit. He would certainly have plenty of both. I wanted him to have something to keep; something to remind him from time to time of me. I thought of the turquoise brooch he had given me and how greatly I treasured it. Had he bought it here? I wondered.

The elderly Italian shopkeeper stood silently watching me, his small black eyes kindly, benignly waiting for my decision.

'Ha qualcose di piu buon mercato?' I managed, pleased with my progress in Italian. I'd been studying hard for the past week. Since Domenico's departure I had not been playing the piano and when I wasn't with Boney, I had plenty of time to read and learn.

Something cheaper, I had requested. Although Calmano's did not look prepossessing to me, Helen had said that some of the most beautiful *objets d'art* and antique jewellery and furniture in Italy were to be found here.

'Perhaps the Signorina would care to look round for something else which takes her fancy?' The old man spoke better English than I spoke Italian. We smiled at each other and he disappeared into a back room, leaving me alone.

The shop was dim, sheltered from the fierce sunlight by blinds, filled with faded splendours of the past. A musty spicy odour drifted from the old wood and leather. A fine dust had settled on the tiled floor but there was no dust on the *objets d'art*, all of which I could see had been lovingly polished.

I didn't much care for the darker, heavier pieces of furniture; nor could I identify the strange types of wood from which it was made. But I loved the tall-backed carved chairs, with their seats covered in lemon yellow, or pale violet, or *bois de rose* brocade. I was fascinated, too, by the painted and gilded pieces and especially by the assortment of carved angel ornaments, the brightness of their gold or silver paint toned down by time.

I touched with nervous hands one beautifully chased mirror and fingered some odd lengths of gorgeous silk and velvet fabrics which had been draped with careless artistry over the back of a sofa.

I knew little enough about antiques but I fell in love with an alabaster figure of a nymph on a fluted marble pedestal, with a tall narrow chest with serpentine drawers, and with the set of Meissen birds adorning it. Most of all I wanted to buy a little gilt cage with a tiny yellow bird perched inside. There was a spring at the base which, when I touched it, released a flood of silvery delicate song from the little prisoner.

The old shopkeeper reappeared silently beside me. He, too, listened to the bird song.

'It is charming, Signorina, is it not?'

I nodded my head. With gentle tact he took my elbow and led me across to a small table on which stood a carved rosewood box, not quite so large as the cigar box I had first wanted to buy.

'If you are fond of music, Signorina, you might like this.'

The carved lid opened silently at his touch. Then the long dim room was filled with the soothing melody of Brahms' *Lullaby*. I was enchanted. How had the man guessed that this was exactly what I was looking for? Brahms was one of Domenico's favourite composers. The little musical box must have been made by a true artist, for the tone was perfect.

'I'll take it!' I cried, forgetting that I might not be able to afford it. I didn't mind. I *had* to have it. I wanted to be able to see Domenico's face when he opened the lid. Here was

190

something he would enjoy even while the bandages were still over his eyes. It would be several more days, I knew, before they would come off.

'How much is it?' I asked nervously.

'I have had it a number of years, Signorina, and although it is very old and valuable, I have not been able to sell it. If you would like it, I would be happy for you to pay half what it is worth.'

He wrote the price down on a piece of paper. I did some quick mental calculation. Five pounds! But that was ridiculous. I checked the currency exchange and saw I had not made a mistake.

'Are you quite sure . . .?' I broke off, embarrassed. I had the feeling that he had deliberately lowered the price for me; that he had guessed I couldn't afford any more. I was touched and grateful. I could not imagine such a thing happening in England.

'It is a pleasure to me to see the Signorina so happy with her purchase from my shop,' he said, bowing. Then he took the musical box out of my hands and disappeared. He returned a moment later. It was beautifully wrapped in silver striped paper and tied with a silver cord, not unlike the golden one that had been round my turquoise brooch.

'Thank you. *Grazie!*' The words seemed inadequate.

He bowed me out of the shop. The hot

sunlight beat down upon my head and warmed my face. I felt so happy I wanted to dance down the streets. Clutching my present for Domenico, and my happiness, close to me, I walked as sedately as I could to the deserted Piazza del Duomo. Most of the Italians who normally crowded the streets would be taking their siesta.

I crossed the wide street to the Cathedral. I had not had time during our first guided tour of Florence to see it as closely as this. Now I spent half an hour quite fascinated by the rose, green and white marble of the Campanile; the red porphyry pillars and the bronze doors of the Baptistry. The vastness of it, the silence, the sacred atmosphere over-awed me.

When I became conscious once more of the time, I saw that it was nearly four o'clock. I took a taxi to the hospital. I was suddenly terribly impatient to see Domenico; anxious to give him his present and at the same time, afraid I would not be allowed to visit him. He might not be well enough to receive me—or wish to do so. The specialist or doctor might be with him . . .

I walked into the hospital in a fine state of nervous tension.

I need not have worried. I was shown at once to his private room. A white-veiled sister announced me. Domenico said:

'*Laura!* What a lovely surprise!'

Suddenly shy, I walked over to the high bed

in which he sat upright, a white bandage covering his eyes. His hands lay motionless on the scarlet hospital blanket. I touched his arm.

'How are you? I was doing some shopping in Florence and had a little time to spare, so I thought I'd drop in and . . .' My voice trailed away. My timidity was so absurd and my lies equally so. If he noticed either, he did not remark upon it.

'I'm so glad you came, Laura. Nonna was here this morning and Helen yesterday evening, but this afternoon no one has come. Just as I was bemoaning my solitary state you appear as if by magic!'

I could see the smile curving his lips. I loved him. Quickly, before I could do anything rash like bending over and kissing him, I thrust my parcel into his hands and sat down on the chair by his bed.

'I thought you wouldn't be able to see flowers and you probably don't like chocolates and someone has already given you fruit, so I chose this. I . . . I hope you will like . . .'

Once more my gabble of words trailed to a silence. Domenico was opening the box; the first charming notes of the famous lullaby filled the room as I touched the spring for him. I watched his lips, trying to gauge his pleasure or otherwise in my gift. To my surprise and disappointment, there was no smile. If anything at all, he seemed to look first of all startled, then sad. I held my breath, anxiously waiting for his praise, but he allowed the music to continue to its conclusion. When the last notes died away, he said very quietly:

'I have been thinking a lot about you, Laura—how strange it was the way you met my grandmother and came into my life when I most needed someone to help me pass the long dull hours—to make the waiting easier. I . . . I am not a very religious man. I am no longer even certain there is a God. But I feel that Fate, if there is no God, sent you to our family when most we needed you. You were there to help me, my grandmother and then Boney. You have somehow become an essential part of all our lives. And now . . . now this . . .'

He touched the musical box thoughtfully.

'You do like it? I could change it if . . .'

'Laura, you could not know this,' he broke in, 'but I myself once gave this same box to someone as a present, to enchant and entertain and please them, just as you have chosen to do for me. You bought this from Calmano's, didn't you?'

Astonished, I nodded my head.

'It was my little nephew's—Tonio's!' Domenico said. 'I gave it to him on his first birthday.'

I gasped.

'This one? The same musical box?' I asked stupidly.

'The same one. I am sure of it. I can feel the

carving of the lid. It is rosewood—is it not?'

'But how could it be—the same one that you gave to . . . to your nephew?'

'Because, when the child died, my grandmother ordered all his things to be removed from the house—everything. Much was given away. His more valuable belongings, such as his gold mug and christening presents were sold and the money given to our Priest for the poor. That is how this box found its way to Calmano's. I dread to think how much you must have paid for it. It is very valuable. It embarrasses me greatly, Laura.'

I didn't know what to say. I told him what the shopkeeper had said to me—that he had had the musical box a long time and was happy to let me buy it at a reasonable price. I'd been so pleased. Now I would give anything for it to have been beyond my means. It could bring Domenico nothing but sadness. I told him so.

'No, Laura! This is only another incident like that of the Bechstein. I think my grandmother is wrong to try to hide or suppress the tragedies of life. One should face them, learn to live with them and find happiness again. Do you know, obedient to her wishes, I have never mentioned little Tonio's name to a living soul since the day he was buried? Now I know my grief should never have been allowed to fester as it has done in my soul. I don't want to forget Tonio. I could not. I loved him, Laura, as if he were my own child. His death turned me against my religion. I could not reconcile myself to the idea that God could allow so awful a thing to happen to an innocent baby who had already endured so much. You know he was crippled?'

'Yes, Helen told me.'

'Poor Helen. She did not love him as most mothers love their *bambini* but I think she cared more about her child than about any other human being in this world. Helen cannot love easily. She grew up learning only to take—never to give.'

'But she loves . . .' I bit back the words but Domenico knew what I had been about to say.

'You think she loves me? I do not, Laura. She is attracted to me . . . she wanted once to possess me. But love . . . I do not think Helen can love as I understand the true meaning of the word. Nonetheless, little Tonio's death was her tragedy, too.'

He opened the lid of the musical box and allowed the Brahms melody to fill the room once more. Suddenly, he was smiling.

'Tonio loved this, Laura. I would go to the nursery each evening at bed-time and so long as I played the lullaby first, he would settle to sleep without any difficulty. Hearing it reminds me of so many happy hours. Thank you, Laura.'

I suppose some people would think Domenico was too soft, too sentimental. I did not. I knew that Italians adored children and the thought of Domenico beside Tonio's cot, playing the lullaby to him, touched me, made me love him even more. I myself was far from being a reserved person, but I shied away from the thought of revealing my love for Domenico. It was not as if he could ever return it. It could only embarrass him. So now, as always when I was afraid to show emotion, I reached for safer ground.

'Your eye—your operation, Domenico? It has been a success?'

'I do not know yet. I hope, of course. But this also I have spoken of to no one but you, Laura. The tone of my surgeon's voice when he last saw me was not, I think, very encouraging. He would not admit failure, but I am trying to make myself face the possibility.'

I felt my heart plunge downwards and bit my lip hard. Domenico might be able to speak calmly of such a possibility but I could not.

'There are other specialists,' I said. 'In England, in America. Brilliant eye surgeons—all over the world. You could go to one of them . . .' I broke off. My voice needed steadying.

'Yes, I know. I have told myself this, too. The man who operated on me is an Italian. He is supposed to be a genius. But one need not give up hope, yet, Laura. At least the thought of failure this time will be bearable if I have your promise not to leave the Villa dell'Alba until I can arrange further consultation. You

197

will give me your word, Laura? It might mean even longer than the month you first promised me.'

I did not hesitate. How could I? If he needed me, I would stay. I would throw up my nursing career, my home, my own people. He alone mattered.

'The hours and days will pass more quickly if we can continue to share our music,' went on Domenico. 'I realise that it is probably a very dull life for you. You are young . . . and Paolo keeps telling me that you are very attractive. You should be having fun, young men to dance with you and take you to parties. I can perhaps arrange for this.'

'No, no!' I interrupted him almost violently. 'I don't want what you call "fun". I love my life at the Villa. I love playing for you, walking in the beautiful gardens, and arranging the flowers in the house where they look so perfect amongst your beautiful things. I am happy in your home. If it were not for . . .'

Once again I pulled myself up too late.

'Go on, Laura, with what you were going to say. I have noticed this little habit of yours of beginning a sentence and thinking better of it. It is quite exasperating and yet I find it intrigues me, too. It is like an unfinished symphony, one needs to hear the ending,' he laughed.

'You'll think I'm being silly again, but as you have asked me to finish what I meant to say,

198

then I will!' I added defiantly. 'I still think someone is trying to kill you. I know it. I ought not to worry you when you are convalescing and have enough to worry about already, but I'm so afraid. You won't believe me, will you? You, who tell me one should face up to life, the good and the bad, won't face the facts yourself.'

'Only because I don't believe they are facts, Laura.' His voice was gentle. 'I think each accident *was* only that, and nothing more. I think it pure coincidence that they occurred within so short a space of time. But you must remember, Laura, I was not blind for long before you came to the house. Someone so newly afflicted may well meet with small catastrophes at first, until they become accustomed to groping around in darkness. Do you not agree?'

I was not convinced.

'Yes, in a way. I wouldn't be so disturbed if you had fallen, or knocked something over and hurt yourself. But these episodes were more sinister, Domenico. The bridge, the car brakes, the big urn that fell from the balcony. Vincenzio agrees with me. I'm not the only one who is worried. I cannot understand why you fail to be in the least bit concerned.'

'But, Laura, your whole basis for thinking as you do, is wrong. There is no one—absolutely no one I can think of who would wish me dead. Once you accept that, you can find plenty of other reasons for those accidents. A murder must have motive, you know.'

'You're laughing at me again!' I was nearly crying with exasperation. Why couldn't he see it? How could I make him see it without having to fling it in his face. His brother, his grandmother, his sister-in-law—they all had motives. But I knew I could not go so far as to tell Domenico so. He'd laugh at me or else tell me to leave him, to go away and stop talking nonsense.

'Well, what plots are you scheming now in that strange little head of yours?' I heard him ask tolerantly.

'Domenico, please! At least consider your sister-in-law, Helen. Whether you believe it or not, she *thinks* she loves you. She must know you don't even like her very much. Even I, a stranger to the house, can detect that fact in your voice when you speak to her. A woman can learn to hate as violently as she has loved—hate to the point of killing. You must know this is true. She takes drugs. That, too, can affect a person; make them behave irrationally.'

'So you know about the drugs!' He sighed. 'I suppose it was inevitable since you are a nurse. I'm sorry, Laura. What with this and the way my brother drinks, you cannot be thinking very highly of the dell'Albas!'

'*You* are a dell'Alba!'

Suddenly he put the back of his hand

200

against his mouth, as if my intended compliment had upset him. I stopped considering anything except that I loved him and that somehow I had just hurt him. I took his hand away from his mouth and pressed it against my lips. I suppose he realised then how I felt about him. He was very gentle with me. He drew his hand away and began to stroke my hair.

'Laura, Laura!' was all he said.

I think I wanted to die. Not because I was sad but because I was so happy. I didn't care that he knew how I felt. I just wanted to stay there for ever, his hand on my hair, touching me.

I don't know how many minutes passed before he said: 'Helen will be here soon, Laura. She is bringing me grapes from the greenhouse—I expect they are probably poisoned!' he ended with a smile.

I jumped up, uncertain whether to laugh or cry. Domenico, I thought, knew just how to bring me back to normality.

'You could, of course, stay and taste the grapes before I do, so that if one of us is to die, it will be you and not me. The Borgias always had a special "taster". However, I feel that would be ungallant for one thing and for another, unnecessary. You see, Vincenzio is coming with Helen. To please you—and only to please you, dear Laura, I will make him be my official taster!'

I was effectively silenced. In the nicest possible way, Domenico had told me what he thought of my fears concerning Helen. He also suggested that I must now go home. I suspected I was beginning to bore him. As I walked to the door, he called after me:

'Give Boney my love, Laura, and tell her I will be seeing her in a few days. I think I should be home by the end of the week. And, Laura, thank you again for the musical box. I shall keep it always.'

With those last words ringing in my ears, I was able to leave him happily.

The shops were open as I walked back through the now crowded streets. People sat in the cafés, under sunblinds, on the pavements. Tourists and Florentines jostled each other and me in one hot continuously moving stream of humanity. I passed a girl and boy clasped in each other's arms, leaning against the stone walls of a bridge, oblivious to the world around them.

'Ti amo, cara!'

How beautiful 'I love you, dearest' sounded in the Italian language, I thought. I myself would never hear them spoken to me but even that could not destroy my pleasure in this day; in my memories; in sheer delight at being here in the heart of the City of Flowers and with the prospect of remaining in Italy, near Domenico dell'Alba, for far longer than I had hoped.

I bought a bunch of pink and violet stocks

from a peasant woman with a walnut brown wrinkled face. She gave me a toothless grin as I paid her what she asked and I knew I had probably been cheated, but I didn't care. Boney would like the flowers. They might remind her of an English garden.

I found myself by the Ponte Vecchio, the subject of so many picture postcards. Now I was a part of it, staring at the crowded little shops full of coral and tortoiseshell trinkets and souvenirs to be taken home to every corner of the world. Below me, the river ran slowly, lazily, in the evening sunlight. It, too, was crowded, the little boats bobbing about or gliding downstream. It was a painter's canvas come to life.

Then the great sonorous bells of the city started to toll the hour of the Angelus. I stood entranced, listening to them. The three deep notes followed by the continuous clanging calling the faithful to the churches. It was exciting and beautiful. I felt a painful longing to be able to transport my father here. This was the same Florence he knew and loved. He had felt a part of it just as I was beginning to do. How well I could understand his longing to share it with me. I would go home now and write a long letter to him.

Home! It was the first time I had thought of the Villa dell'Alba as home. I had done so unconsciously, but now my conscious thoughts made me smile. I must be careful that I did not begin to take all that loveliness, antiquity and wealth for granted. I would have to leave it in the end; go back to my ordinary home; get another job in another hospital. My outings would consist of a drive to Worthing or Brighton for the day, as a special treat, with Father and Betty. Eventually, I supposed, I would marry Pete or some other young man like him and, if we were lucky, we'd get a council house or buy a 'semi-detached' and gradually furnish it with our savings.

I knew it would be so and yet I couldn't believe in it—not standing here on the Ponte Vecchio, the sun hot on my bare head, my arms full of stocks and my heart full of love for Domenico, il Conte dell'Alba. The present— the future; it was as if there was a bridge between them; one I would have eventually to cross. Yet I could not bear to think about it. One was life—one would indeed be a kind of death.

'Now you are dramatising again, Laura Howard!' I told myself sharply. 'You were perfectly happy with the old life until you came here—or *nearly* perfectly happy.'

There had been only an occasional day when I'd link my arm with Father's and lean against his shoulder and say: 'Isn't there anything more to one's existence, Dad?'

Now I had succeeded in making myself miserable. Angry at my own stupidity, I left the Ponte Vecchio and walked determinedly back to the piazza where I could catch the bus out to the Villa dell'Alba. The Contessa had graciously offered to let Guiseppe drive me into Florence in the estate car, but I'd declined, partly so as not to be a nuisance but also because I thought I might see more of the way of life of the ordinary Italians if I travelled as they did. And I was right. That morning, the bus had been choked with people; peasants coming in from the country to shop or have a day out; Botticelli-like babies who, despite the beauty of their cherubic appearance, smelt unwashed when one went close enough; men in labourers' coarse blue trousers and singlets; the odour of garlic mixed with the cheap perfume of the young country girls coming to town in all their finery.

All were laughing, friendly, talkative; pleased to discover I was English; happy to correct my halting Italian; eager to direct me when we arrived at the piazza. It was the same now as I made my way home. One or two people recognised me from the earlier drive and greeted me like an old friend—not boldly but with charming courtesy. I was given to hold a fat brown baby with huge brown eyes. When I got off the bus at the great gateway of the dell'Alba drive, everyone called: '*Arrivederci, Signorina!*' Half a dozen kindly hands helped me down.

The sun was losing its heat as I walked slowly down the long drive. It was cool and

shady in that avenue of cypress trees. As on
that first day, I caught my breath at the beauty
of the great white house, seeming to lie half
asleep in the circle of bright scarlet flowers.
How peaceful it looked! How lovely!

Georgio called out to me as I neared the
flowerbeds where he was still working.

'*Buono sera, Signorina!*'

He hobbled over to me and handed me a
pure white rose bud, the petals just uncurling.
I was touched and thanked him, feeling that he
was as much my friend as the simple people in
the bus.

Today I did not go in by the front doors. I
wandered around the side of the house,
knowing the French windows would be open,
leading to the *salotto*.

I walked into the comparative darkness,
clutching my rose, my bunch of stocks and my
handbag; clutching to me, too, the happiness
of the day.

Suddenly I became aware that there was
someone else in the room. I swung round and
saw Paolo lounging on Domenico's yellow
sofa.

'At last, *carissima!*' he said in a slow drawl.
'I've been waiting all afternoon. At last you
have come back!'

CHAPTER ELEVEN

'Leave me alone!' I cried out sharply as Paolo jumped up and came towards me. Ignoring my protest, he tore the flowers out of my arms. My handbag fell to the floor between us and the contents scattered across the rug. Before I could move, his arms imprisoned me and he was pressing himself against me.

'Let go!' I gasped, struggling to pull away. 'Let go, or I'll call for help!'

Paolo laughed.

'*Nonna* is at her devotions, gone to church. There is no one in the house but us, *cara mia*. Boney is in bed sleeping and the servants will not come unless we ring for them. So you see, you will not gain your freedom by screaming.'

I made no effort to conceal my repugnance for him.

'What is your price for *my freedom*?' I enquired scornfully.

'What will you give me, Laura? A kiss will not do . . . I want more than that!'

Suddenly he was trying to make love to me. I shuddered as I felt his hand lifting the skirt of my dress and touching my thigh. I twisted my body free but tearing my dress from my shoulder, he reached for my breast. There was no gentleness, no attempt to hide his intentions. I knew if I resisted he would use greater force.

'You're crazy!' I said, twisting my face away. I could feel his hot breath, smelling of brandy. Obviously he had been drinking while he awaited my return. I felt sick with disgust and loathing. *'Let me go!'*

I managed to free one arm. Then I caught him a stinging blow across the cheek. He dropped his other arm momentarily in surprise and then, laughing again, caught both my hands. I had not realised how strong he was. I began to be afraid. I struck him again and this time I hurt him, but despite this, his mouth came down on mine. I heard his voice, distorted and horrible, whispering all kinds of filth dredged up from his past experiences. He was truly beastly . . . and he was rapidly beginning to overpower me.

Suddenly I remembered Matron giving the students a talk on how to handle drunken men brought into 'out patients'. She had made it quite clear that in extreme difficulties, we could forget the rules and kick where it would hurt most. I did just that. Paolo crumpled up at my feet with a cry of pain.

I should have left him at once but stupid though it seemed later, I was concerned at that moment as to how badly I had hurt him. I need not have worried. He staggered to his feet almost at once, swearing at me violently.

I backed away from him but now he made no attempt to follow me. He stood in the middle of the room, face distorted with pain, his hair dishevelled, his blue eyes burning with hatred.

'You would not have rejected Niko!' he was nearly screaming. 'You'd have enjoyed a little session with my dear brother, wouldn't you? Don't think I haven't seen the way you look at him. *He* can't see it, but I know you want him. You're in love with him, aren't you? Just like Helen. Just like all the other women. It's always Niko they want, not me.'

I covered my ears with my hands but I could still hear that hysterical voice.

'I'll kill him. I'll get him out of my way once and for all. I hate him, do you hear? Hate, *hate* him! You think I wouldn't dare? *"You'll never dare lay a hand on him, Paolo, because you know what he'd do if you tried!"* That's what Nonna said. And Boney thinks that, too. They forget he's blind now—*blind.* He can't defend himself, can he? He's at my mercy now. I can pay him back for every single fight we've had—all the fights he's won. He always won. He was taller, stronger than me. But I did manage to hurt him once and don't you forget it!'

Paolo seemed to have forgotten he was talking to me. My hands had dropped away from my ears. I listened sickened, horrified but determined to hear it all.

'Oh, yes, I nearly killed him, didn't I? They hushed it up—trust Nonna not to let a public scandal hit the dell'Albas, but she couldn't

209

undo the damage. He lost the sight of his eye and serve him right. I should have thrown the iron bar a little harder, crushed his bloody head in for him. I was only seven years old and I was too small, too weak. But I'm not weak now . . .'

Without warning he burst into tears; harsh, terrible, grating sobs which I could hardly bear to hear. I was a nurse. I recognised genuine hysteria when I saw it. I realised that Paolo was definitely unbalanced. If he had been my patient, I would have called the doctor. He should have a sedative, be watched . . .

My horror outweighed my training. I ran from the room and left him. I could hear his sobbing as I tore up the stairs, my white rose, Boney's stocks, my handbag forgotten. I raced into my bedroom and locking the door behind me, flung myself down on my bed.

When at last I stopped trembling, I got up and bathed my face in cold water, washed my hands and took off my dress. It was torn in three places. I let it fall to the floor, unwilling ever to wear it again even if it could be mended, such was my feeling of loathing for Paolo. I sat down on the side of my bed and tried to decide what I should do. Go to the Contessa? No, I knew that would be pointless. Undoubtedly she already knew Paolo was unstable, even capable of fratricide. He'd shown the tendencies when he was only seven. At seven years old he had hated Domenico

210

enough to want him dead; had actually tried to kill him with an iron bar and succeeded only in blinding him. A thorn bush! That was the story everyone had been told and made to adhere to. I supposed that the family doctor had been well paid to keep quiet about it, too. How many other times had Paolo tried to hurt Domenico, only to have his taller, stronger brother defeat him?

Domenico must know! I thought, my cheeks burning, my hands icy cold. No wonder he had laughed at my wild accusations of Helen and Vincenzio. Why had I never suspected Paolo before? I'd disliked him instinctively. I'd been warned about him by Boney. Even the old Contessa had scarcely succeeded in concealing her dislike for her younger grandson. As for Vincenzio, quite possibly he did not know about Paolo's youthful attempt upon Domenico's life. He had had no more reason than I to suspect him now. I must see Vincenzio—tell him, warn him.

Oh, Helen! I thought. I'm sorry for having suspected you!

But for the ring, I would never have thought it could be her, although she did have a motive. But it was nothing like as strong as Paolo's. I had seen hatred in that young man's eyes—real malice such as I hoped never to see again.

I could not lie there thinking, doing nothing. Restlessly I got up and had a bath, scrubbing

211

my body until it hurt. I was sitting at the dressing table brushing my hair when I heard the sound of a car in the drive. I ran over to the window and saw Helen and Vincenzio getting out of the Ferrari.

Quickly, I pulled on a skirt and shirt and went out to the gallery. Down below me, I could see Helen going into the *salotto*. I remembered my bag and the flowers and wondered what she would make of the disorder; wondered if Paolo was still in there. But I didn't call out to her. She had given me the opportunity to see Vincenzio alone and I took it.

He came up the right hand staircase and I hurried along the gallery to intercept him. He greeted me with his usual little bow.

'Vincenzio, I have to talk to you, at once!' I said breathlessly. 'Can I come to your room? I don't want us to be disturbed.'

There was a momentary hesitation before he nodded and led the way down to the far end of the gallery. He opened his bedroom door and allowed me to go in first.

Like all the rooms, the furnishings were large, comfortable, in perfect taste. The bed had not yet been turned down for the night. On a marble-topped table I saw a Bible and a picture of a young woman, simply dressed and with a mass of long dark hair tied back from her forehead and loose about her neck. I could detect a likeness to Vincenzio in the sharp but

212

handsome features.

'Mia madre!' Vincenzio spoke behind me. I nodded and walked past him to the window. I was finding it hard to pick the right words to begin what I wanted to say.

'Something is wrong, Signorina?' he prompted me.

'Yes!' Now the floodgates were open. A jumbled account poured from me. I told him how I had first suspected Helen and now knew I was mistaken. I told him I'd tried to warn Domenico this afternoon at the hospital and how he had laughed at me. I told him but only briefly of my encounter with Paolo in the *salotto* before his collapse. Then I described in detail, as much as I could remember, of Paolo's outburst.

He did not interrupt me once. When at last I finished speaking, I looked up from my clenched hands to find him staring at me with a strange expression. It seemed to me to be almost one of pity, which surprised me. He had no reason to feel sorry for me. Then he said in a curious hoarse voice:

'You are mistaken, of course, Signorina.'

I couldn't believe I had heard him correctly. Surely Vincenzio of all people, was not going to try to make light of my suspicions this time.

'You are mistaken about Paolo, Signorina Howard,' he repeated. 'He would not dare to kill his brother!' His voice was suddenly filled with scorn. I had never heard him speak with any kind of expression before and I was astounded. 'He is not capable of doing so!' he went on, ignoring my attempt to interrupt. 'Oh, yes, physically he might try, but he does not have enough courage here!' He tapped his head. 'Paolo has always been afraid of Domenico. He knows his brother is the stronger character. He might long to kill him, but he dare not.'

'I don't understand,' I murmured. Vincenzio had spoken with such unusual authority that I found it difficult to argue with him.

'Paolo is weak. He has always been so. He knows what is to be done but he can never achieve it. He is a coward, frightened of his own shadow. If he were to kill Domenico he knows that he, himself, might be found out and condemned to die. Most of all, Paolo is afraid of death. The Contessa has seen to that. Since he was seven years old, Paolo has been told what it would be like in hell. Every night she would go to his bedroom and relate stories of the horrors and sufferings of the eternal flames. She instilled into his young mind not the love of heaven, but the fear of hell. That fear is far bigger than his jealousy of Domenico. He will never kill him now.'

'How cruel!' I burst out. I could see in my mind that old woman bent over the child's bed whispering her dreadful warnings.

'Perhaps!' Vincenzio's voice was pitiless. 'But don't forget, Signorina, the Contessa knew Paolo had the seeds of murder in him. She had to try to stamp them out—to save him from his own weakness. Perhaps you, a young English girl, cannot understand the fierce pride that exists in such a family as the dell'Albas; the lengths to which someone like the Contessa might go to protect the family honour. And who would know better than she how the thread of evil, of madness can run through a great family—even hers! I have read that English noble families, too, have their black sheep—is that not what you call them? In centuries past there have been dell'Albas who have poisoned, murdered, raped; dell'Albas locked away in convents, in monasteries. There have been many great men in the family, too, courageous, good, clever; and women of beauty and intelligence. When a new dell'Alba is born, who shall say whether he is to be great and good like Domenico, or weak and evil like Paolo?'

I stared, fascinated, at Vincenzio.

'You seem to know a great deal about them all, Vincenzio,' I murmured.

He tilted his head.

'More, perhaps, than il Conte himself. He gave me access to the diaries and letters of his forbears, and I have read and studied the family history. I have talked to people who knew his parents, his grandfather. I know the family tree by heart. It has been a great and noble family, Signorina, but not without cost.'

215

'*Has* been?' Somehow those words made me grow cold.

Vincenzio shrugged his thin shoulders enigmatically.

'Who is to say what the future will bring? I do not think Paolo will father more children. Neither will Domenico marry—if he becomes permanently blind,' he added.

'But why not?' I cried. 'Blindness is no bar to marriage.'

'You do not know him as I do, Signorina. He is a proud man. He would never ask a woman to tie herself to a helpless husband who could not protect her and would have to protect him.'

'But she wouldn't care. If she loved him, she wouldn't mind his blindness. She would feel it her privilege to help him.'

'Perhaps *she* would feel that way. But *he* would not.'

The quiet words were unanswerable. I knew he was right. A lump came into my throat and I felt suddenly terrified for Domenico.

For a moment neither Vincenzio nor I spoke. I was still trying to take in all he had said. Suddenly, a thought struck me.

'If it is not Paolo who is trying to kill Domenico, then *who is* it? Can it be Helen after all?'

He did not reply. I stared at his pale face but I could not read what was written in those large dark eyes. I shivered.

'Vincenzio,' I added, 'if we do not know who is trying to harm him, how can we protect him when he comes home—if his blindness persists?'

Vincenzio gave the slightest movement of his shoulders which might have been a shrug. In sudden despair and impatience, I caught him by the arms.

'Don't you care? I thought you loved him. I thought you wanted to help me protect him.'

I was nearly crying. Now, as I looked at him with brimming eyes, I could read pity in the look he gave me.

'You should go home to England, Signorina Howard,' he said. 'There is nothing for you here in this house—nothing but unhappiness. Have you no understanding? Don't you realise that no man can escape his ultimate destiny?'

He turned from me and opened his bedroom door. I knew he wanted me to leave, but suddenly I felt furious with him.

'You can't opt out now, Vincenzio. You love Domenico. I know you do. It's just a lot of rubbish talking about destiny. It's defeatism at its worst. If someone *is* trying to kill Domenico, you and I can stop them. I shall stop them. If you won't help me, then I will—I will find this person alone.'

I ran from him to Boney's room. The old nanny sat propped up by pillows, a crocheted bedjacket round her shoulders, a net covering the wispy white hair. She was knitting a grey wool sock. She looked utterly normal; absolutely English. She was the one person in the world I needed to keep me sane in this crazy household.

'Boney, Boney!' I cried, and like the small girl I felt, I flung myself down on the bed and burst into a storm of tears.

I felt her hand stroking my hair. A large clean handkerchief was pushed into my fist. A voice said:

'There, there, lovey! Don't let on so—you'll spoil your pretty face. Nothing's as bad as it seems, you know.'

I blew my nose, sniffed and said:

'But it is, Boney, it is! Someone wants to kill Domenico and I love him so much, and Vincenzio won't help me any more and oh, Boney, Domenico says his operation probably hasn't been a success and . . .'

I broke into a fresh storm of weeping. I know I ought not to have bothered Boney. She was still weak after her illness. I'd no right to burden her with my worries. But the emotions of the day had been too much for me. Boney seemed to understand.

'You're just overwrought, lovey. It'll all look better in the morning, you see if it doesn't. I know it's very worrying about Niko, but we can't be sure the operation's a failure yet, can we? Helen was here a moment ago telling me that even if it was a failure, there are other specialists. There's no lack of money to take

Niko anywhere in the world where he can find a surgeon who can help him. As to you loving him, I knew that a long time ago.'

Her words dried my tears like magic.

'You *knew*?' I gasped.

The blue eyes twinkled at me.

'It was obvious to anyone as can see!' She saw my expression and patted my hand. 'I didn't really mean that, dear. It's just me that guessed, I dare say.'

'But how?' I asked. 'I tried so hard not to let it show.'

'Well, we've had quite a bit of time together one way and another recently, haven't we, dear? And talking the way we did, I suddenly said to myself, "young Laura is always wanting me to tell her stories of Niko when he was a little boy. Come to think of it, all she really talks about is Niko".' She gave me an apologetic smile. 'And there's that photograph of him when he was a boy—you were always looking at it—not open-like, but whenever you thought I wasn't watching you.'

'Oh, Boney!'

'Well, don't you fret, Laura. I'm not likely to tell a soul. It's our secret. But there's one thing I do want to say—that's that I'm very happy you do love him.'

'Happy?' I echoed stupidly.

'That I am. You're just the sort of girl I'd have chosen for him if I'd been given the choosing.'

219

'But Boney, you don't understand. I'm in love with him but there's no tiny speck of hope that Domenico could love me. And even if such a miracle did happen, he could never marry a girl like me.'

'And why not, may I ask?'

'Because I'm . . . I'm nobody. I come from a very simple home, Boney. We've no money, no titles, nothing.'

'And who's to say Niko would mind about such things?'

I stared at the old woman, wide-eyed.

'Of course he would. He's very much someone in Florence, Boney. You know that. He'll have to make a marvellous marriage with a beautiful, rich girl.'

'That, for a start, is not true. Niko has made a great success of running the estate. His farms bring him in all the money he needs now—he was telling me so last Christmas. He doesn't have to marry wealth the way Paolo did. As to who you are . . . if I say so myself, you couldn't find a better brought-up, nicer, kinder, sweeter girl than you, not even in our own Royal family.'

I hugged her. Her words were wonderfully comforting even if absurd. Of course Domenico could never marry me; as to the chances of his ever falling in love with me— they were so remote as to be non-existent.

I told her about Domenico's request that I should stay on at the Villa until his next operation—if there was to be one. I asked her opinion as to whether or not the Contessa would agree. I didn't worry her with the story of Paolo's attack on me. Instead, we got on to my favourite subject—Domenico when he was a little boy. Before I knew it, dinner was announced and I had to rush off and change.

To my relief, Paolo was not at the evening meal. Helen told me he had locked himself in his room with a bottle of brandy. The Contessa was also absent. Nor did Vincenzio appear. I wondered why. Helen and I dined alone.

'I saw the musical box you gave Niko,' she said unexpectedly, her voice unusually low pitched and thoughtful. 'It . . . it gave me quite a shock to see Tonio's toy again.'

I wasn't sure how to reply to her.

'I'm sorry!' I mumbled stupidly, and busied myself with the *aragosta* I was eating. The lobster was delicious but suddenly I was not hungry any more.

'You needn't be sorry!' Once again, Helen surprised me tonight. 'As a matter of fact, Niko and I had a long talk about Tonio. We never mention his name as a rule, you know—not since the day he died. I'm really rather grateful to you, Laura. You've broken down a lot of barriers in this house—barriers that needed breaking. Do you know, I found I could speak of Tonio without it hurting. I suppose time is a great healer—forgive me the cliché.'

Her voice ended on a note that was almost

flippant but I felt sure she was only trying to mask genuine emotion.

One of the servants took away our half-finished plates of food and returned carrying a dish of *fritelle di albicocche*—which was one of Maria's specialities. Apricot fritters were Domenico's favourite. I'd already obtained the recipe from Maria and sent it home to Betty, forgetting that apricots were not so plentiful, nor so cheap, in England.

Helen and I continued to eat in silence, but it was not in any way strained. I thought suddenly that she was not really so bad and that perhaps after all we could be friends. Poor little rich girl! She was the perfect example. So much money. So little genuine happiness. I pitied her terribly for being married to Paolo although it was obvious to me by now that they saw little of each other. Paolo had his own room. Both led completely separate lives. I wondered if Helen had any idea of what had happened between Paolo and me that afternoon. The memory made me shiver.

I suppose it was coincidence that Helen, too, should have been thinking about Paolo. She said:

'I put your handbag on the table in the hall, Laura. I'm afraid the flowers were trampled on and I told Mario to throw them away.'

I felt the colour rush into my cheeks. I felt Helen's eyes on me. My colour deepened.

'I suppose Paolo tried to force his attentions

on you. I'm sorry, Laura. He's despicable.'

I realised then that it was obviously not the first time Paolo had done such a thing in this house. Probably there had been difficulties with the pretty, young maids. Helen continued: 'He's always having to try to prove to himself what a desirable man he is. Of course, his methods are so abhorrent, he merely proves the reverse. Decent women can't stand him. Girls he picks up in Florence in the night clubs and bars are more his type. They find him—and his money—attractive. But Paolo, although he uses them, isn't interested. What he really wants is to attract the kind of girl who falls for Niko—the intelligent, the intellectual. He never succeeds but some devil inside him forces him to go on trying.'

I couldn't think of anything to say. Helen was making me see Paolo in a different light. In a way, what she was telling me confirmed what Vincenzio had said earlier. Paolo was a psychopath, insanely jealous of his brother.

'He didn't only marry me for my money!' Helen went on. 'He married me because he knew I was in love with Niko. He thought Niko wanted me because of the money. Poor stupid Paolo! It nearly killed him when he found out that Niko didn't give two twopenny damns about me or my fortune. If I didn't despise him so much I might even feel sorry for him. He's quite mad, of course.'

I shivered at Helen's matter of fact tone.

223

But she had given me the opportunity I wanted.

'I know he hates Domenico, Helen. You don't think . . .' I paused briefly but took the plunge. 'You don't think Paolo might hate him enough to . . . to want him dead?'

Helen gave a low, scornful laugh. She pushed away her plate and lit a cigarette, drawing on it deeply before she replied.

'Oh, yes! Paolo would like Niko dead. But don't imagine he would try seriously to kill him. He'd be frightened to death of the consequences. I suppose I ought not to talk to you like this but who's to care? You can't begin to imagine what the early days of my marriage were like . . . Paolo drunk, ranting hysterically in my bedroom, pouring out threats of what he would do to Niko and a few minutes later, sobbing and crying about his fears of hell and damnation. No, Laura, he'd never dare lay a hand on Niko however much he might want to.'

So Vincenzio was right and I was wrong. No one could know Paolo as well as Helen and she had confirmed all that Vincenzio had said. Then if it were not Paolo, who threatened Domenico?

The burning question remained, eating its way into my thoughts. I was sure now that it wasn't Helen. There were times when she behaved like the drug addict she had become, but I knew now that there was good in her; a hard core of practical sense running through her. This strange woman was unlikely to be thrown so completely off balance that she would lose all control. A person who could face facts—the cruel horrible facts about her own life and weakness—with such honesty, was hardly likely to destroy the one person she loved and still respected.

'I'm so afraid for Domenico!' I burst out. 'If not Paolo, then who could possibly want to kill him? Someone does. Whoever it is, will they try again when he comes home? How will they do it?'

'My dear Laura, you are not alone in what you fear. But why torture yourself with such questions? Since the incident of the balcony I've been wondering. Until then I was inclined to agree with the Contessa that you were imagining the whole thing. Now I think you're right.'

I put my hand in the pocket of my dress and drew out Helen's ring.

'I found this!' I said, handing it to her. 'It was . . . it was on the floor . . . in the spare room.'

Helen took it from me and held it in the palm of her hand, staring down at the glittering stones with raised eyebrows. Then she looked up at me, smiling.

'I see! You thought perhaps I . . . oh, Laura, you idiot! I love Niko—you must know that by now. Oh, I've wanted to kill him sometimes—

225

symbolically—times like that first evening when you and I met and Niko made it so plain he preferred your company to mine! But even if in a moment of crazy jealousy I became mad enough to go through with it, I wouldn't do it by shoving a window box onto his head! I'd get a gun and shoot him—a quick clean death. No bungled messy attempt to make it look like an accident. If *he* was dead, do you think I'd care what happened to me? I'd probably shoot myself directly afterwards. No, Laura, you can strike me off your list of suspects. Broken balconies and faulty car brakes are not in my line. They are premeditated. I could only commit such a crime in hot blood.'

She didn't really have to tell me. I knew it now and it cleared the air between us. I felt better. But the ugly question still remained unanswered. If not Helen, if not Paolo, *who*?

'You don't really believe the old Contessa ...?' I faltered.

'No, of course not,' Helen broke in. 'I hate her but I respect her, too. I think she's ruthless and fanatical, but I don't believe she's capable of killing Niko any more than I am. She really loves him, you see. That's how I know she couldn't do it. *She really loves him.* That's why she never put any pressure on him to marry me. One of the grandsons had to have my money for the sake of her beloved family, but she wasn't going to force Niko to ruin his chances of happiness. She's a very astute woman. She knew I was no good. She found out about my past—my affairs—the kind of life I had been leading. She didn't believe I could change, and maybe she was right. Perhaps if Niko *had* been in love with me . . . but what's the use of speculating on the impossible? He never had any time for me and if he'd married me without loving me, I'd have gone to pieces anyway.'

I felt desperately sorry for her now. The last shreds of my animosity towards her vanished. I could see only the tragedy of her life, of the frustrated, wealthy, spoiled girl grabbing all that was offered without thought of the future and then, corrupted and dissipated, meeting the one man she could have loved. Too late then to change the past. Too late then to become the kind of woman Domenico might have loved. Helen never had a chance.

'Let's hope you're wrong, Laura. I'm not entirely convinced you're right anyway, although I fear you might be. I just cannot accept that someone really does want Niko out of the way. I suppose someone outside the household . . . a jealous husband; some man with a grievance; some woman he has hurt . . . but I doubt it, Laura, I really do. I don't know much about Niko's private life but I do know he isn't the sort to play around with married women, nor make enemies of his friends. As far as I know, he's quite incapable of hurting a woman by ill-treatment or by making promises he couldn't keep. He's a good man. That's why it's such hell for me!'

'It has to be someone in the house! Whoever it was must have been in that spare room, watching Domenico, pushing the flower urn at precisely the moment he was underneath.'

Helen stubbed out her cigarette and stood up.

'All the same, you could be wrong, Laura. I'll grant the accidents were uncanny, unnaturally coincidental. But they *could* have been accidents. There isn't anyone in this house who *would* have done it. I'll personally vouch for the servants. They all revere Niko second only to God! I'd suspect myself before Mario, Maria, Lucia, Georgio. They'd give their lives for him happily any day. As to the half dozen others who come in to clean—they are simple country girls whose lives in no way touch Niko's.'

I, too, stood up and we went through into the *salotto* to await the arrival of our coffee. I felt exhausted. The day had been over-long, I reflected. After coffee I would go to bed.

'Play something,' Helen said unexpectedly. 'I'm not in the least musical but I have heard you in the dim distance and liked it. Niko says you have a fantastic memory and expert technique.'

'I'm not professional,' I protested.

'Play anyway—something soothing. The

Brahms lullaby if you like.'

I sat down at the Bechstein and played as she asked. I did not look at her as the last notes died away. If I was thinking of Tonio, her little boy, she must surely be doing likewise. I felt sad and troubled again.

Mario brought in the coffee. It eased the tension. After Helen had drunk hers she began to walk up and down the *salotto*. She seemed unable to relax.

'Laura,' she said, stopping to stare down at me. 'You look terribly pale. You're not still worrying, are you?'

I tried to smile.

'If only I could believe the accidents *were* accidents.' I put down my coffee cup and looked at her helplessly. 'What do you think about Vincenzio Guardo?' I suggested.

Helen sighed. I could see she thought I needed humouring.

'Vincenzio has been with us for years, first as a kind of farm accountant and recently as Niko's secretary. He used to live out—in Florence somewhere—and come to work every day. Niko began to rely on him more and more. Vincenzio's astute, you know, and Niko told me that the success he has made running the farms is as much to Vincenzio's credit as his own. Niko became very attached to him; thought him worthy of a better job than he held. He persuaded him to come and live in. Since then, they've seldom been apart.' She

229

sighed. 'Vincenzio worships Niko and has devoted his life to him entirely. I, personally, don't care for him. He's too smooth, too obsequious. But I can understand why Niko thinks so highly of him. His loyalty is as unquestionable as his discretion.'

I suppose I did not look entirely convinced for she added in that caustic voice of hers:

'Perhaps because I myself was born with a silver spoon in my mouth, I admire people like Vincenzio who started out with nothing and yet still manage to make something of their lives. He was brought up in an orphanage where, so Domenico once told me, the priests thought so highly of Vincenzio's abilities, they gave him better than the customary cursory education the other kids received.'

She paused to light a cigarette and then said:

'I gather the priests hoped their bright boy would one day take Holy Orders but Vincenzio wanted to prove himself outside the Church. He studied at night and by the time he was twenty-one, he was almost as well qualified as a university graduate—a determined young man, wouldn't you say?'

I nodded, understanding a little better now why Vincenzio was always so serious—and why Domenico treated him with a certain respect.

Helen stubbed out her half-finished cigarette and walked over to the door.

'I'm off to bed, Laura,' she said. 'But one

230

last thing before I go—don't underestimate the depths of the affection between Domenico and his precious Vincenzio. Even if you discount all I have said so far, remember that if Niko died, the life Vincenzio has built up for himself here—his job, his very substantial salary—would all go. So what would be his motive for wishing Niko dead? He has none. Paolo would never employ him. They hate each other's guts. Paolo is jealous of him and is aware that Vincenzio despises him. And Paolo is a dell'Alba despite everything. His pride is shattered every time Vincenzio, a mere servant, looks at him with those burning, scornful eyes. Paolo wouldn't keep him in the house for one instant if he had his way, and Vincenzio would never work for Paolo. No, my dear, Vincenzio is not likely to want Niko out of the way, is he?'

I closed the lid over the ivory keys and rested my hands on the cool wood. The night was hot although the sun had gone down several hours ago. Outside the open windows, the terrace was in darkness. There was no moon. The jalousies moved with the air coming in from the garden. I remembered the night Vincenzio had come in from the terrace, the knife gleaming in the moonlight. I shivered. Of course, everything Helen said made sense. It couldn't be Vincenzio. And yet . . .

Suddenly he was standing there,

materialising out of the night, out of my thoughts, like a ghost. No, I thought stupidly— not a ghost but a dark shadow, the light falling on his black hair, glittering in his agate eyes.

He bowed first to Helen, then to me. His olive face seemed pale. I thought he looked ill. I wished he would speak, move, do anything but stand there so silently.

'Good evening, Vincenzio,' Helen's voice was perfectly calm. Obviously she did not find him frightening. 'Have you dined?'

'Thank you, yes, Signora.'

He bowed again to us both, then moved across the room and through the doors which he shut noiselessly behind him.

I whispered to Helen:

'Do you think he heard what we were saying?'

'Who cares if he did?'

'I'm frightened of him. I thought I trusted him but he looked positively sinister just now.'

Helen's eyes were half-closed. She moistened her lips with her tongue. My professional gaze noticed suddenly that she was trembling and agitated and perhaps in need of a fix, or did I do her an injustice? She had seemed so casual and friendly tonight, and so normal.

She spoke to me now in a very different way and with a meaning that I did not really understand. It flung me into as much confusion as Vincenzio's sudden unnatural

232

appearance had done.

'Be careful, Laura. Don't meddle too often and don't ask me or anybody else too many questions. This old house has seen violence and death in the past. It is likely to see it again but neither you nor I can prevent it.'

She turned and walked away, very gracefully for so tall a woman. I was left alone in the *salotto*, trembling, paralysed by a fear that I could not begin to define.

CHAPTER TWELVE

Domenico had been home for a week. We were all reconciled now to the bitterly disappointing fact that the operation had failed to restore his sight. New arrangements had been made for him to go to Rome next month. An important Italian surgeon would operate as soon as possible, but first Domenico must recover his strength. It was arranged that I should stay until he went into hospital again. It meant a respite for me of at least three more weeks—perhaps more. I reminded myself, however, that my dreams must eventually come to an end; that I would eventually return to reality—to England.

For a while Fate permitted me to stay near him—to be relaxed and happy. No further 'accidents' took place. I was beginning to feel, like Helen, that perhaps I had talked myself into imagining that Domenico's life was in jeopardy.

Boney, who was up and about again, remained my staunch friend. I divided my time between playing the piano for Domenico and arranging the beautiful flowers in the Villa. Boney kept saying:

'You do it so much better than I ever did, dear. I just wish Niko could see those gorgeous creamy carnations in the hall. They look wonderful in the old Chinese blue jar. So tasteful. I don't know how you manage it, Laura.'

I wished Domenico could see my flower arrangements, but I know he appreciated the roses I always put on the table by the yellow sofa. He frequently bent his head to the cool fragrant petals and inhaled the perfume. He loved flowers as I did.

Lately we had got into the habit of strolling round the gardens together. He liked me to describe exactly what I saw.

It was July now and very hot. The shutters were kept closed during the day. Indoors it was quite cool but out in the garden the summer air seemed breathless. Lizards lay motionless on the stone walls of the fountain, impervious, it seemed, to the heat. Bees swarmed in the clematis that fought the vine for room on the trellis over the terrace. Huge multi-coloured dahlias and brilliant zinnias filled the flower beds. Georgio's assistant, a young boy, brown body half naked, spent most of his time watering, battling against the Italian sun to keep the lawns green, the flowers alive.

The narrow river that usually ran beneath the new bridge into the lake was a mere stream now, a muddy brown trickle over dry stones. Domenico took me across it to the lake one afternoon. I was reluctant to go but he wanted me to see the swans which now had three cygnets trailing after their graceful parents. I told Domenico how charming the fluffy black birds looked as they sailed towards us across the water. Jasmine and magnolia trees thick with blossom edged one side of the lake and I tried to forget little Tonio and see only the beauty of the pink and white flowers reflected in the water. The cypress, ilex and olive trees provided an oasis from the shimmering heat. We sat down in the green shade and Domenico plied me with questions about England and home. I was afraid he would become bored with the ordinariness of my home life but he seemed to find it fascinating.

'It is so very different from life here, is it not, Laura?' he exclaimed. 'Perhaps only the hospitals are a little the same, except I had no young English nurse to take my temperature,' he added smiling.

I was happy. Most of all, I was happy because we had become such good friends. My love for him was as complete, as intense as ever, but I was learning to keep it well out of sight. I could respond to Domenico's teasing without blushing. I could talk to him as easily as I could to Father in whom he seemed particularly interested. Only yesterday he had offered to have Father out here on a visit.

'He shall come by air to Rome. Guiseppe can drive him from the airport. Do you think he would like it, Laura?'

'Oh, I know he would. He'd be so happy— but he couldn't do the journey, Domenico. He's all but completely paralysed.'

'We could arrange for your sister or a nurse to accompany him?'

Domenico completely disregarded the expense! But I knew it was not possible. Father wouldn't want to come to Italy under such conditions. He would want to be able to go into the city, to walk round the piazzas and streets, the galleries and churches and museums. He would feel even more imprisoned here, where there would be so much he'd want to see and do, than in his wheelchair at home where he sat and remembered it all. Besides, Father was a proud man. He had never owed a penny and he felt badly even about taking Social Security which, in a way, he had earned by contributions from his salary before he was ill. He wouldn't accept Domenico's offer. I could not do so either. I was already grossly overpaid. Doing the flowers, playing to Domenico, was not work. If I did not need the money I was saving to take home, I would have done all these things for nothing. I loved my life here. It was perfect—an enchanted dream world in which I could happily remain for ever.

Yesterday, after siesta, Domenico asked me to take him down to the farms.

'Vincenzio is busy and I haven't been there for so long, Laura. Would you mind? Would it bore you?'

As if I could ever be bored in his company.

We had a perfect hour or two together. Everywhere we went Domenico was greeted with smiles and pleasure. The simple farmers in their rough clothes stopped their work to come hurrying over to us, begging Domenico to take a glass of *vino* with them, offering me figs and plums, or tomatoes, or strong home-made cheese. I noticed that Domenico never refused to drink with the men although, as he told me laughing, if he didn't take care in this heat, he would be unable to walk home.

Through my eyes I made him see his fields, golden with rippling wheat and corn ready soon for harvesting, the olive trees and the almond trees whose nuts were already harvested.

'I really don't need my own eyes when I have you with me, Laura!' Domenico said smiling. But I knew how desperately he wanted his sight back. I had felt the bitterness of his disappointment when he was told the operation had failed. For three or four days after his return from hospital, he had spoken to no one in the Villa. I had played for him on the Bechstein for hours on end until my back ached and my fingers grew cramped. Then the bitterness passed. He became himself again, the Domenico I loved; gentle but firm, kind but never weak, authoritative but never insolent like Paolo. To me he was the perfect aristocrat. People nowadays seldom used the word 'noble', but it suited Domenico perfectly.

This afternoon I was alone. Domenico was shut in his study with Vincenzio, going over accounts. Just before lunch he had said to me:

'Vincenzio has been avoiding me all week. I think he is annoyed because I have given no time to the work he has awaiting my attention.'

'But you shouldn't work. You are supposed to be convalescing!' I told him.

He laughed.

'You know better than I do, that I am perfectly well. I have no headache, no more pain at the back of my eye. I am quite fit to sign the cheques Vincenzio tells me are overdue. Though I would much prefer to spend the afternoon in the garden with you, work I must and shall!'

So I sat on the terrace alone where it was cool and quiet, and wrote yet another long letter home. Letters to me from Father and Betty had been arriving regularly. They both seemed well, though missing me. I was ashamed that I could not with any truth, write back to say I had been missing *them*. I was quite happy to be alone while Domenico was busy. It gave me time to remember the things we had been doing together; every word he had said; every gesture; the touch of his hand on my shoulder as we walked slowly round the farm; his dependence on me. Here alone I had time to dream, to plan the repertoire I would play to him after dinner tonight.

I was flattered that twice the old Contessa had stayed on in the *salotto* after coffee, instead of retiring early as was her custom. She admitted she liked to hear me play. Although at first I was nervous in her presence, I soon forgot she was there and lost myself in my music. I was playing so much better now than when I'd first come to the Villa dell'Alba. I had had so much time to practise, my fingers were more supple and sure. The Contessa congratulated me when I stopped playing.

'You have real talent, child,' she said. It was quite a compliment, coming from her, the more so since she had been so furiously against me touching the Bechstein when she first heard me play.

While I sat on the terrace, pen suspended in my hand, I thought how, with Boney's help, I had made a start on altering some of the clothes Helen had given me. I now had quite a presentable wardrobe, and Helen was generous enough to say that most of her things looked better on me than on her. She and I could never be intimate but we had become friends of a sort. She spent a great deal of time away from the Villa. Her social activities would have exhausted me.

'The more I have to do, however trivial my pursuits, the less time I have to think,' she said.

Mario brought me a tray on which there was a glass of freshly made lemonade. Il Conte, he informed me, had ordered some for himself and the Signor Guardo and had told Mario to bring some to me, too. I was deeply touched by Domenico's thoughtfulness. The gesture was only a small one but so typical of him.

I finished my letter and feeling restless, decided to go upstairs and take that long promised look at the dell'Alba portraits in the gallery. Somehow I had never found time to study them closely—something I wished to do quite alone and unobserved.

Although elsewhere in the house there were portraits of the dell'Alba women, some in low-necked brocade dresses with jewels in their hair, others with plump dark-eyed children grouped at their sides, in the gallery the pictures were all of Domenico's male ancestors. As I looked at them, I recalled Boney telling me that only paintings of the head of the family merited a place of honour here.

There was one which looked hundreds of years old—of a Court dignitary in blue and silver; another of a fat gentleman in the scarlet robes of a Cardinal, seated in a high-backed chair, one hand resting on a huge Bible. I wondered if the big Bible I had seen in the Contessa's room was the self-same one!

As I moved along the row, my eye was caught by a picture of a thin, legal looking man—a lawyer, perhaps, all in black, wearing gaiters and a high winged collar and cravat, a portfolio under his arm. I wished suddenly that Domenico were with me to tell me about these people. A few had features I could recognise in Domenico—the long slightly arched nose, the high forehead, the generous mouth. In nearly all of them was the same proud lift of the head I knew so well.

As I moved down the gallery the costumes became more modern. There was one of a man in army officer's uniform—Domenico's grandfather I guessed. Another beside it had a name engraved on the little plate beneath. It read *Rodrigo Flavio Leonardo dell'Alba*—Domenico's father. His face also resembled those other dell'Albas of the past. I studied it more carefully. It was familiar and yet for a moment, I could not think why. Then I realised that Rodrigo dell'Alba resembled his younger son, Paolo. He had the same full lips, and lacked the strength of character predominant in Domenico's face and those of his ancestors. I stood staring at the late Conte. I knew nothing about him except that he had died of a broken heart after the sudden tragic loss of his wife at her piano on that dreadful day.

I stopped now to consider this. It was strange how seldom il Conte Rodrigo was mentioned. Was he one of the 'black sheep' Vincenzio had spoken of? Sometimes at dinner the Contessa would tell us about one of the past dell'Albas—holding me spellbound with her vivid story of a deed of great courage or a heroic death. But she never spoke of her son, Rodrigo. I wondered if this was because he had been head of the house during its poverty-stricken post-war period . . . a period the Contessa no doubt would prefer to forget.

But I could not keep my eyes or my thoughts on Rodrigo dell'Alba for long. My gaze was drawn magnetically to the painting I had studied often before—of Domenico.

He was wearing white riding breeches, a black hunting coat, with snow-white stock tucked in at the neck. His head was poised at an arrogant angle but the face itself was softened by that familiar half smile which the artist had caught to perfection. He held a crop and riding gloves and the full length portrait showed his long legs in tight shiny black riding boots.

I had asked Boney about this portrait often, for there were no horses in the stables at the

Villa dell'Alba. She told me that all the boys in the family used to ride, first of all here with a groom and later went to an equestrian school to learn dressage and jumping—in fact all the refinements of *haute école*. I recalled a film I had once seen about the famous white horses in Vienna and could imagine Domenico astride one of these beautiful white beasts. Little wonder my romantic imagination was so stirred.

'And so endeth a great dynasty!' a woman's somewhat caustic voice said behind me, startling me. I looked round and saw Helen.

'Oh, Helen, you scared me,' I said, then added: 'You can't say that. You don't *know* that it will end with Domenico's generation.'

Helen shrugged. She looked as smart as ever but tired and depressed. Clearly she had not enjoyed her party, and I knew that her rather brave struggle to defeat her need for drugs was often unbearable.

'*I* shall certainly never have another child. As for Niko . . .' She lifted her shoulders in an indefinable shrug.

I stayed silent. It occurred to me that perhaps Helen who loved him, could not bring herself to imagine Domenico married to another woman. In a way I could sympathise with this but at the same time, I hated to think that this great family line might not be carried on. The portrait gallery was not yet complete. There were empty spaces at the end of the

243

long row—a space beside Domenico for *his son*? He should have a son. From everything I'd learned, I knew he loved children. It seemed terrible to me to think that with Domenico's death, the past grandeur and history of the dell'Alba family would die— become only a memory or even be forgotten.

I turned away from Helen and walked into my bedroom, shutting the door behind me. I felt miserable and not very well. Now and again I suffered from horrid nagging pains in my stomach. This was something new and rather frightening as I could think of no reason for them. I lay down on my bed and fell into a light sleep. When I woke some hour or so later, it was with a moan of agony. The pains in my stomach were now acute. I broke into a sweat as I fought the pain. It raged inside me like some wild beast tearing me internally to pieces.

I tried to account for it—diagnose it. I had eaten nothing at lunch which would account for a very serious attack of indigestion. In any case, I knew it was more serious than that—food poisoning, perhaps. But Helen, Domenico, Vincenzio, Boney—had all eaten the same lunch as I. Could they too, be ill?

I tried to get off my bed to go to Helen's room, but the pain doubled me up and I fell on the floor and lay there gasping. I began to feel the stirrings of real fear. Suppose I could not get help? Suppose this was an incipient appendix; an ulcer? I needed a doctor—and quickly. I had to get help.

Inch by inch I crawled towards the door. It seemed a mile away. The pain was intense. I was barely conscious when at last I clung to the door handle.

I forced enough strength into my trembling body to pull the door open and fell forward into the gallery. There was not a sound. A hushed silence seemed to be holding the house in its grip—a silence broken only by my deep gasping breaths.

Tears began to mingle with the sweat on my face.

'Help me. Someone help me!' I could hear my own moaning voice but it seemed that no one else could. Where was everybody? I did not want to die here, alone.

I was not sure how long I lay there before I became conscious of someone standing by me . . . a tall dark shadow bending over me but making no effort to help.

'Please . . . please!' I begged. 'I'm ill . . . ill . . . a doctor, please . . . '

The figure blurred, moved suddenly into focus and I recognised Vincenzio.

'Call Helen!' I gasped.

Vincenzio's voice—ice-cold, answered on a mocking note:

'Alas, the Signora is out. She has driven il Conte and the Contessa to some friends for tea. There is no one in the house, Signorina

245

Howard, but you and me.'

I was in too much pain to realise the full implication of his conduct. I appealed to him again.

'Get a doctor, Vincenzio! Telephone—*pronto—pronto.*'

'I think that is unnecessary, Signorina Howard. You have a little indigestion, perhaps? I'm sure it is nothing more serious. I will help you back to your room.'

I stared up into his implacable face and felt terror now as well as pain. Couldn't he see how ill I was? That I might die?

I began to plead with him again—raving, shouting when the waves of pain permitted. Vincenzio paid not the slightest attention. He lifted me under the armpits and with apparent ease, carried me back into my room and laid me on my bed.

'Don't leave me!' I panted, sweat pouring down my face. 'I'm going to die. Oh, help me, Vincenzio, please. A doctor—*il dottore!* Or Boney . . . Miss Bone,' I gasped. 'Where is she?'

His voice answered from a very long distance away:

'Just try to sleep, Signorina. I will leave you now.'

Then the pain engulfed me completely.

I returned to consciousness, to renewed agony, when a light suddenly flooded my room.

'Are you awake, Laura? Dinner is served and I thought I should wake you. Vincenzio said you were sleeping but I'm sure . . . Laura, are you all right? My God, she's ill . . . wait, Laura, don't be frightened . . . I'll be back in a minute.'

I recognised Helen's voice but was too ill to answer her. Time and pain were lost in each other.

'Laura, the ambulance is coming—you're going to be all right.' Domenico's voice this time. I tried to hold on to it and to his hand, but energy faded into a red agony. The nightmare was punctuated by crazy bouts of sensibility. I was conscious of metal doors shutting; of bumps adding to my already insupportable pain; of blaring horns, traffic, hospital corridors and the odour of antiseptic. I felt myself lifted into a high bed with sheets cool against my burning body, the prick of a needle. My agony ended but the dream—the nightmare began.

Vincenzio was standing over me, smiling now.

'Of course you were absolutely right, Signorina. I am the one who wants to kill Domenico.'

'But you haven't a motive, Vincenzio. Domenico says no one would want to murder him without a motive.'

Vincenzio began to float away from me.

He seemed to be rising on a white misty cloud. The cloud became a huge white horse.

247

'Now do you see?' called Vincenzio from the sky high above my head. 'I wanted his horse, his horse, his horse . . .'

He jumped on the back of the horse, and came galloping towards the roof of the Villa dell'Alba.

'Mind! You'll hit the balcony!'

But my voice was only a thin scream. Vincenzio's white charger kicked out his back legs and the wrought iron balcony flew into the air. The green flower urn floated slowly, like a feather, towards Domenico's upturned face. Along the drive came the Ferrari; Helen was driving. The pupils of her eyes were pin-points and her handsome face was flushed with the drugs I knew she had been taking. She had her hand on the horn. It was clanging like an ambulance bell. She was warning Domenico to get out of the way of the urn. But the urn melted into green water gushing from the mouth of the bronze horse in the fountain. A sudden paralysing fear caught me by the throat as I realised that Helen meant to run Domenico down. I wanted to run to his help but I was sitting at the Bechstein unable to move. My fingers were stuck to the keys. I could not pull them away. My fear intensified.

'Help me—someone help me!' I cried.

Roney came into the salotto.

'Domenico has just been drowned in the lake,' she said. Tears were running down her cheeks. 'It's not my fault. Why didn't you stop him,

Laura?'

'It's all the fault of her silly intuitions,' said Betty. She was wearing her old blue dressing gown and shabby slippers. She was sitting on the yellow sofa. 'You'd better go back to the ward, Laura. Matron wants you.'

I hurried down the shining clean hospital corridor knowing that Matron would be very angry because I had stayed so long in Italy. She was waiting for me in the Sisters' Common Room. A young probationer who had no right to be there, sat playing the tinny old piano. She was murdering the Brahms lullaby. It sounded distorted and out of tune—like an old barrel-organ.

'All you need is rest!' said Matron, using Vincenzio's clipped, rather high voice. 'I'll help you to your bed, Signorina.'

I felt Vincenzio's arms round me and knew he was about to kill me. He laid me on the bed and forced open my mouth.

'Drink this!' he said, handing me a glass of freshly made lemonade.

I twisted my face from side to side to avoid the glass which had swollen into one of the Contessa's huge brandy goblets.

'No!' I cried. 'I don't want it.'

Vincenzio's black eyes smiled at me.

'But you must drink it!' he said. 'If you don't, how am I going to poison you?'

He forced the liquid down my throat. It was like fire. I screamed. I knew I was about to die.

249

'But you must stay and play to me, Laura!' Domenico spoke. He stood by my bed. 'I can only bear my blindness if you promise to stay and play to me.'

Domenico bent over me and pressed one of my hands against his lips.

'The sooner she leaves this house the better!' said Helen and snatched a diamond ring off my left hand. 'You can't trust her, Niko.'

Domenico flicked a riding whip against his boots and handed me a single white rose.

'It's from Georgia!' he told me. 'You'll feel better when you've eaten it. You must get well, Laura. Ti amo. I love you. Get well for me!'

'She's coming round,' a nurse said. 'She'll be all right now.'

I closed my eyes again and fell asleep.

CHAPTER THIRTEEN

I returned slowly from nightmare to reality. I found that I was in a private room in a hospital in Florence; that I had been desperately ill but was now out of danger. I was too weak to read or write letters. The long days passed slowly. I slept and ate and slept again. Gradually strength found its way back into my body. My mind rebelled against its vegetable convalescence and began to work again. I started to think, to remember, to try to sort the

250

dreams and nightmares from the facts.

My room was filled with flowers. The most treasured, a vase with my favourite yellow roses from Domenico, stood on my bedside table. I lay looking at them for hours, remembering that shadowy figure, that voice saying: '*You must get well, Laura. Ti amo! I love you. Get well for me!*'

I suppose I knew it was just one of the fantasies. It was ridiculous to imagine otherwise but sometimes, when my day nurse left me to doze after lunch, I liked to stare at the roses and imagine it was true. I could cheat a little, telling myself that Domenico would never have stayed all night long at the hospital when it was thought I was going to die, unless he loved me. My nurse, Angelica, had told me about his vigil. Obviously she was greatly impressed that I had so important and illustrious an admirer. She treated me with the greatest respect. I had told her I was a nurse in a hospital in England but I don't think she believed me. She just fingered the edge of the fabulous white lace dressing gown Helen had given me and smiled at me from huge brown eyes as if to say: 'You would not own this if you were not a great lady!' I understood her mistake.

The dell'Albas were extraordinarily generous. My room was like a flower garden and a huge bowl of peaches, grapes and green figs lay on the table by the window. The room itself was vast and I was sure normally used only by the most important patients. The day nurse was mine alone. No wonder the girl thought I was a Princess—I felt like one!

Domenico came to visit me. He did not stay very long but those few moments of having him near compensated for the fact that my dream had been a fantasy indeed and no more. His manner was gentle, concerned, but with no hint of personal attachment.

His main reason for wanting to talk to me, it seemed, was to try to establish what had happened; how I had come to be lying in my room at the Villa dell'Alba without having called for help.

'I know Helen and I were out—with my grandmother—and Paolo, too. But you could have called Boney or one of the servants, Laura. You, a nurse, must have realised you were seriously ill.'

Summoning up my courage, I told him about Vincenzio. Domenico's lips tightened perceptibly. He looked at me anxiously as if he suspected I was once more delirious.

'I find that hard to believe,' he said after a long pause. 'It is inconceivable to me that Vincenzio would ignore your appeal for help. If this is more of your morbid imagination, Laura, I . . .'

'I swear it is the truth, Domenico!' I broke in, tears in my eyes and weakness making me tremble.

He was not convinced. He left me soon afterwards, looking distressed, and said that he was returning home at once with Guiseppe who had brought him, and would question Vincenzio, but only to put my mind at rest.

After he had gone, I lay remembering, half regretting I had told him the truth. I was certain that Vincenzio Guardo had wanted me to die. I was truly afraid of him now. A man who could try to poison a woman was capable of anything. There was no limit to what he might not do to Domenico; nothing to ensure he would not try to kill *me* again.

Domenico had told me it was generally thought I had had a bad attack of food poisoning, but I had not yet been able to find out who had established this theory. If it *was* food poisoning, why was I the only one to suffer? The others had eaten the same food. Neither my nurses nor my doctor would discuss my case with me.

I was aware that I had no proof but I was now convinced Vincenzio had tried to end my life. 'Another silly intuition' Betty would say, Domenico, too, if he knew. I had not dared to tell him anything but the undeniable fact that Vincenzio had refused to call a doctor or get help. As soon as I was strong enough I would demand to see the doctor who had looked after me when I was brought into the hospital that terrible night. I would ask, also, to see the pathologist's report. He must have taken all the usual tests to establish what had made me so violently ill. But I was not well enough yet to insist on anything!

As my strength returned so did my fear of Vincenzio increase. Each time the door of my room opened, I was afraid it might be he. I gave orders to the Sister on night duty and to Angelica, my day nurse, that no one, not even il Conte, was to be allowed to visit me without my being previously informed as to the identity of my visitor.

Helen came to see me. As always, she was beautifully turned out—this day in a rose-pink wild silk dress with a huge peasant straw hat. I was delighted to see that her eyes looked bright and normal.

My little nurse bobbed a curtsey as she showed Helen into my room and left us alone. Helen stood looking down at me for a moment and casually dropped a parcel on my bed. I opened it and found a bottle of expensive French perfume. When I thanked her, she smiled.

'Well, you do look a shadow of your former self! Poor Laura!'

She sat down and with a brief glance to see if I objected, pulled out her gold cigarette case and lit a cigarette.

'How are you, Laura? You gave us all something of a fright to say the least! You know you nearly died?'

I nodded.

'Telegrams rushing between Niko and your father. Niko thought your relations should fly out. Your sister was against it unless it really was the moment of extremis! La Nonna took the unprecedented step of coming to the hospital herself to speak to the doctors! Believe me, Laura, you have been our only topic of conversation lately.'

I smiled back at her. Her green eyes were full of friendly humour. I felt my heart warm to her as it had never done before.

'I'm sorry!' I said. 'I'm afraid I've been a bore!'

Helen's eyebrows lifted in amusement.

'Never that, dear child. Far from it. There have been the most fascinating repercussions. Your accusations about poor old Vincenzio were totally denied by him, you know. After Domenico questioned him, Vincenzio stalked off to the old lady and, as I believe they say, tendered his resignation on the spot. I was in the room so I heard it all.'

'Vincenzio denied I asked him to help me? To get a doctor? But he *couldn't* deny it!' I cried.

'Well, he did! He said you must have been delirious and imagined it. Anyway, to my astonishment, our dear Contessa accepted his resignation; told him to pack and get out of the house quick!'

I felt my heart miss a beat. So now at long last I had an ally. *The old Contessa knew the truth.* She believed my story. She might even have proof from the pathologist that I had been poisoned—and not by food. It would be just like the Contessa to play the whole drama down and to avoid scandal, order the doctors to call it food poisoning. No doubt her influence held good even in this hospital where she was an important member of the Board. But I wasn't going to begrudge her her lies and deception now, if it were true. It was enough that Vincenzio was leaving Domenico's service. Now Domenico would be out of danger and when I returned to the Villa, I too, would have no one to fear.

Helen must have seen the look of relief on my face for she said wryly:

'Don't count your chickens before they are hatched, Laura. Vincenzio's in luck. He's not to be dismissed. Niko flatly refused to allow it. He and his grandmother had a blazing row such as I have never heard before. *"Give me one reason why he should go!"* Niko said over and over again and the old girl wouldn't—or couldn't. I don't know which. *"Then I'm not losing my loyal servant and friend"* were Niko's final words. So our dear Vincenzio is still with us!'

My heart sank. I lay back on the pillows.

'Oh, no!' I breathed. 'It can't be true.'

'And that's not all,' Helen went on. 'There followed a "to-do" about *you.* La Nonna called you an hysterical, unbalanced girl who had

256

stirred up far too much trouble since your arrival at the Villa and said you were to be sent straight back to England as soon as you were well enough.'

I stared at Helen, unable to speak. The blow was too shattering.

'Niko, however, refused to accept that either,' Helen went on. 'He defended you as royally as he had defended Vincenzio. You were very ill, he said; in your delirium it was only natural that you should have mistaken a bad dream for the truth, especially when one recalled all the other accidents that had indisputably happened recently. You were not responsible for what you said and he had no intention of sending you home.'

I let out my breath. I felt like 'the condemned man reprieved'. Tears of relief fell down my cheeks. Helen gave me her handkerchief and with some concern, added:

'I'm sorry, Laura—you're obviously not well enough to take all this just yet. I shouldn't have come.'

'No, I wanted all the news. I'm glad you came,' I told her quickly. I tried to smile.

'Well, there's one other bit of news—good this time,' Helen said, standing up and walking to the window. 'Niko's gone to Rome for his second eye operation. It was a bit sudden but the new specialist had to come to Florence for some reason and saw Niko at the Villa. He said Niko was so well, he'd operate some time

257

this week. Niko went to Rome yesterday afternoon and telephoned us last night to say he had settled into the hospital. I think they'll do the job on Wednesday, subject to the preliminary tests being satisfactory.'

I digested this information in silence. Naturally I was thrilled for Domenico. I knew how impatient he was to have this second operation. But selfishly, it crossed my mind that now I wouldn't see him for days, weeks, perhaps. Even if I were well enough to leave here in a week's time, he would remain in Rome at least a fortnight after that.

Suddenly, I realised that if this short separation could so torment me, what it was going to mean when I knew I would be parted from him for ever. Somehow, lately I had lost sight of the fact that I had to go back to England one day soon. Even if Domenico did not wish it to be immediately, it could not be delayed much longer. I felt like weeping again but struggled against my tears. I had too much I wanted to talk about to Helen.

'Helen,' I broke out. 'Do *you* believe I just imagined Vincenzio refused to go for help and left me to die? Do you think I dreamt it?'

'I don't know, Laura. It's all too odd and really rather improbable. I'm sure you didn't deliberately lie, but it could have been a dream, couldn't it? You *were* delirious when we found you.'

'Yes, it could have been delirium, but I'm

absolutely sure it was not!' I said firmly. 'And I think Vincenzio knew exactly what he was doing. He did not act from ignorance of how ill I really was. He wants me out of the way because he knows that I suspect his attitude towards Domenico. Only I can't prove it.'

Helen looked at me curiously, as though she were trying to size me up, to decide whether I was in fact, 'round the bend', or someone whose opinions mattered.

'I suppose I'd be less inclined to believe you, Laura, mad as your story is, if Nonna hadn't wanted Vincenzio sacked. That's what puzzles me. It's so out of character somehow. He and the Contessa have always got on fairly well and Vincenzio never puts a foot wrong with her; says and does the right things; is the perfect employee. I must admit I did think it very odd she wanted him out of the way, especially when Niko challenged her to give a reason and she couldn't. That wasn't like her either. She usually backs up her arguments with sound logic.'

'Well, then!' I said triumphantly. 'Suppose the Contessa suspects Vincenzio as I do, of trying to poison me—never mind *why* for the moment—what would she do?'

'Try to suppress the facts, I suppose,' Helen said. 'You know her—anything to avoid a scandal.'

'Could she suppress them?' I asked breathlessly. 'The pathologist's tests must have shown up the cause of my illness. Food poisoning is easily distinguishable from something like arsenic, for instance.'

Helen nodded.

'Yes, but *was there a pathologist's report, Laura?* When I found you so ill in your room that night, Nonna insisted we should call in the family physician. He went with you, in the ambulance, to the hospital. You were *his* patient. He could have said anything to the authorities, couldn't he? Even that you'd tried to poison yourself, for instance.'

'But that's absurd!' I broke in. 'Who would believe . . .' I broke off again as Helen opened her handbag and brought out a crumpled sheet of writing paper. Watching my face closely, she held it out to me.

'I found it in your room, Laura, on your bedside table, when I was collecting a nightcase of clothes to go with you in the ambulance. I kept it . . . I thought you wouldn't want it made public. Frankly, I believed you were dying!'

My fingers trembled as I opened the folded sheet of paper. It was part of a letter I had written compulsively to Betty and, as I'd meant to all along, thrown away.

'. . . *I love him so much, Betty. I can't bear the thought of any life in which he has no part. How am I going to come home and leave him? I can't! I can't, I can't . . .'*

260

As the hot colour burned my face, I sat silent, remembering the words that had poured from my pen one hot afternoon when my love for Domenico had been too much for me to bear alone. My sister was my only safety valve. Although I did not intend ever to post that letter, it had somehow helped writing all that I felt on paper.

'Don't look so embarrassed, Laura!' Helen went on sharply but not unkindly. 'No one else but me saw the letter. I was going to chuck it away. Don't know why I didn't except I thought if you *did* die and there were some kind of inquest or something, I *might* have to produce it.'

Now I was angry.

'You didn't think it was a *suicide* note?' I burst out indignantly.

Helen laughed.

'To tell you the truth, I did, once or twice. But the more I thought about it, the more improbable it seemed. Why leave only a part of a letter lying around rather than a whole one? And in any case, suicide didn't seem quite your line. You're really a very strong, straightforward character, Laura. I know you've hit the roof once or twice with your wild ideas about attempted murder and so on, but you've had the strength to stick to your views in spite of furious opposition. Another thing, why try to kill yourself that day? Why not wait until the day you were due to go home to put a dramatic end to yourself? And last but not least, why should you, a nurse, choose such a painful death as poisoning?'

I breathed a sigh of relief.

'Well, I'm glad you now realise I was far from suicidal!' I said. Suddenly a new thought hit me in the solar plexus like a physical blow. 'How did this get on my bedside table?' I asked, holding up the single page. 'I wrote that letter days ago—threw it away in the waste-paper basket.'

I think I knew the answer even before Helen had time to take in my question.

'Vincenzio!' I said triumphantly. *He found it and put it beside me.* He wanted to make it look as if I'd tried to commit suicide.'

Helen came across and patted my shoulder.

'There you go again! One of these days someone will have you up for libel. You're just guessing, Laura. You don't *know* any of this, do you?'

I looked away, resentful because she was doubting me again.

'I can't prove any of it,' I admitted reluctantly. 'But what other possible explanation is there?'

But Helen seemed to have become bored with the whole affair. She stubbed her cigarette end in the ashtray on the table.

'We all have to work out our own salvation, Laura, and you'll have to work yours out, just as I am doing. I'm going away, you know—back to England; into a very Private Nursing Home for a cure—if I can stick it! I've been very good lately but I don't trust myself.'

I forgot my own problems at once and concentrated on hers.

'I'm so glad!' I cried. Her announcement made me genuinely happy. 'That's marvellous news. When do you go? What made you decide to do this?'

Helen shrugged her shoulders.

'So many questions! And I don't know if I can answer any of them except that I leave on Friday. As to why—I really don't know. Maybe partly because of you.'

'Me?' I echoed stupidly.

'Yes, you! Seeing you around all day so . . . so young and untouched and . . . decent, I suppose . . .' her voice trembled slightly as if she were concealing her real emotion beneath the casual tone of her voice. 'I suddenly came face to face with myself—Helen dell'Alba, and I didn't like what I saw. I . . . I don't mean to suggest that I can ever go back to being like you. I don't suppose I ever was like you. The poor little rich girl always had far too much! But at least I could regain a modicum of self respect if I could knock off the drugs. Oh, hell, what's the point in trying to explain when I don't really know myself. Anyway, I'm off. I really came in to say goodbye.'

She held out her hand and gave mine a

quick, unexpected squeeze.

'I'm glad for you,' I whispered. 'I hope it will all work out. What will happen to Paolo?'

Helen sighed.

'He's off, too. Some friends of ours invited him to their house in the Bahamas. He's always full of fads and now wants to try deep sea fishing. He can't get there quick enough. Maybe it'll do him good. He can't drink *and* dive!' She ended with a laugh. 'So that's it, Laura. Maybe you and I won't meet again. Anyway, I wish you luck. Look after Niko for me!'

Her face, that beautifully made-up mask, crumpled just for an instant. Then she smiled brightly, waved her hand to me, and was gone.

I lay back against my pillows exhausted. Even talking, thinking, tired me. I knew I ought to relax—try to sleep. The puzzle could wait. It could all wait. Domenico was safe in hospital and I was, too. There was no danger to either of us for the moment.

I closed my eyes and tried to avoid the recurring nightmare of Vincenzio Guardo's face as I fell asleep.

*　　　*　　　*

One week after Helen's visit I was sitting in the armchair by the window when dear old Boney came to see me. It had been a mixed week for me. I'd had several letters from home, one from Jean, one from Pete saying he was engaged to be married and hoped I'd understand! But no news from the Villa dell'Alba. No word about Domenico, which was what I really craved to hear. But despite this frustration my youth and good constitution came to my aid and I had made a remarkably good recovery. I was well enough now to be allowed out of bed. I was thrilled to see Boney.

'Laura, dear!' the old woman said, coming across to kiss me. I hugged her and we both laughed a little shakily.

'It *is* nice to see you!' I said. 'Like a little breath of England!'

I waited for her answering smile but there was no light in those bright blue eyes.

She took off her white cotton gloves and sat down opposite me. Her brown-spotted, nobbly, old-woman's hands gripped the fastening of her black handbag. I waited for her to speak, some strange premonition of trouble preventing me from inviting her to impart her news quickly, as I might otherwise have done. She opened her mouth once or twice as if she were about to begin and closed it again. At last, I could bear it no longer.

'Domenico?' I asked.

She seemed to relax. Her face broke into a smile.

'Oh, Niko's doing ever so well,' she beamed. 'It isn't absolutely *certain* yet, but the Contessa was telling me this morning, the specialist says there's every reason to hope the second operation has been completely successful. Isn't that wonderful, dear?'

We hugged each other happily. I felt like dancing round the room in my excitement but Boney laid a restraining hand on me.

'Now, sit quiet, Laura. I'm sure you aren't meant to rush around yet, now are you, dear?'

I grinned and settled back in my chair, waiting for her to continue her good news. But another silence fell, was suspended—and increased my alarm.

'What is it, Boney? *What's wrong?* Something *is* wrong, isn't it?'

Her mouth tightened. She sighed deeply.

'Well, dear, I suppose so—that is, I'm rather afraid you won't think it is *good* news. Of course you might very well, but knowing how you feel about our Niko . . . well . . .'

'Boney!' I cried sharply, gripping her arm so hard she winced. I let it go and added: 'Don't keep me in suspense. What are you talking about? What are you trying to tell me?'

Boney, clearly, wasn't capable of imparting the news. She opened her handbag and took out a letter which she handed to me silently. The writing on the envelope was thin, spidery, beautifully formed. I saw at once that it was from the old Contessa. My fingers trembled as I took out the single sheet of expensive linen paper with the familiar crest.

'DEAR SIGNORINA HOWARD,
It is with regret that I have to inform you that your services will no longer be required at the Villa dell'Alba. As no doubt Miss Bone will have told you, my grandson's operation has been successful and when he returns home, he will have many pursuits and little enough time in which to indulge his love of music. You will appreciate, therefore, that your presence would be superfluous.

We all, il Conte included, thank you for the many enjoyable moments your music has given us; and also for your excellent nursing of Miss Bone during her illness.

I trust you, yourself, continue to recover. My physician informs me that you will be quite well in a day or two from now. I am sure you will welcome the opportunity to return to your own family in England to complete your convalescence.

I am enclosing your air ticket from Rome to London, via Milan, in anticipation of your feeling well enough to visit this city as you had originally planned. I also enclose a cheque for two months' salary in lieu of notice. I have already made arrangements for your hospital expenses to be covered.

With every good wish,
FRANCESCA DELL'ALBA.'

I let the envelope, letter and tickets fall to the floor. Boney stooped to retrieve them with a little cry.

'Oh, Laura, dear, you're so white. You aren't going to faint, are you? Shall I call the nurse?'

Her voice seemed to come from a great distance.

'. . . probably all for the best. I know you love him, dear, but in time you'll forget . . . it isn't that he doesn't want you . . . but you must see what the Contessa means . . . she explained it all to me . . . you'd just be hanging around the house with nothing to do all day . . .'

'Boney, don't please!' I couldn't stand the pity in her voice. A little more sympathy and I should break down completely—howl like a kid.

'I'm ever so sorry, Laura. I shall miss you, dear.'

'I'll miss you, too, Boney. Will you write to me?'

'Well, I'm not much good with a pen, dear, but I'll try. Of course I will, and I'll be very pleased to get your letters.'

'Oh, Boney!'

I was crying in earnest now. Her arms were round me and my head lay against her bosom. My tears made dark damp patches against her floral cotton dress.

'There, there, dear! Don't take on so!'

I wondered how often Domenico had lain

his head here, seeking comfort as I did; receiving those same meaningless words . . . *'don't take on so!'*

'I don't mind so much *going!'* I choked. 'It's Domenico not even wanting to say goodbye—to see me just once. I've never seen his eyes—never! You'd have thought he'd want me to stay just for the day he returned home. I wouldn't have minded so much going the day after.'

I blew noisily into a handkerchief and tried to smile as Boney released me. She looked very upset.

'You mustn't think he doesn't care,' she said intently. 'He was like a . . . well, I don't know what . . . those first few days when no one was sure if you'd pull through. Up and down my room like a caged tiger he was, saying: *"She's not going to die, is she, Boney?"* And the number of times he phoned the hospital! He couldn't seem to sleep at night either. It was as if . . .' she broke off, giving me a quick doubtful look and then dropping her eyes quickly '. . . as if he really was feared you were going to die,' she ended. 'Niko's not a heartless boy—he never was.'

'No!' I whispered.

'And it wasn't his idea you should fly straight home!' Boney burst out, still hot in Domenico's defence. 'It was the Contessa's. Niko was in Rome the day she made the decision and wrote this.'

I suddenly remembered Helen's account of what had happened the last time the Contessa had tried to send me home. Domenico had refused to allow it. Hope flared in me.

'Perhaps he doesn't know!' I cried. 'Perhaps when he hears, he'll . . .'

'Oh, no, dear!' Boney broke in. 'Niko wouldn't go against his grandmother in a matter like this, no matter how much he wanted you to stay. He leaves the running of the house entirely to her and he wouldn't go against her orders without good cause.'

I fell back against the cushions in my chair. Without meaning to, Boney had made it clear to me that no one had any use for me now at the Villa dell'Alba—*Domenico least of all*. He might defy his grandmother when he, himself, needed me to play the Bechstein to him. But now he no longer needed even that.

'You do look so tired and pale, Laura. Are you sure you wouldn't like me to call a nurse?'

'Perhaps I would like to go back to bed. It's my first full day up, you know.'

I felt proud of my voice, so much steadier than my trembling hands; my tears seemed to burn my eyelids but did not fall.

'Then I'll leave you, dear. You can have a nice sleep and when you wake up, you'll be able to think what fun it'll be getting home to your father and Betty. Why, there'll be so much to tell them, you won't know where to begin!'

270

She bent over me and kissed me. I wanted to grab her, hold her close to me, old Boney, my last link with the dell'Albas. But I knew I mustn't. Now I was about to take the first step away. They weren't my family. It wasn't my home. Boney wasn't my old nanny. The white rose buds Georgio always saved for me would be given to somebody else. Other hands would play the Bechstein and fill the great *salotto* with beautiful music for Domenico to enjoy. Domenico . . . *Domenico* . . .

'Now, now, Signorina Howard!' Angelica's soft Italian voice broke in on my thoughts. 'Please not to cry. Not a-good for you. See, I take off the clothes and very soon you be nice a-comfortable in the bed.'

Boney was gone. Angelica was gone. I was quite alone. Soon I would be gone, too. My holiday in Italy was finally coming to an end.

CHAPTER FOURTEEN

My train did not leave until mid-day. I had two hours to fill in before I need be at the Stazione Centrale . . . time, I thought, to pay a last visit to Calmano's and choose that brooch for Betty I had been unable to buy the day the Contessa fainted and my unhappy adventure had begun.

I left my suitcases at the hospital and walked out into the blazing heat of the day. My

271

head swam and my legs trembled. I had still not fully recovered. I was also more unhappy than I had ever been in my life before. In two hours I would be saying goodbye to Florence, City of Flowers, the city I loved. In all probability I would never come back . . .

Tears stung my eyes and I brushed them angrily away. It didn't matter. I wasn't going to let it hurt me . . . nothing could really hurt me but the fact of leaving Domenico.

I wandered towards the centre of the town. The streets were crowded and I was jostled and pushed, sometimes receiving an apology although I knew it was I who was not watching where I was going. I tried to concentrate but could think only of Domenico. His operation had been a complete success. In another week he would be out of hospital—able to see; able to do without me. I was happy for him. But his happiness meant the collapse of mine. He did not need me or my playing any more.

I tried not to be hurt because he had no wish to see me—not even *once*; just from idle curiosity. I had wanted so often to see *his* eyes . . . just once . . .

'*Buon giorno, Signorina.* I am delighted that you should be paying another visit to my shop!'

I had arrived without realising it at Calmano's. The old man ushered me inside; into the remembered darkness; the remembered smell of old leather, polished wood and spice. I remembered the musical box

272

and tears welled into my eyes. Since I had been in hospital, I seemed always to be weeping. I knew it was partly weakness due to my illness, but not altogether.

I managed to gulp out that I wanted to see some not too expensive jewellery and he hurried off to search for something suitable. I dried my tears and took a last look round. My eyes became accustomed to the gloom and with a little shock I realised there was someone else in the shop, standing with his back to me. My heart leapt to my throat. I would know the shape of that head anywhere; the set of the shoulders; the profile turning towards me. *Domenico!*

Forgetting everything but that I was to be allowed by a kindly Fate to see him once more, I ran across to him. My second shock was even more intense than the first. It was not Domenico after all. It was Vincenzio Guardo.

'You!' I stammered stupidly. 'I thought . . . I thought . . .'

He bowed.

'Signorina Howard!'

I was still staring at him unable to say a word when he turned on his heel and hurried out of the shop.

Vincenzio Guardo! Vincenzio Guardo! His name hammered in my brain.

'You spoke, Signorina?'

I turned to see the kindly old man looking at me with concern. I must have been

273

muttering aloud.

'No, I . . . I thought that man who was here just now was someone else . . . I thought . . . I thought . . . I was *sure* it was il Conte dell'Alba. I was *sure!*'

My companion smiled.

'Do not let your mistake upset you, Signorina. I, too, have often noticed the resemblance between the Signor Guardo and il Conte dell'Alba. Both come quite often to my shop and I have observed the likeness. It is a natural mistake you made.'

He put a velvet tray of trinkets in front of me but I could not concentrate on them. Something was stirring in the back of my mind—like a bumblebee one could not see but knew to be there because of its angry buzzing. If I could only think quietly, calmly, I would know why the likeness between Vincenzio Guardo and Domenico should so upset me. No, not upset . . . *frighten* me. They were both Italian . . . both dark. Why should they not look alike? No reason. Even the old shopkeeper had noticed the resemblance before. It wasn't just another of my fantasies. The two men were, in fact, more alike than Domenico and Paolo. *They could be brothers.* Surely, I thought, Vincenzio Guardo must be related to Domenico. Perhaps Domenico's father, Rodrigo, had been married before? Had a son by a previous marriage? But that could not be. Vincenzio would be il Conte dell'Alba if that were so. A cousin, perhaps? But would a cousin have been put in an orphanage?

Nothing made sense and yet I was absolutely certain the likeness of the two men was no coincidence. Height, colouring and type were all similar. It was fantastic, now I thought about it, that I'd never noticed it before. Yet I had noticed it, I thought with a surge of excitement, only at the time I had not realised what it was about Vincenzio's face, expressions, mannerisms, that had puzzled me. He had so often seemed strange to me—a little out of character. He was a dark, silent imitation of Domenico. I had thought him unattractive, yet when he smiled, the opposite. Now I knew Vincenzio had Domenico's smile; that same curve of the mouth I had so often watched for and loved.

I tried to still the chaos of my thoughts; to steady them and keep calm. I realised I did not want to think these two were related; that the suspicion both horrified and frightened me. My intuition told me that I had come upon something evil; something to fear; something from which I could only shrink back in horror.

I felt giddy and knew that if I were not careful, too much emotion would bring on a complete collapse. I was still so weak. I knew I had to have help—someone to talk to, to help me sort out my mental confusion—my new terrors.

'Helen!' I thought, but she had gone to England. There was no one at the Villa but the old Contessa and Boney. *Boney!* She had known the family for three generations. She had lived with them for sixty years. If anyone could help me, she might.

I excused myself as best I could to the old man and ran out of Calmano's. It was a few minutes before I could find a taxi and another wasted minute before I could make the driver realise where I wanted to go. I had a sense of terrible urgency. As the taxi ambled with maddening slowness through the suburbs, I begged the driver to hurry.

'Si spicci!' I urged him but he only grinned. Italians, I knew, very seldom hurried. They had no sense of time. *'Si affretti, affretti!'* I tried again.

At last the long drive and the great gates came into sight. I was drenched with sweat, partly from the heat, partly from the tension of the journey. We wound our way slowly up the avenue of cypress trees. I could see old Georgio watering the vine. The fountain still played in the haze of sunlight as it splashed into the stone bowl beneath. The great bronze horse still reared his head beneath the shower of falling water.

Terram Sperno, Sidera Peto! I scorn the earth, I seek the stars. The family motto meant nothing to me at this moment for, at last, I was realising that time stood still at the Villa

276

dell'Alba. In a hundred years from now, the fountain would still be cascading its shining drops on the horse's head; gardeners would still be tending the flowers and the great house would still drowse in the mid-day sun, shuttered against the heat, as it had been doing for centuries.

I paid the driver and ran round to the French windows which were always unlatched. I was no longer part of the household and had no right to come here like this, but my nameless terrors were greater than my fear of the Contessa's displeasure. I hurried across the room and up the staircase. There was no one about. I could hear Maria singing in the kitchen. The gallery seemed interminably long as I made my way to Boney's room. The painted dell'Alba ancestors watched me in proud silence, perhaps with derision. I ignored them and knocked on Boney's door.

The old woman was sitting in a chair by the window knitting. She wore the same blue dress with white collar and cuffs and seeing me, her face broke out in the same smile of welcome she had given me the day I arrived. She too, was timeless. I had the strangest feeling that I was living in some extraordinary vacuum where time had lost all meaning. Perhaps, I thought, none of this was real—the house, the dell'Albas. Perhaps I was a voiceless ghost, knowing them, yet unable to communicate my fear to them . . . When Boney spoke, would I be able to hear her words?

But of course I did.

'What a lovely surprise, Laura. It *is* nice to see you, dear, though you are flushed.' Her face took on a look of concern. 'You're not ill again, are you?'

I flung myself down on my knees beside her and caught her arms. She looked at me anxiously.

'You didn't really ought to be here, Laura. The Contessa said you weren't to come back. I told you, didn't I, dear? That's why Guiseppe took your cases to the hospital. All the same, I'm *that* glad to see you.'

'Boney, I didn't come to say goodbye to you. I came to ask you something—about Domenico; about Vincenzio Guardo.'

I poured out my story. Watching her face, I saw it change from one of kindly concern for me to one of acute fear.

'*Who is he?*' I was almost shouting at her. I was certainly shaking her. 'Who is Vincenzio Guardo? You know, don't you? You've got to tell me, Boney. *You've got to!*'

She pulled her arm away from my grasp and covered her mouth with her hand. She was trembling as badly as I was now.

'Oh, dear, Laura, what a thing! I never thought . . . I never guessed . . . *I can't tell you.*'

'You've got to,' I said again, and added brutally: 'Domenico's life may depend on it!'

'Oh, dear, oh, dear!' Boney whispered and

278

rocked her round little body to and fro.

Very slowly, I wormed the story out of her. She was afraid to tell me because she had sworn an oath to the Contessa that she would never reveal all that she knew. But for Domenico being in danger, even the Gestapo wouldn't have made her talk, she said. But talk she must, to me—for his sake.

Years ago, she told me, Domenico's father, Rodrigo dell'Alba, had fallen in love with Felicia, a young Sicilian girl whom he met on a walking holiday. He was only a young man at the time and it had been the first passion of his life. He was impetuous, headstrong. She was beautiful, simple, ignorant. He told the girl he would marry her and not realising he was one of the great dell'Alba family, she believed him. Unknown to his mother, the Contessa, Rodrigo went back often to visit Felicia. When she told him that she was pregnant, he informed his mother that he intended to marry the girl.

But the Contessa had other plans for her son. She had arranged his betrothal to Sofia de Zacchira, a Contessa in her own right, daughter of the Marchese de Zacchira. Like the dell'Albas, the de Zacchiras were impoverished but a family of tradition and nobility and the Contessa would not consider a daughter-in-law of lesser blood.

Rodrigo, it seemed, was weak. Despite his promise to the Sicilian girl, despite his own wishes, he was rushed into marriage with Sofia, a young, carefully guarded, completely innocent schoolgirl of seventeen. He was not permitted to see his Felicia again. The Contessa arranged everything so that there would be no scandal.

In time, Sofia bore him a son and heir, Domenico. Sofia worshipped her husband and he forgot about his Sicilian love and grew deeply attached to his wife. Another son was born, Paolo, and the past was completely forgotten. Then one afternoon, when Sofia was sitting at the piano, the mail was delivered. Someone (Boney did not know who) had written to the young Contessa. The story of Felicia was unfolded to her and moreover, the *present* existence of a boy, now in his teens, Rodrigo's illegitimate son.

Sofia had never been strong and a weak heart had not been improved by the birth of her last child. This shock and shame were too much for her; she succumbed there at her piano to a coronary thrombosis and died. Rodrigo, distraught with grief and guilt, threw the piano key away and swore that no one should touch it again. The ugly poison-pen letter was given to the old Contessa and no more was heard from the unknown writer. A year later Rodrigo himself was dead.

That was all Boney could tell me. She had no need to put her thoughts into words—they were mine already. Vincenzio Guardo was

Rodrigo's illegitimate son—Felicia's child. It explained perfectly his likeness to Domenico. It explained his easy transition from peasant to aristocrat. It explained, finally, why he and he alone, wanted to kill Domenico. He was the one living member of the family who had sufficient cause to hate Domenico—to resent his position in the Villa dell'Alba. At last I could supply the motive.

'What are you going to do, Laura?' Boney asked me fearfully as I stood up.

'Tell Domenico,' I replied at once. 'I will have to, Boney. You must see that. Now, at last, he will have to take notice of my warnings. He'll see for himself that he cannot go on trusting Vincenzio. He'll realise the grave danger he is in.'

My sense of urgency was greater now than before. If Vincenzio was as astute as I feared, he had probably guessed that I'd realised at least part of the truth when I called him 'Domenico' in Calmano's. It must be obvious to him that I might go to Domenico and warn him. If Vincenzio were to succeed in his attempt to kill his half-brother, he would have to do so at once. He might even be planning now for some ghastly 'accident' to befall Domenico as soon as he came out of hospital next week.

'I'm going to Rome, Boney!' I said. 'I'll catch the next train. If Vincenzio should come back here, you mustn't tell him you've seen me. And most important of all, Boney, you must try not to let him know we suspect him. Your life, too, could be in danger. And, Boney ...' I paused at the door for a last caution '... you *must not* tell the Contessa one word of this. She might try to prevent me from seeing Domenico. If she had meant him to know about his half-brother, he would have been told years ago. She *should* have told him. He had a right to know. And apart from that right, she must finally have realised who Vincenzio was and that all those so-called 'accidents' were actual attempts at murder. She alone of us all knew there might be a motive and where the danger lay.'

'It would kill her if the truth about Felicia was made public. That such a thing should happen after all these years!' Boney said piteously.

'Perhaps!' I said. 'But better that than Domenico's death. The Contessa has risked his life too many times already, Boney—just to keep the family's good name intact. If she really loved her grandson, she would never have taken such chances. She's a fanatic. She may even have guessed some time ago who Vincenzio was, yet done nothing about it until her hand was forced. Even now she has not reported him to the police.'

As I spoke I began to see what a lot made sense now that I had discovered the missing piece of the jigsaw. The Contessa's reluctance to have the 'accidents' investigated; her violent treatment of Paolo when he first showed signs of the same sensual weakness of his father's character; her abrupt dismissal of me whom no doubt she regarded as an enemy when my wild theorising had come a little too near the truth. She probably knew I was in love with her grandson and that nothing she could do would prevent me from bringing up past scandals if by so doing I could save Domenico. No wonder she wanted me safely back in England! It even explained the mystery of Sofia's heart attack and the Contessa's refusal to talk to Domenico about his mother's death.

Boney came downstairs with me and thought up an errand for Guiseppe, which gave her an excuse for sending the car into Florence. I scrambled into the back seat, hiding myself against the cushions in case the old Contessa suddenly suspected something was afoot and came out to investigate.

Soon I was back at the hospital and with Guiseppe's help, collected my suitcases and was on my way to the station. Guiseppe waited whilst I went to the *biglietteria* for my ticket.

'Dove va?'

'Vado a Roma.' I'm going to Rome, I replied.

'Parte fra cinque minuti!'

I was fortunate—only five minutes to wait. Already the train was standing at the platform. A guard was shouting:

283

'*A bordo, a bordo!*'

Guiseppe helped me in with my cases. I was both surprised and touched to see how sad he looked as he said goodbye to me. I realised then that he thought I was leaving for ever— on my way back to England, as had been arranged by the Contessa. I suppose he thought we were unlikely to meet again but he didn't *say* '*Addio*', goodbye. He said '*Arrivederci!*' as if he really hoped he *would* see me again.

There were tears in my eyes as the train pulled out of the station. All too quickly, Firenze, my lovely city, was rushing past the windows. The houses, the churches, the towers, the glorious bridges, the wide lovely Arno—all were receding into the distance. I knew I would never see them again. Like the beautiful, frightening Villa dell'Alba, they had already become part of my past.

*   *   *

At Rome I put my suitcases in the left-luggage office and realising I had had no lunch, forced myself to eat a ham roll and drink a cup of coffee. I found a cloakroom where I could wash and comb my hair. As I made up my face I studied my reflection. I realised suddenly. how much I had changed from the girl who had arrived in Italy such a short time ago. The sunburn hid my pallor and I looked like a fair-haired Italian woman. I wasn't a gauche young English tourist any more. Helen's beautiful dress lent me a new sophistication. I knew I need not feel inferior to any of the smart Roman women around me.

I thought of the ordinary looking, badly dressed girl, Laura Howard, who had begun the coach tour with Jean and Aunt May. Never having been out of England before, the mere thought of being in a strange country had scared me a little. Now, a very different Laura, I could shop, find my way around Florence, give orders to taxi drivers and to the nurses in the hospital; and speak quite fluent Italian.

But nothing could calm my underlying fears for Domenico; nor curb my excitement at the thought of seeing him within the hour. I had exhausted myself in the train thinking about Boney's story and the past. Now I was concerned only with the future; with Domenico's safety.

I took a taxi to the hospital. Though I would never be able to like the Contessa after what I knew about her, I was at least grateful for the generous way she had treated me. I had so much money in my handbag I need not travel the hard way. I hurried into the hospital and demanded to see il Conte dell'Alba immediately. The porter obviously mistook me for someone of consequence. A young nurse was detailed to take me personally to Domenico's room. I had no chance, therefore, to hesitate outside his door; to give way to the shyness, the excitement, the tension of this longed-for meeting with him. The nurse opened the door and announced:

'A visitor for you, Signor Conte.'

This time there were no bandages on Domenico's head. He looked at me with the most beautiful dark-lashed grey eyes I had ever seen. I was so surprised, so moved, I could not speak.

'Signorina?' he asked politely. Then I realised he did not know who I was. He was looking straight at me but of course, he did not recognise me. *He had never seen me.*

'Domenico!'

I uttered only that name but he knew then. His face lit up and he held out both hands to me.

'Laura! Laura! But how beautiful you are. I am overcome. I have thought so much about you and how you would look but I never imagined . . . oh, but yes, I think I did. You are just as the Laura I know would look. Come here, please.' The old imperious voice, I thought!

My heart beat suffocatingly and I felt the colour rush to my cheeks. I was so filled with emotion that I was not sure my legs could take me across the few yards separating us. When at last I could bring myself to take the first step forward, my eye was caught by a movement in the room behind me. I swung round and to my total horror, came face to face with Vincenzio Guardo.

CHAPTER FIFTEEN

All my love for Domenico—the miracle of knowing he could *see* me—was lost in one great rush of fear for him. I flung myself forward and the next moment I was in his arms.

'Domenico!' I gasped. 'You must get rid of Vincenzio. He wants to kill you—I came here to warn you. Domenico, listen to me, *listen to me*, please!'

'Indeed, it really *is* my Laura!' He was stroking my hair, holding my trembling body—and laughing at me. 'Well, Vincenzio, although I had hoped for a different greeting from my little English amorata, at least this makes me feel on familiar ground. I think, since she seems so distressed by your presence, you had better leave. Come back and see me tomorrow, will you?'

My little English love! For a moment, I could think of nothing else, but then I heard the door close behind Vincenzio. I pounded my fists against Domenico's chest, pouring out Boney's story, trying desperately to make him share my fears. I suppose he was listening, but when I finished, he only said:

'*Ti amo, cara mia,* mad though I think you are, *ti amo!*'

Then he kissed me. I forgot my anxiety. The world stood still.

'I love you, too, Domenico. I've always loved you. I don't want you to die. I love you. He can kill me instead—I don't care. I won't let him hurt you. I won't let him!'

'Darling!' How gentle his voice was using the familiar English endearment. He held my face between his hands, 'Such lovely, lovely eyes. Did you know that I've loved you for a long time, *cara mia?* Even when you made me most angry with your wild accusations, I loved you. But I could not tell you. I had to be sure I would recover my sight. Now, at last, my Laura, I can ask you to marry me.'

I stared at him speechlessly. Even Vincenzio Guardo was forgotten. Nothing on earth mattered but that Domenico loved me and wanted to marry me. *He loved me.*

He smiled.

'You look so surprised, Laura. Did you not guess I was in love with you? That night when I was so afraid you were going to die, I did in fact confess it. I was very angry with myself for my weakness and so afraid that when you recovered, you would remember my declaration.'

'I thought I had dreamt it!' I whispered. 'You showed no love for me when you came to visit me. I don't understand!'

'Don't you, darling? It is so simple really. I was aware that *you* loved *me*. It made me happy and tormented me at the same time. I knew I could not ask you to marry a blind man. If this operation too, had failed, then I would have had to send you out of my life for always. I thought the parting would be much more difficult for us both if we each knew how the other felt.'

'But I wouldn't have cared, Domenico—about you being blind,' I cried. 'I loved you as you were then. I'll always love you!'

'And I shall love you, Laura, as long as I live!'

Those words brought me back to my senses, my awareness of his danger. I pulled away from him although he still imprisoned one hand.

'You must listen to me, Domenico. If you love me, then promise me you will do something about Vincenzio Guardo,' I begged. 'He is not what you think. You always refused to acknowledge the truth about the attempts on your life. You kept assuring me they were accidents. You said you knew of no one who wanted you to die. Well, *he* does! Vincenzio Guardo does. He hates you and wants to kill you.' Without pausing for breath, I launched into my story. This time he listened, but from his expression I could see that Domenico was still not convinced.

'Laura, Vincenzio loves me like a brother,'

he said quietly. 'Indeed, if all you have told me is true, he is my brother, my half-brother. And if *that* is true, it explains why I have always felt so close to him—so *sympatico.* I think he feels it, too. You are on the wrong track, my dear little detective,' Domenico ended with a tolerant laugh.

I drew a deep breath. Even now, when I had been so certain I could convince him, he refused to realise his danger. I made yet another attempt to make him believe me.

'He is illegitimate, Domenico. He has a grudge against you. You must see that. *He* was the first son, but *you* were legitimate and acknowledged. Your mother took *his* mother's place.'

'A grudge against my father, perhaps, but not against me. I have never harmed Vincenzio. On the contrary, I have helped him make his way in the world. Now that I know the truth, I shall alter his status so that he lives with me as an equal. It was not his fault that my grandmother forbade my father to marry Vincenzio's mother. He deserves to be recompensed for that wrong. You are a kind person, Laura. I'm sure you want me to put things right for him now.'

'Oh, Domenico,' I said helplessly. I knew I was right, that he was wrong. But Domenico was unanswerable—I had no proof of my suspicions beyond Boney's story. I could not prove that it was Vincenzio who had made those other attempts on his life. I had only my wretched intuition and that was stronger than ever.

'Why was he here? How did he get here?' I went on desperately. 'He was in Calmano's this morning—that *is* a fact. Why should he come rushing here to Rome to see you so suddenly? He came because he was afraid I had found out who he really was; he had to get here before me, in case I managed to convince you. He can't have wasted a minute.'

'Laura, *carissima*! Stop a moment and consider. He arrived here before you, yes; you have come, as you said, to warn me. In what way has his arrival prevented you from telling me all about him? It was not specifically arranged that he should visit me this afternoon, I admit, but I expected him at any time. When I received my grandmother's letter telling me you had decided to go back to England to recuperate, I wrote to Vincenzio asking him to go and see you at once. I wanted him to beg you on my behalf, to visit me here in Rome before you flew home. He was to bring your reply in person.'

'And what was I supposed to have replied?' I asked harshly.

'Vincenzio told me just before you arrived that you had refused to see him in hospital.'

'That is a lie!' I cried. 'He never asked to see me. And it isn't true that I decided to go back to England to recuperate. Your grandmother dismissed me, Domenico. I have her letter here. I was given no option to stay. Don't you understand? Your grandmother wanted me out of the way. I knew too much.'

Now, at last, Domenico was unsure of himself.

'Possibly la Nonna was afraid you'd start a scandal, Laura. She would want to avoid this at all costs!'

'And Vincenzio?' I asked fiercely. 'What excuses can you find for him? I *know* he wants to kill you. I think your grandmother knows it, too. Boney does. She's on my side. If you will agree to do nothing else, will you let me engage a private detective to watch him; to guard you?'

Domenico looked dubious, but I warmed to the idea.

'He could pretend to be a sort of attendant—like a male nurse, to take care of you until you feel perfectly fit again. Oh, Domenico, if you won't do this for yourself, do it for me. I am afraid for you!'

He drew me back into his arms and kissed me. Watching his face which I knew so well now, I could see that I had at last made some impression on him. He looked strangely troubled. When he spoke again it was with the old commanding air of authority which had once so intrigued—and scared me.

'Very well, Laura. For your sake, I will engage someone to watch my interests until I can look into all this when I go home. But you are to tell no one, least of all Vincenzio. I shall treat him as I always do and see him tomorrow. Unlike you, I am by no means convinced he wishes me harm. I will believe it only when there is proof.'

He refused to discuss the matter further. I was to stay the night in a hotel in Rome and return to the hospital in the morning he insisted. I must promise him that I would forget my worries about his unfortunate half-brother, and since the hospital visiting hours were limited and I could not stay longer with him, I should make use of my time by seeing the sights of Rome.

'You will find them far more rewarding even than Milan,' he assured me with a smile. 'Now kiss me before you go, *cara mia.*'

As his arms drew me against him, I knew that my love for him was far more than the sentimental dream of a romantic girl. I felt a deep passionate desire for the man I loved and I was aware that Domenico was as deeply aroused as I. His searching kiss left us both trembling and we clung to one another in breathless urgency.

'So many times I have imagined this!' he whispered. 'You cannot know how often I have longed to hold you, kiss you, make love to you, *mi amore! Ogni minuti t'amo di piu!*' he added huskily.

And *I* loved *him* more every minute, I

thought as I drew away from him, flushed and breathless. Then he smiled at me with the deepest tenderness and taking my hand prisoner, placed it over his fiercely beating heart.

I wondered how I would ever find the strength to leave him but at that moment, a nurse came in and told me it was time for me to go. As I walked out of the building into the brilliant white sunlight, my heart was singing with happiness although I wished I could have remained with my beloved Domenico a little longer. Momentarily, I forgot all my fears and forebodings for Rome lay before me basking in the sunshine and I remembered that Domenico had demanded that I should explore this wonderful city.

Then I saw Vincenzio! He was leaning against a stone pillar smoking, watching me, a wide brimmed hat tipped over his brow to shade his face from the sun.

I had been afraid many times since I had come to Italy, but never so totally and completely as now. For a moment we stared at each other across the stone steps leading up to the hospital. Then he started to walk towards me. I turned and ran. I ran up the steps and around the side of the hospital into the street.

There was no taxi in sight. I jumped on to a passing bus without looking to see where it was going. Gasping, I sat down between an immensely fat woman with a brown baby on her lap and an elderly man with one arm in plaster. It was several minutes before I dared turn round to see if Vincenzio had followed. There was no sign of him. I relaxed. The brown baby grabbed my finger; its mother apologised but I allowed it to cling to me. Its hot sticky fingers were strangely comforting. The mother, all smiles now, began to tell me that he would soon be two years old. It reminded me of Helen's baby, Tonio. He, also, had been two years old when he died. I still did not know who was responsible for *his* death. Vincenzio Guardo? *Could it be?* I worked out the dates, trying to recall how long Vincenzio had been with the family. He had started outdoors in a menial capacity. He might have been in the gardens that day—might have left the gate open . . .

Then I saw him again. He was riding alongside my bus on a motor scooter.

Terror set my knees trembling. I had thought of getting off the bus but now I stayed put. If necessary, I would go with it to the terminus. After that, I dared not think. I was in no doubt at all that Vincenzio was following me and I understood why. He was sure now that *I* knew he was guilty. He must kill me first if he was to go through with his plan to murder Domenico. I alone, stood in his way.

Having accepted this fact, I don't think I felt quite so frightened. I had only to outwit him— lose him somehow in the crowds—to be out of physical danger. I hoped he was already held up by a traffic light, lost in the traffic.

But I saw him again waiting at the bus stop for our vehicle to continue its journey. Fear returned. It increased as the minutes ticked by. Sweat poured down my back. I could feel my thin dress sticking to me.

I stayed in my seat all the way—as far as the bus travelled. At last, exhausted, I saw that we were at Fiumicino—Rome airport. The other passengers were alighting. I must not be left alone in the bus. I would be too easily spotted by Vincenzio.

I pushed between two men, each carrying suitcases, and ran into the building. There was no sign of Vincenzio as I mingled with the crowd. I came to the main entrance and looking up, I saw on the Solari departure board, that a plane was leaving for London in ten minutes' time. I remembered the air ticket in my handbag. I had been booked on the three o'clock flight but if I hurried, I might be lucky enough to get a seat on this one. I could be through the barrier, on board and airborne before Vincenzio guessed my intention.

'Flight 479. London. Departing at 16.50.' There was no red light winking beside the announcement warning passengers it was time to board the plane. I could still change my ticket. Two hours from now and I could reach the safety of London. But for what purpose? My life would have no further meaning if I left

Domenico. Of course I could not go.

It suddenly occurred to me Domenico might only have agreed to engage a detective to quieten my fears; that he never seriously intended to do so. He had not been convinced Vincenzio had any evil intentions and might well have thought to calm my hysterical imagination with promises he felt it unnecessary to keep. I had money, plenty of it. If *I* engaged a detective, it could do no harm and at least I could be sure Domenico was out of danger. Moreover, I myself needed protection from Vincenzio. I was absolutely sure of that now. My immediate course of action must be to find someone to watch Vincenzio's every move.

My mind made up, I turned and walked out of the building. There was a taxi standing there.

'*Desidero Ufficio Informazioni!*' I said.

The driver nodded as if he understood and knew of such a bureau. I pulled open the door and with a sigh of relief, I got in. At the same moment, Vincenzio pulled open the opposite door and climbed in beside me.

I tried to get out but he forced me back against the seat and told the driver to proceed. I struggled but Vincenzio was ten times as strong. I shouted to the driver but he only grinned as he saw us in his mirror. He was, I suppose, used to quarrels in his taxi. This was Italy.

297

'*Aiutarmi!*' I shouted continuously, but the man only laughed at my calls for help.

'It is no use, Signorina,' Vincenzio said in English. 'He will not help you. Before you came out of the building I told him about you.'

'About me?' I echoed stupidly, and stopped struggling. I was trembling violently.

'That you are my wife; that we live in Florence and that it came to my ears this morning that you had gone to Rome to meet your English lover. He, the driver, was very much concerned for me. He told me in a fatherly way that if I must marry a foreigner and a non-Catholic, then I must expect trouble. He agreed to help me. I told him that if you saw me in the taxi, you might try and run away; that therefore I must hide myself and give him a sign when you came out of the building. It worked perfectly.'

'How did you know I *would* come,' I asked, too astonished at the cleverness of his story to feel anything much but curiosity. 'I might have caught the plane to England.'

'I know you love il Conte,' he said drily. 'A woman does not leave the man she loves.'

I pulled a handkerchief from my bag and wiped my face and hands.

'And now?'

'Now we are on our way to my "aunt's" house. It is out in the country, or so I told the driver. There I will be able to talk a little sense into you, "my wife", make you see the folly of your ways.'

'And this house? It doesn't exist?'

'No! We are going to the quarry *dei pietre.*'

'Quarry!' My worst fears now returned but I was outwardly calm. I would not give him the pleasure of seeing how scared I was. 'Then you mean to kill me—as well as Domenico?'

'I regret, Signorina, but it is necessary. I hoped it need not be, but . . .' he shrugged his shoulders, 'you should not have interfered.' His tone of voice was not threatening or violent, but conversational.

'You tried to kill me once before, didn't you?' I asked. 'You tried to poison me but you failed.' My voice too was astonishingly calm.

'This time I shall not fail,' he answered quietly.

I suppose I could have pleaded with him. I could promise to leave Rome at once; get on a plane for England; give him my word not to try to contact the police. But he must know I would not keep my word. I had had my chance to leave Rome and had not taken it.

I do not know how many kilometers we covered, Vincenzio watching me closely all the time in case I tried to jump from the taxi when it slowed at traffic lights or a junction. His face remained implacable. Now that I sat so close to him, I could not see any likeness to Domenico. His face was much more like that of the Contessa—severe, fanatical.

I felt it would be useless to plead with him.

299

If he let me live, I could and would prevent him from carrying out his intention to kill Domenico.

We were well out into the country when Vincenzio ordered the driver to stop. For the first time, the man showed some sign of indecision. There was not a house nor even a human being in sight. No one could live here. We were on a wild, desolate plain, uncultivated, rocky. The entire landscape was barren, unfriendly. The only living thing I could see was a white ox browsing under a solitary olive tree.

The driver was looking at Vincenzio doubtfully. My hopes revived.

'*Aiutarmi!*' I begged. 'Help me, please!'

But when Vincenzio spoke to him, the man smiled again and nodded his head. The two men dragged me out of the car.

'I told him the house is not far from here and that a walk might help to cool you off!' Vincenzio informed me in his quiet voice.

He paid the driver who turned the car and drove off towards Rome. My heart sank. Vincenzio and I were alone.

He took me by the arm and began to pull me off the road along a rough cart track. I could see now where he was taking me. A few hundred yards away the overgrown rocks and humps of a disused quarry sweltered in the sun. Lizards ran across the hard baked ground in front of us and vanished under the hot stones.

I was terrified. I tried to think calmly of Domenico, of Father, Betty—the people I would never see again.

Once or twice I made a desperate attempt to pull myself free but Vincenzio always caught me. The heat of the sun and my intense fear were making me dizzy. I knew I could never outrun him.

We reached the quarry. Vincenzio was sweating and stopped to mop his face and neck. My face, too, was burning and my forehead damp. I guessed I might have a temperature but it seemed silly to worry about it when in a few moments, I was to die.

I suppose my calm acceptance of approaching death was partly due to the fact that I was ill. None of this seemed to be very real. I hoped I was having one of my nightmares and would soon wake to reality. But the nightmare went on.

'How will you do it?' I asked once, quite coolly. We were standing side by side, a few feet from the edge of the quarry. 'Are *you* going to shoot me and throw my body over . . . over *there*?'

I could not look down into that horrible chasm.

'A shot might be heard. In any case, it is not necessary.'

I realised then that he intended to push me over alive. I felt sick with horror. To gain time,

I said:

'Vincenzio, let me say a prayer first? I know I am not a Catholic but I have sins I must confess to God. I can't die in a state of mortal sin. Please, please, let me pray.'

If he was surprised he did not show it. He nodded and showed no sign of anxiety until I began to open my handbag. Then he reached forward and took it from me.

'I haven't a gun!' I told him scornfully. 'I only want a cross from my bag . . . a silver cross I always carry with me.'

He returned the bag and stepped back a pace. Unnoticed by him, I took out my small purse mirror. Then I walked forward and knelt down at the very edge of the quarry.

It was, I knew, a kind of Russian roulette I was about to play. I had only the smallest chance of success and yet I had to try. At least I would have made an effort to save myself. It was better than waiting meekly for death.

I began to speak aloud, reciting the Lord's Prayer in a loud, clear voice. The words came automatically. I held the mirror in the palm of my hands which I had raised just above the level of my shoulders—a strange way to pray. *But it enabled me to see Vincenzio behind me.* So long as he did not realise it was a mirror I held, I had my one chance to anticipate his next move. I was trusting that the sun's reflection on it would seem to him to be the silver cross I had told him about.

'. . . *forgive us our trespasses as we forgive them that trespass against us. Lead us not into temptation but deliver us from evil, for Thine is the Kingdom, the power and the glory, for ever and ever . . . Amen!*'

I guessed he would pick that second when I said 'Amen' and he did. As he lurched forward, hands outstretched to push me, I flung myself sideways. I felt his legs hit my body as he hurtled past me; heard the scream as he went over the edge, carried by his own momentum. I lay there paralysed, listening to that terrible scream which seemed to go on and on and on; then fade to silence.

Suddenly I realised that it had begun again. Sickened, I forced myself upright and peered over the edge. A hundred feet down, Vincenzio lay in a twisted heap. His fall had been broken by a rocky ledge. He was still screaming.

My first instinct was to run—to run away from him; from the quarry; from that terrible noise. But I was a nurse—a human being. I couldn't go. I knew I must somehow try to climb down and help him if I could. No matter what he had tried to do, I could not leave him like that, screaming until he died.

The sides of the quarry were not as steep as I had feared. But the quarry itself was deeper than I had imagined. Only once did I look down to the very bottom and its distance so terrified me, I dared not look again.

Concentrating as I was on my descent, I was not aware at first that the screaming had stopped. When I at last reached Vincenzio, he lay there quite still and quiet. I knelt beside him. I was sure he must be dead. But I could feel his pulse still beating. As I tried to straighten out his twisted legs, he said:

'Do not try to move me, Signorina. No one can help me now.'

I looked down into those dark eyes, immense with suffering, his face cut and bleeding, blood pouring from his scalp. I knew then that he was right. He couldn't live much longer. Under my fingers, his pulse fluttered. His breathing grew more rapid.

'Stay with me!' His voice was filled with urgency. 'Don't go. I know I have not the right to ask you after . . . after . . . but I want to talk to you. Listen to me, please!'

All fear of him had gone. I felt only compassion. I eased his head on my arm and said quietly:

'I won't leave you, Vincenzio. I'm listening.'

'You know who I really am?'

'Yes! You are Domenico's half-brother.'

He sighed, his lips twisted with pain.

'My mother was a beautiful girl and good. She was very bitter when my father deserted her. After the disgrace of my birth, no man would marry her. Her father threw her out of his house. She was alone . . . always alone but for me. I loved her . . .' he broke off gasping.

304

I tore a strip from the hem of my dress with which to wipe the sweat from his forehead. There was nothing more I could do to relieve his agony.

'. . . when she was dying, she asked me to prove my love for her. "A promise, Vincenzio," she begged me. "A sacred vow". "Anything in the world, Mama," I told her. "Anything." '

I waited while he fought for the strength to continue.

'. . . my vow . . . I made it over the crucifix without knowing what it was she wanted of me.'

He lapsed into semi-consciousness. His voice was almost a whisper now. I had difficulty in understanding him.

'Mama!' he cried suddenly. 'I would have been happy to kill myself for you. Why wasn't it *my* life you wanted?'

I stared down at Vincenzio's tormented face, pinched and grey now as death came one step nearer. But suddenly his eyes held recognition again.

'It wasn't my life she wanted, Signorina Howard. It was that of every male member of the dell'Alba family. "*You will avenge me, Vincenzio!*" Those were the last words she spoke.'

'Oh, Vincenzio!' I cried. 'She was ill, dying. She could not really have meant . . .'

'Yes, she meant it and I had to keep my vow, Signorina. I did not know it would be so difficult. The little one . . . Tonio first. That was bad . . . but not too bad. I could tell myself that crippled as he was, his life would never be properly fulfilled. I didn't have to hurt him. I waited my chance to unlock the gate. The child found his way down to the lake.'

He paused, a shudder passing through his body. He seemed to be in excruciating pain but after a moment's silence, he somehow managed to continue:

'Paolo was to be the next. I *wanted* to kill *him*. He was a disgrace to the dell'Albas. But I saw that if I waited, I might have no need to commit a second mortal sin. With his drunken driving, he would surely kill himself in his car before long, I told myself. So . . . so it was to be Domenico.'

'Domenico!' I echoed. I tried not to edge away from the dying man. My loathing for him returned in full force.

'Yes, Signorina, Domenico!'

There was such love in Vincenzio's voice as he spoke that name, it confused me.

'I love him, Signorina, more than I thought it possible to love any man or woman. He is truly a great dell'Alba. You must make him understand that I did love him. That I died loving him.'

'You can say that—*you*, who were trying to kill him!'

Vincenzio's eyes were clouding. They looked desperately into mine. With a

306

superhuman effort, he inclined his head.

'*Si, si*, Signorina! That was my great difficulty. I should have killed him at once—before I began to know him; to respect him. But I was curious to find out what went on in the big house. I wanted to meet the great Contessa who had ruined my mother's life . . . I wanted to see the portraits of the dell'Alba ancestors—mine, too, do not forget. I wanted . . . to see how my father had lived; to discover for myself how corrupt were the children of such a man . . .'

I was beginning to understand at last.

'And instead of hating Domenico, you found yourself liking him?'

'It may sound strange to you, Signorina, to hear that I would gladly give my life for him . . . but I had made my vow. Do you understand? To a Sicilian, a vendetta is a matter of honour. I could not leave my mother unavenged.'

His head fell sideways over my arm. For several seconds, I was afraid he was dead, but suddenly he whispered:

'I had to do it . . . I tried to find a way that was indirect . . . I could not face the look that would come into his eyes if I, whom he trusted so implicitly, held a knife to his heart . . .'

'So you weakened the bridge? Tampered with the car?'

He nodded.

'I hoped the brakes would fail on our

307

descent from Fiesole and we would die together . . .' His voice was so weak I could barely hear him. But I had to know everything. 'And that night . . . the night I found you in the *salotto* with a knife in your hand . . .?' Everything made sense now. Vincenzio admitted he had been trying to find the courage to kill Domenico when I came downstairs and prevented him. I looked at him with pity. His life must have become a living hell—committed to killing the one person who meant everything to him.

'I'm not sorry that it is ending like this,' he whispered. 'I could not kill myself . . . but this way my mother's spirit can rest in peace. I am happy . . . happy that it is Domenico who will live.'

His story was tragic. His life had been doomed from the beginning. I bent over him.

'I'll tell Domenico that you loved him . . . like a true brother. He loved you, too,' I told him gently.

Vincenzio smiled. He was still smiling when he died.

*   *   *

Domenico and I were married very quietly in Florence. I wore a white suit and a tiny white hat made of roses. I carried a small posy, also of white roses, wrapped in silver lace.

Betty and Father were there to support me;

308

Boney and the old Contessa for Domenico. As we came out of the church it seemed to me all the bells in Florence were ringing for us. We had a small celebration lunch but no proper reception. Neither Domenico nor I wished it. All we wanted was to be alone together at the Villa dell'Alba. Boney would not intrude and the Contessa seldom left her rooms now. She had grown old suddenly—the stiff upright figure bent, like Boney's. I knew that she had given way at last. She had made no attempt to fight Domenico when he told her he intended to marry me. I was not afraid of her any more. In fact, I thought that in time we might grow fond of each other. She was very frail but Domenico said that by sheer will power she would live long enough to see us produce a new dell'Alba heir.

It was hard to believe only two months had passed since Vincenzio's death. I still dreamed occasionally of that terrible afternoon when I had staggered along the road from the quarry in search of help. A car had driven me to Rome where I was promptly despatched to hospital. The shock and strain of Vincenzio's attempt to kill me and the awful consequences following so close on my illness had caused a relapse and I was put to bed in a private room adjoining Domenico's. During the long weeks of my convalescence Domenico and I had planned our wedding and our family. I wanted a child as much as he did.

But now my illness, my nightmares were all in the past. Domenico had seen to that. He no longer doubted me—how could he?—and told me he would never discount my 'intuitions' again.

He and Father got on famously. Betty was still a little in awe of il Conte, but Father was quite at ease. I had felt almost jealous last night when they had forgotten me during a discussion about Italy in the days when Father knew it! But it made me happy that they liked each other. Domenico was wonderful to Father—accepting his opinions as though they mattered, and making him feel important instead of a useless old man in a wheelchair. He had been generous, too, sending Father and Betty the money for their fares, arranging a special ambulance plane to bring Father to Rome and on to Florence. Now Father and Betty were to remain as Domenico's guests for a further three weeks, staying in one of the best hotels. Domenico had hired a wheelchair so that Father could get about with Betty whenever he wished. Guiseppe would bring them out to the Villa for lunch or dinner . . . but not yet. Not until we had enjoyed the first week of our honeymoon alone together, Domenico and I.

'You are happy, *mi amore*?'

I looked up at that face I would never tire of seeing, and sighed.

'Completely, perfectly, wonderfully happy!'

310

I told him.

We sat side by side in the back of the car, holding hands, as Guiseppe drove us home. It *was* my home now, I thought with awe as we turned in between the gates and moved slowly up the long drive. I saw Georgio bent over the roses. I saw the beautiful white house ablaze with bougainvillea, asleep in the sun. I saw the water falling over the head of the bronze horse. I thought of the dell'Alba family motto—my motto now.

'I scorn the earth, I seek the stars'! It did not apply to me, I knew, for I had found my stars already.

We hope you have enjoyed this Large Print book. Other Chivers Press or Thorndike Press Large Print books are available at your library or directly from the publishers.

For more information about current and forthcoming titles, please call or write, without obligation, to:

Chivers Large Print
published by BBC Audiobooks Ltd
St James House, The Square
Lower Bristol Road
Bath BA2 3BH
UK
email: bbcaudiobooks@bbc.co.uk
www.bbcaudiobooks.co.uk

OR

Thorndike Press
295 Kennedy Memorial Drive
Waterville
Maine 04901
USA
www.gale.com/thorndike
www.gale.com/wheeler

All our Large Print titles are designed for easy reading, and all our books are made to last.